AF167446

The Other

The
Other

Sandy Hogarth

Copyright © 2023 Sandy Hogarth

The moral right of the author has been asserted.

Apart from any fair dealing for the purposes of research or private study,
or criticism or review, as permitted under the Copyright, Designs and Patents
Act 1988, this publication may only be reproduced, stored or transmitted, in
any form or by any means, with the prior permission in writing of the
publishers, or in the case of reprographic reproduction in accordance with
the terms of licences issued by the Copyright Licensing Agency. Enquiries
concerning reproduction outside those terms should be sent to the publishers.

This is a work of fiction. Names, characters, businesses, places, events
and incidents are either the products of the author's imagination
or used in a fictitious manner. Any resemblance to actual persons,
living or dead, or actual events is purely coincidental.

Matador
Unit E2 Airfield Business Park
Harrison Road, Market Harborough
Leicestershire LE16 7UL
Tel: 0116 279 2299
Email: books@troubador.co.uk
Web: www.troubador.co.uk/matador
Twitter: @matadorbooks

ISBN 978 1 80514 054 2

British Library Cataloguing in Publication Data.
A catalogue record for this book is available from the British Library.

Printed and bound in Great Britain by 4edge Limited
Typeset in 11pt Minion Pro by Troubador Publishing Ltd, Leicester, UK

Matador is an imprint of Troubador Publishing Ltd

For my lovely mother, Jessie

'Rhea and Rhoda were the same girl. They wanted it that way. Only looking from one to the other you could see they were two.'
Heat, Joyce Carol Oates

'And when we have our naked frailties hid,
That suffer in exposure, let us meet…'
Macbeth, William Shakespeare

1

21st June 1974

They reached out for each other in the wet warmth of their mother's womb.

Mother's zygote was slow to divide, eight or more days, developing from the one, to form two embryos. The two were head down, eyeballing each other in the warm sac of amniotic fluid, each existing solely for the other.

*

One autumn evening, a few days short of nine months back, their father had put down his brush, turning, with some regret, from his easel, descending the stairs that led down from his eyrie at the top of the rundown cottage, and carried her, in his paint-splattered hands and arms, out the door and into the forest. She had clung tight, hiding her head in his chest, and the susurration of the trees had quietened her. She closed her eyes against the moonlight.

He spread his jacket on the soft grass beside the pond, and laid her on it, dropping his trousers down to his knees, not bothering with his shirt but pulling the band from his dark hair so it fell across both their faces. She didn't open her eyes, even when he entered her.

Now, while eating his breakfast, the shouting began. He paid little mind until the word 'hospital'. He stood, in no great hurry, and helped her down the stairs and into his car, leaving her at the hospital doors. She sobbed, holding both hands twisted tight across her belly, her face ashen.

He strode away.

The next day, having deemed enough time to have passed, he parked among the dozens of cars and made his way, unhurried, to the double doors at the front of the sprawling red-brick building. Inside he stared, nonplussed at the signs, the arrows, the corridors, sighed, and half turned back towards the double doors.

At a desk, a young woman raised her head at his request, irritation in her eyes, and pointed to a corridor, instructing him to follow it until the sign on the left.

He walked too far, so retraced his steps, the sign now on his right. He passed people sitting alone, staring into the distance, and some minutes later he pushed open the doors to a ward. His shoes were heavy on the hard floor. Nine beds on each side. Mothers raised their heads from their babies. She was in the very last bed, her chin held high, triumph in her eyes, and a baby in each arm, remarkably alike, although his glance was fleeting and his smile, a poor thing.

'Helen, the most beautiful woman in the world,' he murmured as he looked away from the creatures, and from her. 'And Clytemnestra, mind you, she came to a bad end as did the other. The mother, Leda, impregnated by Zeus, the King of the Gods, disguised as a swan.' And he laughed.

'Leda,' she murmured. 'Helen, the most beautiful woman in the world,' and a flush rose up her neck to blanket her face, as she gazed intently at one, then the other.

She held them out to him.

'Who knows,' he said, his hands and arms pinned, unmoving, to his sides. He permitted his gaze to linger a few seconds on the same patch of dark hair on each scalp, the blotches of red on their cheeks, their exquisite full, small, pink lips, and wrinkled hands and feet. And their eyes seemingly gazing into his, then around, exploring.

He would not be coming back to her, or to them. He did not regret her, but the two? He hesitated, then turned and left.

He had got it wrong, always too hasty, for Helen and Clytemnestra of Greek myth had not shared one egg, but these two beauties, Helen and Clytemnestra Richards, born in the north of England on midsummer's day, 21st June 1974, in the swamp of the Watergate scandal, indubitably had.

Clytemnestra was born thirty-five minutes before Helen, fighting to be first out. Would she be as ruthless as her namesake? Helen had held fast to her in their mother's womb, to stop her leaving. They had been safe in there, just the two.

A birthmark on Helen's right shoulder twinned Clemmy's on her left, their shoulders had kissed. A hundred per cent match. What a freak show. Genetically closer to each other than to their mother, or to their father, but he counted for little.

The midwife had pointed to the small kiss on each of the girls' shoulders and said, 'Special,' wonder in her voice, so Mother had brushed off her despair and put out her arms for the two. 'My girls.'

2

Three years earlier he had left the London he hated, eager to be back among his giants in the far north. His exhibition had gone well – 'a great success' were his agent's words, no doubt his own commission filling his head.

It was a long way but he hated trains, and people. On the long drive back he had grown bored and cross, the trunk roads full of trucks, seemingly endless. He only enjoyed the radio when painting so it remained silent. After enduring a couple of hundred miles he wandered off in no particular direction, while acknowledging to himself that he was not usually a risk taker, and followed a road that became ever more narrow until it was a dirt track in the depths of a forest where the trees grew close and dark, so it was a relief – for he was a man from the high, bare mountains – when it opened out a little. He stopped, stared around. The forest had invaded the garden on all sides, its picket fence surrendering, yet its rotten remains defiantly still circling the cottage, mostly fallen or somewhat overgrown, the wooden gate jammed permanently closed, easy to bypass and hints of a one-time rose garden, strangled by tall, lank grass. He was a little afraid of the dark trees, yet his fingers itched for a pencil, for a brush, for change.

And there stood a cottage that reminded him of his childhood drawings: rough stone with four windows, a door in the middle and a steep roof with a single chimney, painted white long ago, now peeling and grubby.

He turned off the engine, sat still a moment or two, and all the turmoil of the drive vanished, as the silence of the forest wrapped itself around him, curiously calming.

The worn front door slipped open. From the hall a large kitchen led off to the left with a front room opposite, and behind it an even smaller dining room, thick with dust. The cottage was old, perhaps a couple of hundred years, with stone-flagged floor downstairs and stone stairs. It was cold, but that had never bothered him. He climbed to the first floor then on, up the stairs, twelve narrow steps on which his big feet stumbled, to a north-facing room at the back of the cottage, that spread itself across the two bedrooms below, its large windows overlooking the broadleaf forest. It was this space, with its light and beckoning treetops, that made his heart thump in his stout chest.

No street lights, only shadows, which suited him although he knew little of trees.

The track widened beyond the cottage to allow parking and turning, but after that the forest had won, taking over the narrow lane. An electric wire sagged its nervous way from the road to end at a pole outside. There was no phone line, something that pleased him.

He enquired in the nearby town and offered the owner a good price, not intending to stay, a little puzzled by his decision.

He wrote to his agent and small vans delivered replicas of those things that languished in his studio up north: paints and easel, brushes, paper, canvases and more. His strong hands took time to adjust to his new tools. He had need of few clothes; his one suitcase held the essentials.

A year after moving in, he had been passing time in the only café in the nearby small village that liked to call itself a town, idly scanning the newspaper and puzzling over people marching to Aldermaston. He understood little of the world, and of atomic weaponry, was waiting for the light, waiting for his hands to find what was in his head, the puzzle of colour, and how to render it in the manner his imagination was demanding. His eyes painted even when his hands held no brush.

The town, with its one high street, a few scattered shops and café, had changed little over the years, and was a little old-fashioned, reflecting the customers. A big, tall man, he had hurried to a table in a corner, ignoring the stares and the whispers, and nodding, almost imperceptibly, to Jack, the owner, a short bald man with stained, crooked teeth, delicate features, soft voice and a large belly straining to escape its white apron.

It might be a small town, a very small town, but the locals were loyal and the café usually busy. Long fluorescent tubes threw out harsh light and the menu on the wall rarely changed, yet it gave the customers what they wanted so they minded little. The linoleum floor was worn in places, and the wide windows allowed them to observe passers-by if they were bored or wanting some gossip.

Jack was the closest he had to a friend, although he

acknowledged it was an exaggeration to call him that. He had never indulged in friends.

The townspeople left him alone. He liked it that way, had forgotten small talk and casual encounter. Although he could not put it into words, even into clear thoughts, he was perplexed about life, about himself, believing he should not be thus at forty-two.

He shuffled his feet, rubbed his beard, picked at the blobs of paint among the black hairs on his knuckles, impatient to run back to his eyrie above the treetops, to the canvas he had scrubbed clean with turps. His painting had failed him or he had failed it and he'd walked away from his studio, to distract himself and wait.

He watched her stroll in: petite, with high heels that made her lean forward a little, or was it the weight of her generous breasts? She wore a sleeveless, close-fitting red dress, her blonde hair swinging above her shoulders, and she carried an overlarge bright red handbag.

*

She waved to a table of young women, acquaintances. Their laughter was bouncing off the café's hard walls, seeming to increase when their heads turned towards her. Perhaps she'd join them, perhaps not, for the talk would all be about boyfriends and they would guess she had been dumped. She regretted his car, a flash MG, more than she regretted him yet her need for a laugh right now was overwhelming. She was twenty-two and broke, stuck here where nothing ever changed. She had left home years back, left her pig of a father and the many other kids. She wanted fun, wanted to dance, to real music, not the old-fashioned crap they played at the occasional socials in the hall here. She had gone once and left early after a quick drink or two.

As her gaze travelled the room, she saw his deep-set brown eyes run over her, with their invitation. He must be the painter with his boring clothes, his long hair and beard. Word was that he was rich, even famous. Did painting count? He didn't get up when she stood beside his table, but pulled out a chair.

'You're the painter,' and she sat, placing her bag on the table. 'Coffee, please.'

It was a cold house; the surrounding forest embracing it with darkness. She had been expecting something grand, gates that swung open like in the films, and the next day she stood in the kitchen, asking herself what she was doing here. It was a large room, the central table covered in grime, with four old chairs scattered around. A fridge took up one corner and she creaked its door open to find bottles of beer, butter and cheese. An electric oven and hob and cupboard and shelves, one of the cupboards full of old saucepans, and a drawer of mismatched cutlery.

A battered leather sofa languished in the sitting room, and an open fire offered heat that was more symbolic than real. Against one wall stood an upright piano. She played a few notes, pointed to it and said, 'I play.'

Upstairs, the bed complained when she threw herself onto it, so she replaced the cold nylon sheets with Egyptian cotton, and his old army blankets with soft, warm, woollen ones and insisted on new furniture for the bedroom, sitting room and kitchen. And a new set of saucepans (not that she cared much for cooking), cutlery, and an electric radiator that always sat close to her feet.

She cleaned one side of the wardrobe ready for her new clothes. It was soon full but she had nowhere to go to show them off. He gave her his car keys once a week to go into town to shop but she bypassed it for the nearest big town and filled her wardrobe with the latest fashions – exotic, fanciful, expensive and it groaned when she opened the door. He liked her to look good and she took full advantage.

A couple of years ago, she'd fallen in love with a silver teapot in an antique shop. 'Georgian,' the owner said. '1780s.' That sounded really old and had cost a fortune so she took great care of it. Now it stood on its special shelf, in the never-used dining room.

He did not mention love, which did not bother her.

'You can stay if you want,' he'd said that first morning at breakfast, and had smiled. 'We can get your things.' That smile had been his best. And when he touched her, he was gentle, often intense. He had led her by the hand into the forest, naming the birds and the trees. Close by the pond, he had laid her down and made love, tenderly, wordlessly.

He had taken her the next day to the supermarket outside town, given her notes and told her to buy whatever she wanted.

She had believed she might be happy with him. He had only taken her once more into the forest.

After a few days, he left her when breakfast was done and climbed with his flask and a snack to the room at the top. She followed.

He turned to her at the door. 'This is where I work; it is

only me and my paints. I'm sorry.' He locked the door after himself and stayed the day long there, with his flask of coffee and a snack.

He never spoke of his painting and none of his work hung on the walls of the cottage.

She shouted from the landing below, bawling to know if he loved her. He never replied, and mid-afternoons, the piano, loud, brutish, sent him a message: he had been upstairs too long. Evenings, he scrubbed the paint from his hands and led her upstairs to their bed.

Neither of them spoke of her swelling belly, and each blamed the other.

3

The day after the two, (it was them he pictured, not her), he was seated at the foot of his oak, his trousers rolled up above his ankles, a thin, somewhat ancient shirt covering his chest, the sleeves revealing pale white arms and small blobs of paint nestling amidst the dark hairs.

He took out his sketch pad and pencils from his shoulder bag and drew the asymmetric-limbed trees, the branches of many hung with lime-green petticoats of lichen. He was certain that the trees spoke to each other, sharing the secrets of the forest and its lore, just as his paints and brushes spoke to him. The forest had enfolded him in its ever-changing arms, sharing itself. It was not yet 7am and a pink-breasted chaffinch perched nearby, its head moving from time to time. Approval? Perhaps.

His oak was scarred deep into its trunk at shoulder height, surely an attempt on its life many years back, marked perhaps for Nelson, for one of up to 6,000 oaks that it took to build a warship. A survivor. Far up, in its green top, the air buzzed with insects, and below, its roots spread twice the distance of its crown. It had been a mast year for the oak, so it had set millions of seeds. They were clever, the oaks, with their leaves of bitter, toxic tannins, some years holding back, to defeat the predators. Their acorns fed the voles, mice and squirrels, pheasants and pigeons. He had occasionally glimpsed the white bottoms and tails of roe deer as they scurried away. Pigs no longer roamed, and wolves had vanished aeons ago.

Most mornings he had made his way, shortly after dawn, through the trees: larch, birch, hazel, sycamore, ash, beech and oak. They welcomed him and the forest unpeeled itself. He breathed in the smell of wild garlic wafting down the bank, a dense colony with its elliptic green leaves and white flowers and, around his feet, a pool of bluebells, the queen of the forest floor gifting the air with a blue haze. An intermittent soft rustling, perhaps mice, and the fluting of blackbirds. Nuthatch ran headfirst down a nearby tree, and the ugly caw of crows made him search the treetops. A grey squirrel on the tip-end of a branch swayed up and down in its private fairground. The scream of an owl startled him.

Beyond the forest were steep, bare hills scattered with sheep, and a single row of may trees in full blossom, an etiolated *corps de ballet* in white tutus, dancing up the hill, their white glory lighting up the green fields. Did they miss the bustle of the forest? And a solitary silver birch, in winter and spring its trunk glowing eerily white.

Now, midsummer, the forest was fully robed in every shade of green. Many of the flowers had faded but not the purple, soldierly foxgloves.

He packed up his pencils and paper and followed the

narrow path deeper into the forest, to his pond. Rocks jutted out on the south side about eight feet, disturbing the watery image: four small, flat rocks, each a couple of feet square, then two more, much larger. He had grown to love the trees, and even more, the pond.

Seated on its edge, his shoes almost in the water, he selected a pencil from his tin box – his treasure from his boyhood, a defence, back then, against loneliness. Perhaps still. His hand moved quickly, even carelessly, and he soon had the image he wanted, a mere beginning. It would be his last sketch here in the forest.

He stood, gazing around, filling his head, his memory bank, then turned and strode back through the trees, along the meandering path, purpose in his steps. The blackbird sang farewell.

The forest was his loss, for he was returning to his high mountains where the few trees stood in soldierly rows, dark, grim, bereft of life in their shade. He had loved those giants once, would again, but for now, it was the jewels of the forest that cosseted his painter's heart.

He hadn't noticed her for a long time, had forgotten how to translate what had once been in her eyes.

And the two small creatures. She would be expecting him, would thrust them out, demanding what he could not, would not, give. He had been a fool. There was only one thing in his life that mattered and it wasn't her, and not babies, although he smiled a little, for their soft eyes and their vulnerability had scarred him. He'd always walked away, the few occasions when he had been careless. He crossed his arms over his chest, his heart beating a little faster and the skin beneath his beard flushing.

He picked up the flask filled with black coffee. His hands shook a little so he grasped it tightly and moved up the stairs, climbing the small steps more slowly than usual, his big feet clumsy. He prided himself on his fitness, standing at his easel for eight, ten hours a day, the cigarette stubs tracking the time. She would be back from hospital in a few days. He was done with her, had been for some time; she would not miss him, only the money.

He unlocked the door and locked it again from the inside. Habit. He strode to the windowsill and put down the flask. The trees, his friends, beckoned, his blackbird on the chimney pot sang a welcome. He took two long breaths and turned away. In the corner, on a small table, was an old paint-splattered radio. He switched it on and Mozart quietened him for a minute or two. As soon as he picked up his brush, the music would fade.

A wide chest with shallow drawers stood against one wall, holding his paper, sketches, some failed paintings and drafts that remained just that. On its top a folio filled with drawings: hope and failure, and beside it, a plastic basket of half-empty tubes of paint, a jar of turps, a couple of rags and three old mugs holding brushes, perhaps twenty in all, some stiff with age, unused for a long time, others silky smooth. His favourite eight or ten were in another pot on the table beside the easel, with his palette, which was dotted with small blobs of paint, his pets, burnt umber, raw umber and burnt sienna, prominent at the front. The position of the colours rarely varied. On the opposite wall was a battered leather sofa and, in the corner, a small washbasin.

He lit a cigarette and turned back to stare out of the window, smoking slowly, filling his mind with colours and asking himself how he could paint without the forest. He was going home.

He stubbed out the half-smoked cigarette as the morning light fell directly onto the canvas and he used his right shoe to push off his left, then his bare toes for the right. He liked the feel of the paint-splattered wooden floor beneath his naked feet, and when the going got hard he curled his toes. He tied his apron around his waist. At the foot of the mountains the original pristine thing of twenty or more years ago waited, becoming its own creation, an abstract of splashes of many paints. The tying of the apron emptied his mind of frippery, of anything except his colours, even of fags for a time. He stood at his easel, rolling up his sleeves to above the elbow. Outside, the branches of the trees oscillated encouragement.

The lightly painted outline, head and shoulders, on his primed canvas, threatened. Unusually, he was nervous of his brushstrokes. A mirror, about twenty-four inches square, was propped next to the canvas and turned toward him.

He had done the preparatory work, more than was his custom: charcoal drawings, too many. Some were stuck to the nearest wall. In them, his head was turned slightly to one side, not full profile, looking away a little, or was it back? He had roughly sketched the man in the mirror, a man in his forties. He had trimmed his beard and was the man he had been before he left the mountain in the north, eyes brimful of hope. His mouth was sensual. Women liked that. His ears were surprisingly delicate.

He wasn't a portrait painter. This would not be his best work.

He placed his hand on the bulge in his trousers, lingered there a time, doubt and excitement mingling.

He ran his fingers over the brushes, his lushes. He would select his favourites while letting the others feel cared for. He placed a brush between finger and thumb of his right hand and it hovered over burnt sienna. He did not have long. He dabbed on the paint, a beginning. Colours, brushstrokes, looking into his own eyes.

He walked away from the easel, from failure, lit a cigarette. Two puffs and he ground it out. He would remix his colours, wait for them to work their magic.

Twice he took a turps-soaked rag and wiped the canvas clean, starting again, his canvas face lit by a sprinkling of sunbeams, his thick fingers selecting a different brush from time to time.

Too much haste. He could not rid his mind of the two. And yet. They were girls; boys might have made it harder. He was an only one, had been a loner, even at school, not much liked, but he hadn't cared, even preferred it that way. He had never wanted a sibling, had barely known his father. It did not escape him, the pattern, and he dismissed it.

He stood back from the easel. It wasn't working.

Then a small miracle and hints of the man he was accustomed to seeing in the mirror began to emerge, determination in the set of the mouth, and in the eyes, something he had not intended, a sadness.

As he worked, the sky brightened until, much later, the lingering sun warned of dusk. Many hours passed and he peered out of the window into the limpid dawn light, behind him the portrait, perhaps of a man he did not much like.

He turned up the radio, lay down on the sofa, and closed his eyes.

Ten minutes later he sat up, scrabbled for a pencil and

a piece of paper, wrote a few words, and pinned the note to the easel's legs. He picked up his brush one last time, touched its tip into the paint and gave the eyes some softness, a little more light.

He had turned away from her burgeoning belly, and now the two. A god, not him. It was his sperm she had sucked into herself for she was always greedy. There had been no rape and he was no swan. Six feet plus an inch or two; strong, big, square hands; body on the hairy side, not feathers – and thick dark hair and a beard that he trimmed from time to time.

Why hadn't he sent her packing long ago? He couldn't fly but he could flee. The two puzzled him, threatened. They were his. She had sucked up his money too greedily to risk a dalliance. He knew nothing of children, of babies, and wanted it to continue that way. His need to run was grave, to blot them out, to save himself, to paint.

The loss of the forest was the price he had to pay. He would carry it in his painter's hands and head. Was it the two or the forest? He didn't care to investigate. He'd not let others' lives change him, yet worried that this might be the exception.

Had he been bewitched by the forest, the trees? He was not one for fairy tales. Bewitched by a forest. His laugh was deep, loud. His paints and brushes had also fallen in love with it. And yet his life was not like those of others, not that he knew many. The profit-and-loss ledger, that was how he summed up his life, not that he understood what that was but they were colourful words, profit far outweighing loss. Indeed, his imagination did not stretch to any real loss, if you deducted his childhood.

The window was open. Were the trees applauding?

'Fool,' he said, out loud.

Yet lack of children had always been an item in the profit column. Money, there was no shortage of that, especially after that last London exhibition and his forest paintings.

He shifted in his seat, tried and failed to stretch his legs, cursing his car.

The two. He understood little of genetics, but he must be in the two even if they were girls.

Their eyes.

He could ignore her, had done so, had never understood love.

He cleaned his brushes and packed them into a small bag with his paints. His palette was still sticky with half a dozen blobs of paint ready-mixed. He should clean it, take it, but would not. His life here was over, done with, he would start again further north. It would not be the forest. He now saw that this room was scruffy, second-rate. His other easel and a multitude of brushes and paints languished in the far north, awaiting him. He'd not take much with him, was impatient to be gone. Had this sojourn here been a mistake? He had never been adventurous. Yet the forest had served him well. His agent had been astonished to receive the paintings and even more at how well they had sold.

A painting leant against the wall: the pond lit by a glimmer of moonlight and, on the jutting-out stones, with a shadow of a man. He picked it up and leant it against the legs of the easel. Two gifts for the two.

He left a blank canvas leaning against the wall in its place.

She would never bother to climb the stairs. Would the two one day?

He took his sketches down from the walls and carried

them downstairs with a couple of finished paintings, the bag of paints and brushes, and a half-full bottle of malt whisky, leaving them by the front door, then climbed the narrow stairs one last time, to walk regretful steps to the window and gaze out over the trees.

Despite his success, how little he had explored himself or people. And now... He breathed deeply and locked the studio door.

He gathered up a few books and clothes. There was little he cared about in the way of possessions, including his ten-year-old car. He didn't bother to lock the cottage.

In the driver's seat, slammed the door shut, turned the key and let out the clutch. The wheels spun. One brief glance back at the cottage lit by the early afternoon light. And the forest.

*

Settled again at the foot of a Scottish mountain, in a hamlet he knew well, and in love once more with his giants, he wrote, saying he would send money once a year on the girls' birthday so they could be brought up decent. She must send photographs every June, though he wasn't sure he wanted them. He gave a PO Box address sixty miles away. He could count on her greed.

He packaged up and posted a cheap camera.

The first photographs came less than a year later. Two babies in identical dresses, identical smiles, Helen and Clemmy written on the backs, innocence in their eyes, as far as the indifferent photographs would allow. The world had not yet tarnished them. His regret surprised him and he sent a cheque for a larger sum than he had intended.

He would have liked to paint them, beauty doubled.

4

As her belly had grown so had her resentment of him, and she had wished away the thing inside her.

She had not minded that he had not returned to the hospital, for many wandered to her bedside to marvel at her girls.

Back at the cottage she walked through the unlocked front door, a baby in each arm, triumph in her eyes, and glanced around the kitchen. She laid the two on the carpet in the sitting room, stood at the bottom of the stairs and bawled, again and again.

She ran outside. His car was gone.

'Bastard,' she shouted at the air.

She sat at the kitchen table, head in hands.

She ran upstairs. The door was locked, silence inside. She hammered on the door with both fists until they hurt. Downstairs in the kitchen she found the key in a drawer.

She cursed him; she had slipped up. She hadn't intended

staying and didn't usually have to resort to old men – she was young still. The sex had been good, for a time, he had been hungry for it. Best of all she had left her job, an office drudge, although she claimed to anyone who would listen that she was a secretary to an important man.

She had cooked and cleaned and longed for the town, for people, not to be stuck out here with the forest leering at her. Her twenties would not last forever. She had called him the old man. It was not affection. She had cooked food she liked and he often hated, and bawled at him, demanding more money than he wanted to give. She played the radio loudly, music he despised.

The twins scared her. She had never wanted to be a mother. Clytemnestra was too much of a mouthful, even for the child of a god, so she called her Clemmy, called one of them Clemmy.

She did not tell the social worker about his money so the state stepped in. Vans delivered everything the twins needed, or everything the magazines insisted upon. Two cots with exquisite bedding, pink and flowery, but the twins bawled if separated. She bought pretty baby clothes and painted the walls of their room pink. No one could call her a good mother for no one ever came to the cottage with its cold stone floors.

The two drowned her with their demands. Double everything. Feeding them took hours, even when they abandoned her breasts, and the spoon flashed from mouth to mouth. Double the mess, the stinking nappies, the baths, double the guilt. At first, she was determined to be a good mother, whatever that was, waiting to be rewarded with their love. That did not come and it puzzled her. She might as well have been a robot. Their eyes turned solely to each other, turning away from her kisses.

She waited for their first steps to her, waited for them to put out their arms to her, and she called to them, 'Twins, come to Mummy.'

And they ran to the arms of each other.

She pushed the pram along the track to the bus stop and in town she paraded them. Strangers marvelled at the two, lying side by side, dressed in identical exquisite dresses, pretty socks and shoes, and the same colour bows in their hair.

'How do you tell them apart?' strangers asked, taking liberties.

'Oh, a mother knows,' she would reply, with a toss of her head, and saw that she was no longer noticed, only them.

She hated the trudge along the track in all weathers so she bought a cheap car on hire purchase. She did not like it but she felt free.

Their hair grew until two small copper plaits swung across each back. She bought two new beds, was stern, insistent, one in each bed, and in the morning, they were in one bed, arms wrapped around each other.

'Clemmy,' she said to the one with the defiant eyes, and freckles on the right cheek. They shrieked, 'Helen,' and giggled. She asked herself why they did it, refused her, confusing her deliberately with the names. I am their mother, what is wrong with them?

'Come to me, girls, a cuddle,' her voice soft, pleading. Helen and Clemmy held each other tight. Sometimes Helen started forward, a small step, and Clemmy dragged her back and they ran out of the room, laughing.

They insisted on the same clothes, ran away if she tried to dress them differently. On the sofa they sat away from her, crushed into each other, swinging their legs to the same rhythm, sighing, laughing at the same moment. And sometimes they wrestled like small boys.

They whispered secrets to each other, often not needing the spoken words.

At night, from outside their bedroom, there were giggles, then silence when she entered the room.

At first, they had shrunk away from the shrill call, 'Twins,' and then laughed at her and pretended deafness. They were fleet-footed and learnt to read her face, especially when a slap was coming.

She took them into town from time to time, for a treat, to Jack's café.

'They're special,' Jack said.

'Trouble, nothing but trouble,' and she clenched her fists.

He smiled and, with a touch of sadness in his voice, offered them their special cake, two small sponge cakes iced in pink with an outline of a girl in white.

Helen and Clemmy chorused their thanks and gave him their Jack smile.

Customers were startled, filled with wonder, some later swearing they must have been dreaming.

A week before their birthdays she took two photographs with the camera he had sent and wrote their names on the back of each. She would not use the camera again for another year.

A cheque arrived shortly afterwards.

More birthdays, more photographs. She forbade them the forest, certain that wolves roamed it. And worse.

Then she broke, hauling them apart, shoving one screamer through the door leading down steep stairs to the cellar, and dragging the other up to the bedroom, locking both doors. Singing and laughter drifted down and screams and banging roared up. She flung open the door to the cellar. Darkness. She had forgotten to switch on the light.

'Stop that noise,' and she hauled the howling girl upstairs to her twin, then returned to the kitchen, sank on a stool, put her head in her hands and sobbed.

The next day, she left the girls with Jack and returned bearing a kitten, a white, fluffy, mewling thing. She held it out to Helen, the one she believed she had shoved downstairs. 'For you, a present.'

Helen hugged the creature to her small chest while Clemmy tried to put her small arms around them both. Helen pushed her away. They stood, facing each other, pain in their faces, bewilderment and anger. Helen clutched the kitten tight. 'Mine,' she said, and her eyes shone.

Not long after, Mine disappeared. Helen bawled, Clemmy grinned, and Mother pointed to the dangerous forest, where monsters roamed its depths.

'You did it,' Helen shouted at Clemmy. 'You did it. Where is she? She was mine.' She stopped and listened to that word bounce around: mine.

Clemmy turned away.

*

25

'You start school next week, girls.' The leaves in the forest had begun to litter the track, and the cottage was cold.

'With other girls?' Clemmy screwed up her face and chewed on the skin below her left thumbnail.

'And boys. You'll like it,' Mother insisted.

'Both of us, together?' Helen said.

'Of course.'

*

'What will it be like Clem?' Helen whispered as they sat on Clemmy's bed.

'Dunno, Hel.'

'Will we like it?'

'Dunno.'

'We'll be together, won't we, Clem?'

'Of course, Hel.'

5

1979

Early morning sun sprawled itself across the chest of drawers and the wardrobe, and over the two beds that took up most of the space in the room; one crumpled, the other pristine, with two dolls, with blonde plaited hair and blue eyes, wearing the same pink dresses and pink ballet shoes, perched on its pillow. Mother had bought them many toys: teddies, rabbits, bears, but all, except the two dolls in pink, were thrown into the bin or torn to pieces.

Piles of clothes littered the floor.

The two stood, hand in hand, dressed for school in yellow dresses, black shoes and white socks, and yellow ribbons on each plait. Fair-skinned, their faces were small and hopeful, with wide-set green eyes, high cheekbones and full lips, tall and long-legged, and set to grow and blossom.

They knew little of people or towns, which mattered not to them.

Mother ran to them and pulled them into her arms. 'You are my two little girls.'

They wriggled free, giggling.

She went with them that first day, offering a hand to each, but they screwed up their small matching faces and ran ahead. On the bus they sat, bodies bound together. With wide, wet eyes, Helen stared out of the window as they wound around the streets, stopping frequently to let children and mothers on and Clemmy studied the other children while her feet jiggled and swung.

The bus was almost full when it finally stopped outside a large building with children running around an asphalt playground.

Clemmy turned to Helen, grinned, slid off her seat and, pulling Helen after her, ran to the front and jumped down from the bus – the first ones out.

'A small school,' Mother had told them.

'It's big,' Helen whispered, perhaps to herself.

Clemmy gazed around at children and mothers, huddled together on the pavement, waiting. She pointed to the far end of the playground, to strange lines and a tall pole and board with a ring and netting. She imagined throwing a ball through the ring.

They stood, hand in hand, a little apart from the others, breathing hard, trembling with excitement and fear.

Children clung to their mothers, others ran, shouting and whooping, into the playground. More hurried to join the crowd and the noise ratcheted up. Helen held Clemmy's hand tight, and both hopped from foot to foot.

A bell rang and a tall woman strode towards them. 'Miss Bailey,' she said to Mother, stopping a few feet away. 'I believe you are Mrs Richards and these two are…'

'Clytemnestra and Helen,' Mother said, too loudly, redness covering her neck.

'Clemmy,' Clemmy muttered, 'and this is Helen.'

Miss Bailey offered a tight smile.

Some children stopped talking and watched, giggling and pointing.

'Clemmy it is,' Miss Bailey said. 'And Helen.'

Helen examined her shoes.

'Come along now,' and Miss Bailey moved Helen and Clemmy, so that one was either side of her and they could no longer hold hands. 'Say goodbye to Mummy.'

They sniggered at that word and did not turn around.

Clemmy ran to the other side of Miss Bailey to take Helen's hand.

In the classroom, they ran to the back.

Their desks nudged each other, their pencil boxes matched, as did the ribbons in their hair and everything else.

When asked a question in class, either one answered.

'Clemmy,' the teacher said. 'Can you tell me…'

'Yes, Miss,' Helen answered.

'Weird' was the word they heard most often. Clemmy liked weird, Helen hated it. Some laughed, pointing and gawping, others wanted to be friends. Mostly they were just called twin. They did each other's homework and Clemmy took care to copy Helen's writing, so they got the same marks.

'Strange,' Miss Bailey said. 'I don't suppose you copy each other's work.'

Clemmy rolled her eyes, smirked behind her hand, Helen dropped her head, and the rest of the class laughed.

Miss Bailey gave them separate projects. Helen helped Clemmy but the grades began to change.

Some fought to be with Clemmy, the noisy one, to be best friends. Clemmy swore to them they were the only one.

Helen, standing a little apart, watched her wave her hands, heard the laugh, not the real one. Neither needed a best friend.

They continued to grow taller than their peers, learnt to read, and brought books home, Clemmy clutching adventure stories and Helen fairy tales of woods and forests, wild creatures and witches.

The other children talked endlessly about their favourite television programmes so they demanded a television. 'Makes us look stupid,' Clemmy shouted at Mother. 'Everyone else has one.' And Helen pleaded, 'Please, please.'

'We can't afford it,' Mother said, yet again.

The twins were sick of her saying that about everything, but they did not give up so she bought one on hire purchase, the biggest in the nearby town's shop.

A van pulled up outside the cottage, and a man got out.

'Too tall,' he pointed to the surrounding treetops. 'No signal,' and did not unpack the van.

'I'm sorry, girls,' Mother said, regret in her voice. 'It won't work. It's this awful forest.' She stamped her foot, and Helen and Clemmy clutched each other and ran to their rooms crying and shouting, 'It's not fair.'

At school the chatter about *Animal Magic* on television was endless so Helen pretended it was her favourite programme too. Clemmy saw herself as a swashbuckling pirate, convincing herself and the others.

Mother overheard the girls talking about the shows and hurried to the bookstore where she found *Animal Magic*, and *Mr Men*.

Then *Wind in the Willows*. Mole, Ratty and Mr Badger, Helen loved them all. Clemmy sneered at her when Helen, face full of excitement, told her the story. 'You would like it,' Clemmy scoffed. 'Woods and all those silly animals.'

*

Clemmy invited boys to the bushes behind the bicycle shed. They came, ten-pence pieces in their sweaty, grubby hands.

Helen watched them disappear round the shed, saw their excitement, heard Clemmy's quiet laughter as she turned back to her, finger to her lips.

Clemmy lay down on some rough grass, pulled up her skirt and dragged down her knickers. Four small heads peered, their faces moving closer, their laughter loud.

'No touching,' she hissed, clutching in her closed fist four ten-pence pieces.

They drew back.

She closed her legs, pulled down her skirt.

When Clemmy returned she slipped two ten-pence pieces into Helen's hand.

'What are you doing? Can I do it?'

Clemmy giggled, 'I don't think you would like it.'

*

'Hey, Twin.'

Helen, red pencil in hand, pad on her knee, sitting on the corridor floor, drawing, waiting for Clemmy's detention to end, saw a round-faced girl with soft, happy eyes.

'You're Helen, aren't you?' and the girl lowered herself to sit, with a thump, beside Helen. 'Thought you were,' she breathed hard. 'Waiting for Clemmy? I'm Abby.' She wriggled on the hard floor. 'Bet you're sick of it.'

'What?'

'The twin thing. I'm an only one. My mum, dad and me.'

It was the word 'dad' that hit Helen, in a wave of shame and loss.

The door to the classroom was flung open and Clemmy flounced out, saw Abby and ran down the corridor.

Helen scrambled to her feet and Abby got onto her knees. 'Don't go,' she called after her. 'Let's be friends.'

When Helen reached the school gate, Clemmy was not there.

*

At break next day, Abby took four biscuits from her lunch box and handed two to Helen. 'Mum made these, she's great at baking.'

The love in Abby's voice flooded Helen.

'We bake at weekends. You can come over if you like, Mum will teach you. What about your mum?'

'She doesn't cook much.' Helen flushed and promised to go to Abby's next Saturday.

On the other side of the playground, Clemmy watched.

Back in the classroom, a large sheet of paper was stuck on the classroom door and on it in red capital letters: 'Fatty Abby.'

*

'We waited for you, me and my mum. You never came.' Abby's round face was screwed up, flesh almost covering her eyes. 'We were going to bake a cake.'

'Sorry.' Helen bit her bottom lip, looked away.

'It's that sister of yours, isn't it? Wouldn't she let you?'

Helen flushed, put her hand over her mouth and fled.

Clemmy was not home and Helen's whole body still trembled with Abby's scorn. She stood on the track, peering into the trees and along a narrow, overgrown path. Perhaps she'd find Mine and bring him home. She shivered, recalling her only time in the forest. Not long ago.

*

They were running into the trees, into the dark recess, in their best dresses, black shoes and white socks up to their knees, their plaits swinging, their laughter and shrieks glancing off the branches of the trees.

Mother had forbidden them the forest, warned them of evil spirits.

Helen and Clemmy's hands parted and they raced, in opposite directions, Clemmy to hide, Helen to wait and count, hands over her eyes.

Clemmy ran, and ran faster. Helen would never find her.

The trees towered above her, the brambles tore her and her best dress. She spun round and round. It was all the same, trees imprisoning her. She screamed, 'Helen, I hate you,' and fell into the silence, the brambles tightening around her neck. Darkness loitered and, in the shadows, large, menacing giants.

Much later Helen found her and laughed. 'Coward,' she'd jeered, as Clemmy screamed, 'I'm never coming here again.'

*

Helen took a few steps along the path, forcing her way through brambles and bushes, her heart beating too fast and her head now filled with Mother's stories of the creatures that lived in the forest, that might hurt her, kill her even. She would tell Clemmy later. And Abby. That would show them. She hadn't changed her shoes, and they were already dirty. Mother would know. She bit her lip.

Shadows moved among the trees and loud noises frightened her. She saw birds high up, silent, watching her. She stopped in front of the biggest tree she had ever seen, an oak. It was hundreds of years old, she was sure, and had a deep cut at the height of her head. She dug her fingernails into the cracks in the trunk, picked at the moss and gazed high up, trying to find its top, then snuggled at its foot among its roots, frightened to go deeper into the black recesses.

She stood and followed the dark path a little further, caressing the buds along the sides of the path, gently, so as not to damage their growth.

Clemmy had never been this brave and Helen smiled. Hearing birdsong really close, she looked up. It was a small and beautiful creature singing just for her. She promised she would come back soon.

Back home, the cottage was empty and she cleaned her shoes of the mud.

'There are lions and tigers in our forest,' she told any at school who would listen as she imagined the big cats licking her face with their rough tongues.

'Don't believe you,' they chorused.

No one came to their cottage. Helen's only friends, the animals, lingered in her head. She drew the lions and tigers with her coloured pencils – sheets and sheets of them – and hid them away.

She asked Mother for some paints.

'No. You'll make mess all over the place,' Mother said. 'We can't afford it. They'll be expensive.'

She tiptoed into the forest, early mornings, before Mother and Clemmy were awake, each time going in a little further, lingering, believing this was her special place. Only hers. She was happiest in spring and the melancholy of winter made her uneasy so she stayed away from its deep, dark heart. Sometimes, in late summer nights, she disentangled herself from Clemmy's arms and crept out of the house to stand in the blackness, perforated only by stars, her stars.

The forest was her secret.

6

1984

'You decide.' Mother examined them, as if for the first time. They had turned nine a week ago. She banged down one plate of spaghetti in front of Clemmy. She was sick of them thinking they could fool her. Especially Clemmy. She would stop their game.

The two sat side by side, their long copper hair in neat plaits, their green eyes indecipherable, their full lips tightly closed.

Clemmy shoved a spoonful in her mouth, then divided the pasta in two, leaving a clean line down the middle of the plate. She pushed it over so it sat between them.

'One of you is going to have your hair cut. You decide.'

'No,' they screamed in unison and clung to each other. Clemmy shoved the plate across the table and both watched it slide onto the floor and the spaghetti spread, then pulled their plaits over their shoulders and held them tight. Helen put the end of one into her mouth and sucked it.

'Stop that,' Mother snapped at Helen. 'A hairdresser in

town.' She clenched both fists tight, her long nails biting into her flesh.

'We won't go,' Clemmy shouted, and dragged Helen off her stool. Hand in hand they ran up the stairs.

*

Mother pulled the two through the door of the small salon at the end of the high street.

A woman walked toward them, a big smile on her lightly freckled, small face. 'Hello girls. Which one of you is getting into that big chair over there?' Her voice was soft, friendly.

Helen's grip on Clemmy's hand tightened.

'Me,' Clemmy said.

'Are you Helen or Clemmy? Lovely girls, I've seen you running past.'

'Clemmy.' She wanted to touch the woman's hair to see if it was real. She couldn't suppress a small snigger and Mother raised one hand.

'I'm Sally.' She turned to Helen. 'Would you like to sit next to your sister?'

Helen nodded.

Sally pulled over a small stool.

'Are you sure?' Sally held a bunch of Clemmy's hair in her hands as she turned to Mother. She had undone the plaits and brushed out the hair. Light flickered in its wavy copper-gold.

Mother, tight-lipped, nodded.

Clemmy sat utterly still, except for the finger of her right hand picking at the skin below her left thumb, her chin raised.

Helen sat, stiff, tearful, clutching her two plaits.

Mother stood near the door as if to block escape, spots of blood on the palms of her hands.

Clemmy began to hum, tunelessly, blurring the sound of the snipping scissors, watching the waft of copper hair floating to the floor.

'Lovely hair,' Sally said.

*

Mother sent them to bed, glancing briefly, with an inward sigh, at Clemmy's cropped hair. Occasionally she had dressed Helen and Clemmy in their best clothes, sometimes in her own dresses and gave them her handbags to carry, put make-up on their faces, and hats on their heads and bundled them into her car and paraded them down the street, arm in arm, herself in the middle. The girls sulked and onlookers stared and laughed. Some, always women, turned away.

Those days were done. She no longer paraded them in town, where she'd looked a dummy, and strangers had ooh-ed and aah-ed over the girls only. She was a good-looking woman, if a little on the plump side, yet no man seemed to want her now, and she might as well have not existed as far as the twins were concerned. She would like to take back these last nine years of her life.

*

Helen waited until the house was in total darkness and silence, then led Clemmy downstairs to the kitchen, holding her hand, shushing her protests. Shutting the door quietly,

Helen switched on the light and found the scissors in the drawer. She held them out to Clemmy.

'Short, Clem,' she whispered and tears found paths down her cheeks. Later she ran her hand through what was left, then took the scissors and snipped and snipped.

Before creeping back upstairs, Clemmy scooped up a thick lock of Helen's hair from the floor and folded it into her fist.

In bed they wrapped their arms around each other, their shorn heads feeling strange.

The children cheered when Helen and Clemmy returned to school with their hacked hair.

'We did it,' Clemmy said and their status rose.

Mother found hair spread across the kitchen floor, and slumped in a chair, leant her elbows on the table, dropped her head and wept.

She had been willing to give them everything. Well, almost. She couldn't take it, their meanness and, worse, their indifference to her. She had tried. She had failed.

7

1986

The blackbird's song was mellow. 'Shut up,' Mother shouted to the sky, for she could not see it perched on the chimney pot.

'What are you two doing up there?' She could not miss the sound of their feet running across the floor of her bedroom. She crushed her anger. 'Come down. I have a surprise for you.' After a few minutes, she shouted again, excitement in her voice. 'Twins.' She was not demanding love – knew the pointlessness of that.

They descended the stairs slowly, hand in hand.

'I'll teach you to play my piano. You'll like that.'

They turned to go back up the stairs.

'Here you are,' she said, dragging the cover off the piano. Many times she had forbidden them to touch it. She ran her fingers, a little clumsily, over the keys, then sat on the piano stool and began to play.

Helen and Clemmy put their hands over their ears and screamed.

Soon afterwards the piano disappeared.

Jack gave her a job at the café. When she heard customers murmuring 'Beauty and the beast,' she laughed and put her arm around him for he paid her well. She was out of that house at last. The girls now left early and returned late afternoon from a high school the other side of town.

The annual cheques continued to arrive, the sum each year a little larger than the previous one. The twins were a disappointment so she gave up trying, the little devils.

She had loved their father once, well, she must have done. Perhaps that was the story hindsight told her. And she had hated him for abandoning her with those two, but now she had found life at the café. People talked to her, complimented her and she laughed, startled at first by its sound. And she changed the colour of her hair: blonde, black, red or a mixture.

The two fascinated Jack. They switched their necklaces with quick, practised fingers and he let them believe. He watched them taunt their mother, and trick strangers. One chewed her thumb when angry or sad, and tossed her head so her hair flew as she opened her eyes wide. It was the eyes that revealed most, the pretence, and he heard the other quietly call her Clem. The other's eyes were often dreamy. He suggested Mother bring them in more often and they ran to him, calling him Uncle Jack. He laughed and held them against his belly and gave them all the cakes and hot chocolate they wanted.

Then he had to cut some of Mother's hours. 'There's no money out there. It's her, she's killing us in the north. "No such thing as society." Easy for her to say.'

Mother had loved the Iron Lady.

41

Often, she came home smelling strange to the girls, or stayed out late. They did not need her and life was not what it should be, and she was getting fat.

One evening the twins came to the table bare-breasted, their thin bodies, their taut young breasts mocking her.

Mother fought back, tearing off her pretty blouse and her capacious bra, letting her tits flop, almost onto the table.

Their chairs crashed backwards onto the floor as they fled.

8

June 1988

They stood naked, side by side in front of the mirror, large green eyes examining themselves, or was it the other? Perfection of nose and cheek, and full lips. The face of Helen of myth although they knew nothing of that. A symmetry of cheek freckles, and shoulder kisses. Each ran a hand down the other's body, over soft, smooth skin, from the shoulder, over the incipient breasts, over the waist and down the hips. Hands paused, above the thighs, and they giggled. Their legs long and slim.

In a few days they would be fourteen.

There was no sound from Mother's room. They ate jam on toast, packed biscuits for lunch, and left for their big school on the other side of town.

They walked the lane, hand in hand, sometimes chatting but mostly quiet and content, breathing as one. Helen walked with her eyes a little down or wandering into the forest, her free arm swinging gently. Clemmy's heels punished the track, the surface of anything she walked on.

Their desks were no longer jammed together but side by side, a small distance separating them. The teachers had insisted. They did the same classes, sat together for lunch. Sometimes Clemmy broke away, responding to the demands of one of her so-called friends. She was good at pretending so she gave them someone as changeable as the sky and liked it that way, playing with them. She was sometimes as splendid and opaque as the blossom trees on the edge of the school yard, at other times, the leafless winter trees. She laughed in the playground, boisterously, and some laughed with her but the uncertainty in their eyes told that they did not understand what they were laughing at.

Helen didn't laugh. Clemmy did not expect it.

In class Clemmy sat quiet and sullen, rolling her eyes from time to time, her thumb to her mouth, dreaming of the day when the two would escape, across the ocean, away from the forest. She had a good memory and usually got by with exams. 'Why bother?' she told herself if she didn't.

Her first lie had been accidental, sort of. Few kids believed, yet admired her skill, so it became a game. She told them she lived in a tree house, that their mother was a witch and their father was rich but absent. One day he would return and they would have everything they wanted. She flung her hands about in front of her, a windmill gone crazy. They had nothing better to do so hung about for more.

They turned to Helen, who stood nearby, listening. She said nothing.

'So when is he coming home, this rich guy?' Ellen said, the one who always sneered at Clemmy's stories.

'Soon.'

'What did he do? Steal his money?' She grinned.

'He's a painter,' Helen butted in. 'He's famous.'

Ellen swung around and stared at her. 'So she talks after all.'

Clemmy stepped closer to Helen.

*

'He's famous,' Mother had told them a few years back when she had heard the banging and found them trying to get into that room. She had found the key in the drawer and hidden it where they would never find it. 'There's nothing up there, it's just a room. The key's lost. Forget it.'

'Then we can have it, it would be great up there.' Clemmy's feet jiggled. Twice they had climbed the trees trying to peer into the windows. And failed.

'When is he coming back?' Helen said.

'He's not.'

'Why, why?' Helen almost cried.

'He ran when you were born. Didn't have time for you.'

'I don't believe you; you're lying.' Helen stepped back, a hand over her mouth.

'What's up there?' Clemmy's chin stuck out and her arm was wrapped around Helen.

'Nothing now. He painted, all day, that's what he did up there.'

'If he's famous, why aren't we rich?' Clemmy waved her hands.

'Stop doing that.'

Clemmy's flung her arms and hands even more wildly. 'Why?'

Mother laughed, 'You might ask that.'

'Where is he, where is he?' Helen stepped close to Mother, trembling a little.

'Somewhere way north. He won't want to see you.'

'We don't want him.' Clemmy ran from the room.

Helen stayed, eyes pleading.

*

The north. Helen had read about the mountains and the wild seas. She dreamt about him: a youngish man, tall and beautiful, wearing bright, smart clothes.

Clemmy told her she was daft when she recounted the dream. 'We don't need him. We've got each other. I don't want to talk about him ever again.'

Was he up there, painting, hiding? Helen had to find a way in. At school Miss Wood praised her drawings and her paintings, told her she was exceptional. She would be a painter too, perhaps famous.

*

'Come on then.' Clemmy was longing to do anything but hang about for Mother. 'It's got to be somewhere. We can have fun up there.' They slung their school bags down in the hall in the late afternoon and threw off their blazers.

Clemmy pulled Helen up the stairs and along the passage to their mother's bedroom where they went often, to examine her dresses, riffle her underwear drawer, try on her make-up. Clemmy stood still, in the middle of the room, staring around. They had searched through most of the drawers and cupboards at one time or another, in here and in the kitchen.

Helen bit her lip.

'Ah,' Clemmy murmured and walked to the windowsill. She picked up an ugly blue vase that had never been bedecked with flowers and turned it upside down. A clatter of metal on pot and a key hit the carpet. She threw the vase to the floor. It cracked, then shattered.

Helen dived for the key, was first up the stairs to the secret room above. The lock was stiff. It surrendered; she pushed on the door, took a step back, almost treading on Clemmy.

'It stinks.'

'Hurry up.' Clemmy nudged her, trying to squeeze past.

Helen took two steps in, Clemmy's hand on her back pushing, and stopped. Loose sheets of paper were scattered over the paint-splattered floor, an ashtray replete with stubs, half-used tubes of paint and a piece of cloth with a little liquid at the bottom of the jar sat on the table beside an easel. Miss Wood in art class had an easel like that.

Helen's quick steps carried her to it, some ten feet. She stretched out a hand, her fingers stopping short of the canvas.

A man, head and shoulders, bearded, long, dark hair and brown eyes.

From the table, she picked up the palette and inserted her thumb through its hole the way Miss Wood did, then noticed three grimy tubes near where the palette had been. She picked one up, took off its cap and squeezed it hard. Nothing happened. She squeezed again. A bright red bubble on the tip of her finger. She sniffed it and her joy almost frightened her. She scratched at the small hillocks of paint on the palette. They were hard. She turned slightly. There was a bare canvas leaning against the easel leg. She picked it up, breathing hard, and placed it back down. She would be a painter, famous even, just like him.

'It must be him.' Helen grabbed Clemmy's hand. 'We'll find Daddy.'

'Says who? You're mad.' She pulled her hand away. 'If he is our father, he didn't hang around, did he? Why should we care about him? Anyway, he's probably dead.' She laughed, a thin derisive sound. 'It could be anyone. Whoever it is, I don't like him – he's a tramp.'

'It's him, it's Daddy.' Helen's face was almost touching the painting.

'Not my Daddy.' Clemmy strode over to the windows, kicking papers on the floor.

Helen stepped closer to the easel and pulled off a piece of paper that was attached to one leg. '*For my beauties,*' she read out loud, separating each word, then gazed back at the face in front of her, wanting his arms around her. She'd never wanted anyone's except Clemmy's. 'His beauties.'

'And you believe him. He left us.'

'She lied to us, he loved us.' Helen shouted across the room, waving the piece of paper.

Clemmy strode back. 'Give it here.' Clemmy's hand shot out.

'No.' Helen carefully folded the note and placed it in her pocket. He loved them, she was as certain as if he'd spoken the words to her.

Then she noticed a painting leaning against the easel's legs: a pond with a small stone pier, reeds, trees and a shadow of a man. 'Daddy.' She reached out again. Why had he left them? She had a father. Her eyes filled and she gave him her best smile. She would tell everyone at school.

She shook her head, a very small movement and smiled. Perhaps she would find him one day or he would come back to them. She examined the man in front of her and laughed out loud to see his dark hair down to his shoulders. 'Daddy.'

'Your father.'

Their mother's voice from the doorway startled them both. She was still in her outdoor coat with her handbag hanging over her arm.

'So you found it, the key, clever girls.' Her lips curled. 'Well, he left it in a mess, he was like that, didn't care. I got sick of cleaning up after him everywhere else in the house. He never would let me in here, said it was private.' She took a few steps into the room. 'It can stay like this. I'm not cleaning it after all these years.'

She looked into the eyes of the man she had first met about seventeen years back. He might have loved her but he was already betrothed.

'I'll clean it, I'll clean it.' Helen squatted to pick up paper off the floor.

'Time for tea,' Mother said, carefully placing one foot on the first step and carrying on down.

Clemmy stood, a second or two, then crossed the room and followed her, shouting back at Helen, 'I hate it up here. It's disgusting and I hate him. You can have him.'

Helen scrabbled in her pocket for the piece of paper, stood a few moments, then crept down the stairs, grabbing her coat and running out the back door, into the forest in the bright June evening.

Brambles bloodied her and the undergrowth wrapped her in a tight embrace. She scrambled past her oak, then crawled on her knees, bumping into trees until she fell onto the skinny path, stood, ignoring the blood and scratches, and ran on. He would be there, he'd left her a message.

A glint of water: dark, tranquil. She dipped her hands in the water, then picked her way round its edge. At the far end a stream gently trickled down a steep valley, through tree roots and over a tumble of rocks easing into the pond, barely nudging it into small ripples.

A crow cawed, a fox barked and scuttled from the pond's edge and a pheasant screeched and flew over her head, heavy, close. She wrapped her arms around herself, sat on the stone pier and wept. He was not there. 'Crybaby,' she hissed.

The fox crept out as the light was fading and sprawled himself on the opposite bank. He smiled at her, and the pheasant, a few yards away, nodded, flapping admiration for the newcomer. The crow chuckled.

She searched the trees around.

This was his pond, she was certain. She waited, starting at the sounds around, trembling. Hours passed. Years, perhaps. Darkness fell, a glint of moonlight, then the stars. She grew colder, wrapping her coat tight around her. He would come, would show her how to paint, give her an easel just like his.

A baby rabbit lolloped along the edge of the pond and Helen fell asleep and dreamt she held it in her arms, and her long, soft hair, occasionally lit by the last shafts of sunlight cunning enough to find their way through the summer foliage, nestled on her shoulders and green cardigan.

*

'She'll be back,' Mother said, and not much later Clemmy heard her mother's whisky-laden snores echoing around the room.

She found the bottle, took a mouthful, spat into the sink and poured the rest away, watching it gurgle down the plughole.

She climbed the stairs in the half-light to the room at the top and stood in front of him.

'Fa-th-er,' she sniggered, stringing out the letters. He looked stupid with that beard and hair. Perhaps he wasn't their father. She scowled, stepped closer, raised a fist towards the canvas, close, then Helen's voice, one word, filling her head. 'Daddy'. Well, she didn't want him. She lowered her fist. He'd never loved them.

She looked around the room, one last time. She would not be coming up here again.

She picked at the skin of her left thumb, before searching for her handkerchief.

Early next morning Clemmy rang the police and Mother snatched the receiver from her just as Clemmy was explaining to a kind man at the other end that Helen had disappeared.

'A pond in the forest,' Clemmy said to the tall policeman standing in the kitchen. 'That's where she is.'

Mother sighed.

'Come, I'll show you.' Clemmy ran out of the room. The policeman stood a moment then followed her up the stairs.

In the room at the top, Clemmy pointed to the picture of the pond. 'That's where she is.'

'God knows where it is, in the forest somewhere.' Mother was out of breath.

The policeman rubbed his chin. He had already asked about the child's father. 'Do you know it?'

Clemmy shook her head and her plaits flew around in front of her face.

'I might,' he said, after a long silence.

'Can I come?' Clemmy asked.

'No,' Mother said.

Clemmy tugged at the man's jacket.

'Sorry, love.'

She tumbled down the stairs, into her room and crawled into bed.

*

'Wake up, love,' the policeman said, and bent to gently shake Helen awake.

Helen opened her eyes, took deep breaths. It was not the man with the long dark hair in the portrait. She scrambled to her feet.

'It's alright, love, you must be cold.' He took off his jacket and placed it over her shoulders. It reached close to her knees. He led her back along the path.

9

Eleanor Wood strode around the school grounds, corridors and classrooms, in long floral skirts, smart boots, plain blouses, and cardigans, if the weather was cold.

She loved the children and they mostly loved her back, doing their best for her with their paints and pencils. Clemmy called her Shorty for she was taller than her. Eleanor accepted that Clemmy was one of the few who did not like her, or like the way Helen was praised for her work.

Miss Wood's classes were noisy, for she did not mind the chatter, indeed, it cheered her.

She gave of her time when requested, and most days was one of the last teachers to leave, getting into her small, fast car with a smile in her eyes.

At thirty Eleanor Wood sometimes pondered on what she had missed out on. Time enough. For what? Children? Doubtful. A man? Also doubtful. She was difficult to please. There had been gentleman friends. She liked those two words and she had stood as tall as she could, borne the kisses, thrown her head back and adopted a romantic posture, her hair loose, her body trembling, but had not liked it when they touched her in places she considered private.

Eleanor lived for great literature, words from another time, a gentler time, and great art, and, from a young age, had believed she was destined to be an artist, something her mother encouraged. She would exhibit in London's best galleries, perhaps New York, had talent, real talent. She tapped each finger of her right hand, starting with the forefinger, against the palm of her left hand, as if counting. But... she had a mother to support, a mother who needed her, lived for her – as her mother told her too frequently, in their house on the other side of the forest. Eleanor brought her to the school on special occasions.

With good A levels she had been accepted into two well-known art schools, but had gone instead to teacher training college, safe and respectable, her mother proud of her. London galleries were never mentioned and the school holidays were spent at home, despite the stack of brochures in the drawer of her bedside table. (She took care that mother did not find them.) She lay in bed with her imagination and brochures for company, reading them closely, sometimes believing she had taken the holiday (escaped, not that she dared to use that word), revelled in the hot sun of Italy and Greece, and strolled through the Musée d'Orsay in Paris and the Doge's Palace in Venice. Number one on her list, (she liked making lists), was St Petersburg. The Soviet regime had crashed and Boris Yeltsin was in charge. Perhaps Moscow too, with all those glorious buildings that she'd seen on TV.

It took some years for Eleanor to abandon her dreams of greatness and her travels.

She had the children in the classroom, and she loved them, perhaps more than she should. Most of them were not the least bit interested in great artists or in their own messy imitations, yet she tried to make it fun for them. With each new intake there was usually the one, rarely more than one. Helen was the one and Eleanor noted her burgeoning talent early, although the girl was overly diffident and shy so her work suffered. The girl had spoken to her, in their first class, excitement making her voice tremble. 'I'm Helen,' she'd said, while the other had scowled and walked away. Eleanor had no trouble telling them apart.

'Daddy left us two paintings,' Helen told Miss Wood, excitement bubbling its way through her words. She loved to say that word, 'Daddy,' out loud, said it in the forest often, talking to him, telling him about her day. She had hung around in the classroom until all the others had packed up their paints and mess and left.

She breathed in so deeply that she had to hold the edge of the desk. 'I am going to be a painter like him. He left us when we were babies and I've found his studio with a portrait of himself and a note.' Her voice unusually loud and excited.

'It's like yours, the painting you showed us, Miss.' Helen paused for breath. 'I want to paint like that. Can I?' She looked away, biting her lip. Then back. 'Will you help me?' The shy voice had returned, her voice was barely audible. 'He called us his beauties.'

'And so you are, and your work shows great promise.' Already the girl's work was way beyond that of anyone else in the class and she had never mentioned a father. Eleanor wanted to stretch out her hand and touch the shy, eager face.

Her painting was remarkable, even with the rudimentary paints they used in the classroom. She had to do something for her.

10

Day after day Helen returned to the pond, sitting on the stones, dangling her feet in the water and giggling as the small fish nibbled them with their soft mouths. Overhead, big black birds cawed.

Beeches dipped their branches into the dark, still water – supplicants; a wren and a pair of blue tits flew in and out of the bushes, and a male pheasant squawked and flapped, ungainly, from the water's edge. Trees preened across the flat surface: trunks, branches, foliage, a sheet of music, each note distinct on the water's surface. Boles encrusted with ivy or lichen and green algae littered the shallow edges of the water. A mallard clambered out to peck at the grass nearby; another dozed in the water, his head tucked into his feathers. Silver birch stood proud on one edge, and in the middle a small island, covered with dense bushes and rhododendron.

The birdsong was muted.

She sat, dreaming, planning, hesitating, then wandered back along the path and sank into her seat in her giant oak's generous roots, leaning back against its trunk in the speckled shade, gazing up at its high green crown. She had once brought her mother's tape measure, tried to measure its girth, and failed. The boughs creaked, rubbing against each other in the chattering wind, and the rust-red and grey chaffinches flew around her. She picked at the lichen on the trunks with her slender fingers.

The forest was hers, no one else's. Clemmy hated it, was somewhere away from the forest, on her bike. She had never liked the forest, not since that time she was lost. Mother didn't like it either, but that didn't matter.

They had shared everything, she and Clemmy, always, just them. Until now. Mention Father and Clemmy's eyes flashed, her fists curled.

Helen bit her lip, wiped her eyes. Clemmy was her life, nothing could change that. She leant forward and clasped her hands around her knees. 'Clemmy, Clemmy.' Her words were soft and replete with love.

Much later, she stood and laughed to see her heart flip-flop along the forest path in front of her.

'Wait for me,' she shouted.

The summer was ending and the acorns began to plummet down to the carpet of earth below. The swallows had fled the autumn's chill and spiderwebs glistened in the early morning frost. The robin would still be somewhere around the pond; he would not desert her. Wind teased its surface, making an old woman of it. It was female, surely, with everything it nurtured beneath its surface. The trees waved, rustled, and twigs fell; leaves floated, rocking with the caressing wind or drowning deep. Water half in shadow, the light of the sun as it climbed forcing the shadow to retreat. The blackberries had ripened and Helen carried home bagfuls for Clemmy.

Then, one day, she abandoned her oak and the pond and climbed the stairs to the studio, carrying pebbles from the water's shallow edges in her pockets. She arranged them on the windowsill, then was disappointed when, on drying, they lost their lustre. She got out her paints and gave each stone its own small forest creature: rabbit, fox, bird, duck.

She had cleaned the studio thoroughly weeks back, locked the door and pocketed the key, just like him, then unlocked it. Clemmy had vowed she would never come up.

She pressed her nose against the glass, turned and walked back to the easel, a small step at a time. Then to the window again, biting her bottom lip.

At the easel, she tied back her hair with a rubber band and leant forward to examine the portrait, trying to read the signature. She could make out David but not much else. She said the name over and over, her voice soft and loving.

Mother had refused to tell them his name. 'Not important,' she'd said with a toss of her head. 'And why do you want to know? He ran when he saw you both.'

After many minutes Helen, carried the portrait from the easel and leant it against the wall, replacing it with a sheet of paper from the pad he had left behind. Pots of paint on the table and beside her, the drawing she had made of the pond.

'No, not that colour for the water.' Her father pointed to another colour and holding her hand in his own, dipped the brush into the paint.

'What do you think? More white?' he said.

She had paint under her nails and on her hands. Excitement, joy. And failure.

She scoured the library for books on painting. The librarian, a kindly, grey-haired woman, enjoyed her enthusiasm and ordered in books for her.

Time stolen from Clemmy.

And when the next school year started, Miss Wood, in their first art class, led Helen to a small easel and placed some tubes of paints and brushes on the desk beside it.

'See how you get on,' she said, and walked to the front of the room.

The other students swung around to stare at Helen, so she shrank down, trying to hide. Clemmy was no longer in the class.

*

Last term, Clemmy had shouted at Miss Wood, 'I hate it,' pointing at the paintings around the room, and the concentrated faces of the other students, avoiding Helen's stricken eyes. She had thrown down her brush, splashing paint over herself, Miss Wood, and some of the desks and other students. All movement in the classroom stopped and silence took over except for a couple of sniggers.

'Then perhaps this class is not for you, Clemmy.'

'Teacher's pet,' Clemmy spat at Helen and ran from the room.

Helen's lips had trembled and her eyes had filled.

11

'I hate him,' Clemmy said, 'he didn't want us.' Her eyes brightened. 'Perhaps he wasn't our father anyway.' Her legs jiggled. They were sitting side by side on the old sofa. Helen had been painting when Clemmy barged in and Helen had immediately put down her brush.

Helen stared at her. 'He talks to me.' She never stopped, trying to work out where he was, why he had left them, when he might come back for them.

'Talks,' Clemmy snorted. He didn't talk to Clemmy, and she hated it up here. The forest was trying to break in through the windows; it followed her everywhere. Clemmy's scorn came out as a high-pitched squeak, 'You're barmy.'

'He tells me how to paint.'

Clemmy stood and thumped down the stairs and out the back door to where her bike was leaning against the front fence. Mother had bought them second-hand, one bright yellow, the other red. Clemmy had tied two red ribbons to her handlebars. As she rode towards the town, she used one hand to wipe her eyes.

At school she now kept apart from her usual crowd, wandering to the far, empty spaces of the grounds. No one seemed much interested in her now. Helen followed her, but was rewarded with a sharp, 'Go away.' At home Helen was always upstairs pretending to be him, so Clemmy played loud music or left on her bike when Mother objected. And never mentioned him.

They didn't even know his name and he was supposed to be their father. Yesterday Helen had been called 'special' by the Head in assembly, told to stand up in front of the whole school. She had blushed furiously and stared down at her feet as the Head gave her a prize for painting; a rising star, she had called her, said the school was proud of her. Everyone clapped and Clemmy made her hands clap louder than anyone else, while something inside her was breaking.

The days were too long and she hated the radio, books (not that she was much of a reader), Mother, and now Helen; and even her bike with its two red ribbons.

Who was she? Not that she'd ever given much thought to questions like that. Pointless, like everything else. School was no longer fun, her teachers were horrible, and Helen called him Daddy all the time. Some of his money would be good.

Helen had abandoned her for him, had abandoned their lives together.

So Clemmy bunked off from school and went to Jack's when her mother was not there, stuffing her school blazer into her bag and putting on her bright red jacket.

Jack welcomed her, but his voice was uncertain. 'No school today? Problems?'

'The usual,' and Clemmy shrugged away his question.

'Not a good idea to bunk off too much. Come on, treats. Where's Helen?'

'At school, or up there painting, that's all she cares about now.'

He placed her favourite cake on a plate, poured Coke into a glass and led her to a table away from the few customers.

'I knew him, your father, not well. He was a bit of a loner but lived for his painting. David someone, he never told us the rest. He was like that.'

'Don't talk about him.' Clemmy put her head down and shovelled up her cake. She couldn't paint, didn't want to, couldn't understand why Helen spent all her time messing about up there. They had once been two poppies: tall, bright red and beautiful. No longer. They had done everything together, always. Now she was ugly. Alone. She had to find something, something big, special, just for her.

She knocked the tumbler to the floor, got to her knees to touch the shards of glass, watching her fingers bleed, small red circles, so she pressed harder, into the pain. Blood the colour of poppies.

Jack knelt and put his arm around her.

It was autumn and time for the school play, *Sleeping Beauty*. Clemmy sloughed off her anger and sadness. She boasted that she would be the star, the princess. All the bells in the land would toll at the news of her birth and she would feel the prick to her finger sixteen years later just as the fairy Maleficent, the mistress of all evil, had predicted. Clemmy sat, chin up, picking at her left thumb as they all waited. She had to be the princess. She could be anyone she wanted to be.

The other students had laughed when she was given the

role of Maleficent. After some long, tearful days she decided it would be fun, better even than being the princess. Helen helped her learn the lines, and Clemmy practised them, over and over. Someone in the café told Mother and she offered to help and was refused.

The other players talked about actors on television and at the cinema. Clemmy hadn't heard of most of them but didn't care. She would be the special one.

Rehearsals started well, and she threw herself into the role, waving her hands wildly in the air, already hearing the applause. Not all knew their lines like her and it grew a little boring with much waiting as others rehearsed. Impatient, she started to do things her own way, changing her lines and missing rehearsals.

'A shame,' Mrs Thompson said, when she told Clemmy she'd been replaced. 'A bit of discipline and you'd make a good actress.'

Clemmy smiled her way through the schoolyard, that special, brave version, and once on the track threw herself into Helen's arms. Only one word stayed with her: actress.

'I was a great Maleficent. I'm not going back to that crummy school.'

Helen held her close, Clemmy's head on her shoulder, tears wetting Helen's shirt. 'You must. You are brave, you can do it, my Clem, you can do anything.'

'I will show them; one day I'll be a famous actress.'

'I believe you, Clem. We won't tell the cockroach?'

The play went ahead without Clemmy and many laughed and jeered when the news got round, as it did, fast, in the school ground, with her boasts of being the star.

Clemmy had loved her role, loved being someone else, had believed she could do it, would do it.

Mother did not find out until the play was about to open, one of her rare encounters with another parent. Shamed, she had rushed home and found the girls in the kitchen, eating buns.

'Why do I always have to find out things from others? The play, I hear you made a mess of that and got thrown out. You'll never succeed at anything. Discipline, that's what you need.' And with that she stormed upstairs.

*

A year passed and summer came round again. The hawthorn was covered in berries and the wood sorrel had come and gone.

Helen carried her pad and pencils to the pond. Later she would paint the reed-edged water with its hint of green slime on the surface, backed by trees smudged with lichen, showing only their trunks, their lower backbones. She sat, a packet of crisps in one hand. She would take her drawing back and clip it to the top of her easel while she painted. Miss Wood had given her some paints, sketching paper and brushes and she loved the buttery feel of the paints, losing everything else except translating the colours from her hand, finding her way through, often too impatient. She had cut up an old dress for rags to clean off her many mistakes and start again. She cursed her ignorance and persevered. All else vanished, which perplexed her a little.

She put down her pencil, needing Clemmy's arms around her so she hurried home.

12

21st June 1990

Navy skirts caressed their slim hips and navy ties circled the collars of their white school shirts. They wore knee-length socks, and their blazers with its crest on the right-hand pocket. Their exams were over.

'Happy birthday to us, sixteen.'

Clemmy half turned and ran her slim fingers over the cloth covering Helen's swelling breasts. 'One day a man will touch you there, you will like it, perhaps love him.'

Helen ached a little for the sadness in Clemmy's voice, pushing her hand away, asking herself how Clemmy knew these things.

'Birthday cake tonight,' Mother called after them as they walked hand in hand, out the front door. 'Don't be late.'

'The insect,' Clemmy whispered.

Helen had read about cockroaches, creatures of the night, and when she and Clemmy heard Mother come in late at night, they whispered to one another, 'The cockroach is back.'

They turned left out of the gate, towards the bus stop and school. Helen's steps were quick; she had a painting in her bag to show Miss Wood.

Clemmy lagged until Helen tugged her forward.

*

Mother sighed. *They play with me, the little devils, just when I get it right they do something different. Helen's always up there, thinks she's her father and the other one is God knows where, and the school complains. What can I do? I longed for their love, tried my best but it was no good. It's always been just the two of them.*

Sometimes she chastised herself for not trying harder. She reached for the bottle of pills: *Mother's Little Helper.* When she couldn't be bothered with her make-up, something was wrong. She should have been a beautician, had a natural flair for it. Her face had lost some of the perkiness that made men look at her a second time and speculate, her smile had become fixed in lines that travelled downwards and her small snub nose seemed ordinary. She was forty, had given sixteen years to those girls. For what? And to the dark anger of the forest.

She hadn't wanted motherhood but once her belly began to grow she had dreamt of an exquisite child who would adore her, would hold her when she was sad, make her laugh. No one could say she hadn't tried. She'd made sure they had a good breakfast and looked decent before they ran down the lane, hand in hand, giggling, their hair flying and their school bags bouncing on their hips. She'd been home when they got back from school, the first years anyway. Their clothes cost her a fortune and she had begun to ask herself why she bothered. They didn't speak to her; she might as well have been in a nunnery.

She ran one hand through her hair, recently dyed platinum blonde, as she told herself that she loved them, always had.

A few men had offered her the promised land, but somehow it had never materialised. She'd stopped bothering about anything much, she had to think of herself. Those years when she had first brought the twins home and he had buggered off were faint dreams. At least at Jack's she could have a decent chat, laugh, dress up a bit, be herself. She would have been a good mother if they had let her.

She set the table for three. It was a long time since they had eaten together. The girls simply ransacked the fridge. There had been a time, years back, when she had cooked good meals, slaving over the stove. Clemmy had always been greedy and Helen had picked at her food.

It was their sixteenth birthday and she'd lashed out on the birthday cake, a farewell present. She carefully pushed sixteen candles into the cake's white icing and placed a box of matches beside it. The macaroni cheese, their favourite, was ready to go in the oven.

She would get the camera, send a last photo, tell him she didn't need his money anymore. She pulled back her shoulders and smiled: she wouldn't bother with the photos. The yearly ritual was done: she would never be short of money again. She had gone to the bank earlier that day and drawn out much more than she had intended. No one could accuse her.

She poured herself another glass of wine, switched on the telly, put her feet up, hitched up her short skirt and admired her slim legs. She was small-boned, delicate even, although of late she had over-indulged, and a small roll of flesh eased itself over the waist of her skirt.

She settled down to wait, opening a bottle and selecting her best wine glass.

An hour later she opened the front door and shouted at the trees, 'Where are you?'

At 7pm she threw the cake into the bin, wrote a note, tucked it under the bread bin, then turned back and pulled the note out a little more.

She could not hang about. He would not like it. The girls would not starve and Jack would look out for them. He had promised.

She climbed the stairs and stood, gazing around her bedroom, taking it in for the last time: the satin pink bedspread and the matching curtains and ruff around the dressing table, and she decided they looked a bit cheap. She'd kept the room clean, when she had time, bothering little with the rest of the house. Why should she eternally pick up after them? They could live in their own muck. She sat on the stool, leaning her elbows on the glass of the dressing table and played, many minutes, with powder, rouge, lipstick. She smacked her lips tight together, smiled a little, and sighed with satisfaction, then stopped. Her eyes had faded from their startling blue and her hair looked like farmer's straw, not that she had ever seen any. She picked up a bottle of perfume and sprayed her wrists and neck generously, then pulled open drawers and slung back wardrobe doors. She would not be taking much. She flung clothes onto the bed, scrummaged through them and selected, not many. She pulled out knickers and bras and a few other things, ran her fingers over the make-up, decided it was cheap, and left it there.

Downstairs, she carefully lifted the silver teapot from its shelf in the dining room. When the twins asked her about it, she'd always said, 'Never you mind, it's worth a lot.' She didn't really know but it was her precious thing. She wrapped it in tissue paper, slipped it in with her clothes and carried the case to her car.

She had to get away, hated this shithole, always had done; the house falling down, and the forest brooding over it. After sixteen years his money didn't buy much, not the way she liked to spend, and she had another man, a good one, a reliable one. He was rich, older, a lot older if she was truthful, and he didn't want the girls. He had walked into the café, clearly not from around here, wearing a smart suit, carrying a briefcase. He had said little but left her an extravagant tip and returned a week later, taking her to a hotel some miles away. A southerner, he promised her a new start, promised that she could have anything she wanted and chucked his money around.

She'd always had her stories of her own life, dressed and oven-ready, an orphan, or perhaps run away from home when a slip of a thing. She wasn't from these parts, but from where the wind blew strongly most of the year. A multitude of brothers and sisters and not enough food or love had driven her away.

Perhaps she was making the same mistake but she didn't care.

'They sound like two little devils,' he'd said. 'You'll have to choose.'

Perhaps she had complained too much about them.

She had the right to her own happiness and he would not wait forever.

She threw the empty wine bottle into the bin.

13

Clemmy had pinched a couple of notes from Mother's purse, and they ran to the cinema straight after school.

'Come on, it's starting.' Clemmy pulled Helen to the stairs. 'It's Julia Roberts, she's great.' The kids at school had gone on forever about this film so she had to see it, didn't much care how good it was. She was sick of pretending. '*Pretty Woman*, everyone is raving about it.'

Helen looked puzzled, then nodded.

They ran up the wide staircase and into the dimly lit cinema. A girl at the door smiled at them and said, 'Sit wherever you want.'

There were only a dozen others there and Clemmy chose a seat away from anyone else and close to the front.

The lights dimmed and Helen bit her lip. 'It's a bit dark.'

The silence was broken by loud music. They both jumped and Helen grabbed Clemmy's hand. The screen was enormous, a different world, outer space even.

Clemmy didn't jiggle her feet or fidget but sat absolutely still, leaning forward, her elbows on her knees, her chin in her hands.

'A whore. So what, she's famous. He loves her,' Clemmy whispered a few minutes before the end; she was in love with Julia Roberts, had lost her own world, was her.

They stayed in their seats until the girl stood in the aisle beside them. 'Your first time,' she said, her voice smiling.

An hour later they banged their way through their front door, clutching their small bellies full of fish and chips, their hearts bursting with love for Julia Roberts, and ran straight upstairs to bed, Clemmy singing '*Pretty Woman*' as loudly as she could.

Overnight a storm broke the trees, snapping off branches and leaving them strewn across the forest floor like derelict, homeless old men or women, and they watched the lightning pirouette across the sky, pointed, shouted and laughed, clapping their hands, their eyes shining.

Next morning Clemmy was first downstairs.

The fridge was emptier than usual, no birthday cake anywhere. Cupboards banged and slammed. They had been promised.

She swung round, grinned. Sticking out from under the lid of the rubbish bin was a small wedge of white icing. She opened the bin and thrust her hands deep, pulling out a chunk of cake, almost half, and dumped it on a plate on the table. She dug again, deeper. The next bit had something old and smelly attached so she brushed that off and stuck the piece of cake to the first piece. Once more, and she had an almost-whole bedraggled cake. Most of the candles had fallen off so she left just two, pushing them into the big section, then lit the candles, and shouted up the stairs, 'Come on, lazy bones. I've something to show you.'

Helen skittered down.

They sat, arms around each other, singing 'Happy birthday to us,' and hugged and kissed and ran round and round the table, their bare feet slipping on the stone floor. It didn't much matter that it was a day late.

Breathing hard, they perched on the stools, each grabbing a handful of cake, Helen's mostly icing. She threw the candles into the sink where they hissed indolently.

'Where is she?' Clemmy looked around, expecting to see Mother in the doorway. She liked to do that, catch them unawares. 'Early for her to be gone.'

All was quiet upstairs. No footsteps.

'Perhaps she's dead,' Clemmy laughed, and ran into the dining room.

'She's gone,' she said, skipping back in. 'The teapot's gone.'

Helen put a hand to her mouth. 'Gone, she can't be. What will we do?' Her voice trembled.

'We'll be all right, we don't need her.'

'But…' Helen closed her hands tight, fingers entwined, still expecting Mother to shout at them for the mess, the bits of cake everywhere. She shoved back her stool and ran the few steps to the bread bin, always light-footed. White paper stuck out, demanding to be plucked from its hiding place. She lifted the bin. A folded piece of paper and two stacks of notes. She picked up the first £10 note, rubbed it between thumb and forefinger and held it up.

'Dozens of them.' She pointed to the two piles.

Clemmy stood. 'Give them here.'

Helen pushed one pile towards Clemmy and began to count the other.

'We're rich,' Clemmy shouted, jumping from foot to foot, and hugging Helen.

Helen stared up at the ceiling. 'Where's she gone?'

Clemmy grabbed the piece of paper, unfolded it, and read, her lips moving, her finger following the meandering writing, then she went back to the beginning and read out loud.

> *Clemmy and Helen*
>
> *You are sixteen, young women now. You don't need me; you never did except as babies and even then you turned to each other, not me. I was sixteen when I left home to find my own way, you can do the same.*
>
> *There is enough money for you to get by for some time if you are careful. I am going far away and I am not coming back.*
>
> *I have done my best these past sixteen years. You will not miss me so I am going to live my own life.*
>
> *Look after yourselves girls. I have told the school we are moving so you can't go back.*

Clemmy whooped. Helen wiped her eyes and held out her hand for the note.

Clemmy read on.

> *If you need help, go to Jack. He will help you sort the bills, perhaps even give you a job.*
> *Mother.*

Helen stood, absolutely still, slow tears running down her cheeks. No more school. Mother. She bit her lip.

Clemmy laughed, opened a drawer, took out a pair of scissors and ran into the hall. She grabbed her blazer and carried it back to the kitchen. 'School's over,' she shouted, and she laid the blazer on the table and cut round the school crest on the breast pocket, then threw the blazer onto a chair. 'No more school,' she crowed, and counted her pile of money again.

She ran up the stairs, two steps at a time, to their mother's bedroom.

The wardrobe doors stood wide open and clothes were strewn across the double bed.

Helen stood and watched as Clemmy hauled the remaining clothes from the wardrobe, sorting them and those already on the bed into three piles, chanting: 'Yours, mine, rubbish.'

'Mother's gone.' Clemmy took Helen in her arms and dragged her around the room until they fell, giggling and breathless, among clothes.

'We'll move in here,' Clemmy said.

They perched on the stool in front of the dressing table, opening drawers, finding make-up and perfume and other bottles and tubs. And nail polish, so they painted each other's nails, different colours and badly. Patches of rouge blotted their cheeks; mascara stung their eyes.

Clemmy plastered her lips with the brightest lipstick she could find then put it in her pocket.

'Here,' Helen said, and sprayed Clemmy's wrist with perfume the way Mother did.

'Sex,' Clemmy said, and Helen blushed.

The shoes were too small so they went into the rubbish with most of the clothes.

An hour was all it took to ransack the bedroom. It had been exciting for a time, then the rubbish bags filled fast.

Clemmy took her own clothes from her bedroom to her mother's. Helen couldn't be bothered. She was longing to go upstairs, to solace, safety.

That night they sprawled together in the double bed, giggling and a little restless.

14

'More cake, we need more cake.' Clemmy slung her plate into a sink already overflowing with dirty dishes. 'We'll go to the bakers.'

Helen had eaten all the icing off what remained of the cake and as she fingered a ten-pound note, joy in many colours flooded her head. Paints.

She dropped the note and grabbed Clemmy's arm. 'The camera, no photos.'

Clemmy ran upstairs and minutes later was back holding out a small box. 'Under the bed.'

Helen tore open the box. An envelope fell to the floor, landing with a clunk. She picked it up and took out a card, and read it out loud, Clemmy looking over her shoulder, her arm around Helen's waist.

You must be five, my beauties. You are now so different from the first photograph. I am a fool, of course you are. I'm thinking of you both too much sometimes, and it stops me painting. It's the photos she sends. Without them I can banish you into the forest where I left you both. That day in the hospital, I couldn't know then, who could have, that you would grow into such beauties.

What has she told you about me? Does she care well for you, spoil you?

I left you a portrait of myself, not my best work but I wanted you to have it, although I could not allow you to share my life and you are probably better off without me. Is there a shadow of doubt in that sentence? I would not make a good father. Does she make a good mother? I doubt it. Painting is my life, that is why I left. Did I get that wrong? My beautiful Helen and Clemmy, the names on the back of the photos, you will not be able to read this but perhaps she will read it to you. I bribe her richly. She will explain.

Helen put her head in her hands.

Clemmy guffawed. 'A bit late, took him five years.'

Helen turned furious eyes on Clemmy. 'He is our father.' She picked up the envelope, replete with cards.

'Much good it did us.' Clemmy hopped off the stool. 'Give them here,' and she held out her hand.

Helen clutched the cards to her chest, pulled out the one on the top, read it then handed it to Clemmy.

1984

Your hair, my beauties. What has she done? The last photograph, your beautiful hair all shorn. Why did she do it?

79

What games do you play, not the ones I played as a child, too many years ago? Sometimes I believe I might rescue you from her, my beauties, but I don't suppose I will.

'She hid them from us.' Helen placed the cards on the table. 'Perhaps he'll come and find us.' Her voice trembled.

'Fat chance, 1984, seven years ago. Where is he?'

Clemmy scanned the next card, slammed the others down on the table and stood. 'You read them. It's too late, I don't want to talk about either of them,' and she ran out, her heels slamming the floor.

Helen sat for a time, absolutely still, before picking up the next card.

1986

You are growing up, and your beautiful hair is back. I'd like to paint that, to paint you both.

One of you has shy eyes and the other's a little defiant with seven freckles on the right cheek. Am I right?

Sometimes I plan to drive down, spy on you from the shadows of the trees, then my paints and brushes claim me. I am their prisoner.

Do you like school? You will have plenty of friends there. I think I was lonely as a schoolboy.

And the forest and all that lives in it. Are they your friends?

'Yes, yes, yes, Daddy,' Helen almost shouted. 'I love the forest and the birds and the rabbit and the fox and the trees.'

1987

I am fifty-four. I think of myself as your father. Do you? I am your father.

How can I say I am proud of you if I don't know you? Questions, questions. And another. Does she give you these small notes?

Perhaps you will never read them.

Helen dropped the card on the table and started reading the next, longing for his words, his love.

1988

You are fourteen. Will we meet one day? What will we say to each other? Your photographs are on the wall of my studio here.

Do you go into the forest? I hope so. I had a special oak. If you follow the path in for a few hundred yards, you may find it. You will recognise it by a deep cut in its trunk from many years ago.

I miss them in these grand mountains.

I have enclosed a small painting of my favourite bird. If you find the pond it will be there. It is done from memory. It is too cold here for the goldfinch.

'I have found it, and the pond, I have found that.' She held the goldfinch in her hands for a long time, almost believing it to be real.

She searched for another card: on the floor, the tabletop. She sobbed and replaced the postcards in the envelope, except for the goldfinch, and ran upstairs and hid them in her treasure box, everything tumbling into each other, the way her paints did, becoming something else. Who was she? A goldfinch?

Running footsteps in the hall and the front door slamming. Helen peered out the window. Clemmy was on her red bike, with rouge on her cheeks, wearing one of mother's dresses. She dug in her pocket and waved a ten-pound note.

Helen prepared her palette and waited, biting her bottom lip. Then she dipped the tip of her brush in her crimson alizarin mix. Her father's goldfinch perched on the bottom right-hand corner of the easel.

*

The sun was at its highest, the days eroding the nights.

No photographs. His paints and brushes lay untouched, forlorn. He had missed few people in his life. He would not send money, he would play her game.

His giants were calling him, their vast slopes beckoning, so he climbed high up, seating himself on his rock where he rubbed his beard and messed with his hair. His hands did not enjoy idleness.

He had not missed her for one moment, but the beauties, they had filled him more as the years passed, with regret, perhaps love. He was not overly familiar with either. Each year the two had taken over his head as midsummer grew near, a meagre path through their lives. He would like to walk them up his giants, take them by the hands, one either side of him. They were too old for hand-holding. Sixteen.

Two eagles circled, idling, high up, across the blue sky. Had he done right by them? He did not often ask himself that sort of question.

He was not a wordsmith. His fingers and paints did the speaking, surprising him sometimes. He did not paint people, did not understand them. He loved best the big, lonely mountains, each its unique self, yet sometimes now he found himself painting odd, abstract pictures, paint splashed here and there.

He had never held a baby. It had not bothered him for he had nurtured his painting as tenderly as any child – or so he imagined. And he had watched them grow into young girls, an annual glimpse. Had their childhood been like his? They had each other. He had often asked himself these questions, especially in early June.

When she had bawled at him or demanded more, he had cursed himself for a fool. He had been sensible, honest, to step away, for his life was a wasteland without a brush in his hand, colours in his head. The two would have changed all that. He had been an absent father. The word father shocked, and he permitted his tongue to try out the word again: father.

Had the photographs been a mistake? It might have been easier just to forget them.

Back home, he found his pen and a card.

*

Helen heard the smack of the letter box and ran downstairs. On the doormat lay a white envelope.

She stood totally still, breathing hard. The writing was the same: strong, cursive, clear. *My Beauties.* She reached for it with fingers stained with crimson paint.

You are sixteen. Have I got that right? No photographs.

Have you left the forest? A small death. Are you proud of me? How could you be, you don't know me. I dream that one of you is in my studio. Perhaps both of you. Gazing out over the forest.

Do either of you paint? That is my prayer, that you feel life in the colours.

My beauties.

Perhaps I will come and find you one day.

She slipped the card into her pocket.

15

They lay side by side, hand in hand, until they fell asleep at the same moment. On hot nights they slept naked, the breeze from the open window caressing, their hands resting on themselves or on the other.

They bought cakes with exquisite thick icing, and exotic ice cream that melted on its way home so was chucked. They ran into shops they'd never been in, ones that Mother had always declared too expensive, not for the likes of us. And fish and chips. And crisps, chocolate bars and Coca-Cola. They cycled home with full baskets and more bags hanging from the handlebars.

Clemmy made sure the biscuit tin was never empty. There was a large sack of flour in the larder so Helen made bread, one of the few things Mother had taught her, loving the silky dough, massaging, shaping, watching it rise. They could live on that for months, with butter and jam.

Yet they kept running out of boring things so it became less fun.

Helen left everything to do with money to Clemmy. It was easier that way. She cooked, such as it was: heating up tins of soup or beans, occasionally frying eggs.

Jack called after a few weeks, standing awkwardly at the front door. 'I could give you both a job. You must be lonely out here.'

Clemmy turned to Helen, grinning, 'Both of us?'

'Well,' he hesitated.

'I couldn't,' Helen whispered. 'Don't leave me,' and she clutched Clemmy's arm, and did not look at Jack.

Clemmy's fair skin flushed. 'What do you do every day? Leave me.'

She swung back round to Jack, breathing deeply. 'Sorry Jack. Later perhaps.'

'Come to the café then, for your cake,' and he reached out to touch Helen's arm. She had not raised her head.

They did not come so he brought them treats.

*

They passed many hours at the cinema, sitting there all day if they could. Helen closed her eyes or put her hands over her ears when sex or violence came on, and sometimes she crept out and waited downstairs. Clemmy stayed, in another world, living someone else's life, her own dream becoming more certain. And her plans.

They often didn't file out after each show but slipped low in their seats until the next film started. They cried together, laughed together and came home to a cold, dark house.

Helen tried to drag Clemmy across the track into the trees. 'It's magical,' she cried out, and pulled Clemmy's arm. 'Don't be afraid, nothing will hurt you, I will keep you safe.'

Clemmy pulled herself away.

Letters arrived, none addressed in that bold, cursive handwriting. They kicked them into a pile on the floor behind the front door. Ten-pound notes were still in the kitchen drawer, no longer in two piles and much diminished. Summer was ending.

'You're always upstairs, boring,' Clemmy pronounced, and set off on her bike, returning with food and a blonde wig that made her look a bit like Mother.

Helen was sure he would come for them; he would know they had been abandoned.

*

When Helen didn't return to school, Eleanor Wood waited, then drove along the unmade road to the cottage. Her mother, Eleanor knew, would be sitting by the electric fire, waiting for her to come home and light the real one. She didn't make demands, priding herself on that, although Eleanor guessed that she would like her daughter married, especially for the grandchildren.

Helen's painting had developed and surpassed Eleanor's own, her skill quite remarkable for one so young, and her beauty made Eleanor catch her breath, made her want to place her hands on the girl's breasts.

*

Clemmy half turned from the woman in the doorway.

'Shorty's here,' she shouted over her shoulder. She had never liked the art teacher; her face was too angular, like some crummy statue. And Helen was her favourite, everyone knew that. Clemmy swung back and, making no effort to dissemble, ran her eyes up and down the tweed skirt, mauve woollen sweater with complicated stitching, a Peter Pan white collar showing at her neck, and on her feet, boots she might have liked to wear. Her hair was not in the bun she always wore at school but hanging loosely on her shoulders. Clemmy noted the annoyance in Miss Wood's slightly tightened lips.

'Clemmy,' Eleanor said, with little warmth in her voice, and peered past her. She shifted from foot to foot as the girl blocked the doorway.

'Who?' Helen called out from the dark end of the hall.

'Shorty.'

'Miss Wood,' Helen said, her voice trembling a little, hurrying to the door, still holding a brush in one hand. 'Miss Wood.' The summer holidays had passed. Helen still lived a school timetable. She had missed her teacher, her advice, her kindness. She looked down at her own trousers, at her blouse. She'd meant to change them days back. She crossed her arms, endeavouring to cover the worst.

Miss Wood placed her hand on Helen's shoulder. 'I've come to see how you are getting on. I was so sorry to hear you had left. I was told you had moved but did not believe it.' She added, turning to Clemmy, 'Both of you.'

All three stood moments, unmoving.

'Your mother?'

'She's out,' Clemmy didn't bother hiding the sneer.

'May I come in?' Miss Wood's voice was firm but warm as

she took a school-teacherly step inside the door, so Clemmy had to step to one side.

'Gone,' Clemmy said, her voice loud. 'She's gone, we can look after ourselves.' Her hands at her sides made small fists.

As Clemmy slammed the door shut, Miss Wood's boot knocked the pile of mail on the floor, and she started to say something and stopped.

Clemmy scooped the letters into her arms, stormed into the sitting room and turned up the radio.

'Would you like to come upstairs?' Helen's voice trembled. The studio – she loved that word but did not often speak it out loud – was a mess, but she didn't care. She started up the stairs and Miss Wood followed.

Miss Wood stopped in the studio doorway, looking around. 'You've not given up then.'

Leaning against the wall were three completed paintings of an oak: Autumn, Winter, Spring, and on the easel, the same tree, resplendent in its summer finery.

Miss Wood walked across the room to stand in front of the three.

'You love the trees, don't you, Helen? So do I.'

'It's my oak, Miss,' Helen said. 'It's special.' She had finally measured its girth, nine feet eight inches, and its roots spread far. In winter it was bare, showing off a different kind of beauty to its lush summer wear. Long-tailed tits and goldcrests took its insects and the treecreeper probed the bark and roosted at night under its ivy. The mistle thrush announced spring from its crown and on the ground, bluebells created pools of colour, followed by wood anemones and wood sorrel. The thirsty tree could drink tens of gallons of water a day to support its leaves and seeds, and the acorns fell to the forest floor in the autumn. The older oaks, and this one was very old, were clad in ivy and lichen. Helen was frequently kissed by the falling leaves as she sat at its foot.

'You have great talent,' Miss Wood said. 'You must not waste it. I will help if I can,' then both turned toward the door at the sound of Clemmy's snigger.

'She's not going back to school.' She took a few steps into the room and pointed at the easel. 'There's Summer,' she said, her voice replete with pride.

Helen stood, completely still.

'You could still take your exams and go to art school. There are scholarships, I could help.' Miss Wood ignored Clemmy.

The answer was on Clemmy's face.

Clemmy turned and skipped back down the stairs, singing at the top of her voice.

Helen and Miss Wood both stood, waiting for the song and footsteps to fade.

'You must miss your mother.'

'Not really.' Helen bit her lip and studied her shoes.

'My mother, you could meet her one day. Please call me Eleanor.'

Helen flushed.

Eleanor started to walk to the windows, stopping in mid stride. 'This is your father? May I?' And she bent to pick up the portrait, carrying it over to sit on the back of the sofa, propped against the wall.

Helen held her breath.

Eleanor leant forward and gasped. 'It's good, very good.' She peered at the bottom of the portrait.

'David? I can't read it. Is it Richards?'

'She never told us.' Helen paused, looking hopeful, 'Perhaps you know his work?'

Eleanor shook her head and carefully placed the portrait back against the opposite wall. 'I could come again? And help you?'

'I'd like that.'

Eleanor picked up a book, the only one in the room. '*The Little Prince*,' she said. 'One of my favourites. The rose and the sheep.'

Helen nodded, but it was not the rose and sheep that had possessed her but a small planet somewhere big enough for only Clemmy and her. She had hoped, once, to see in the forest a laughing little man with golden hair, or at least the fox, shy and wild.

Eleanor came every few weeks. When Clemmy recognised her knock, she shut herself away with the radio, playing it at top volume, and dancing fast and with abandon, around the room.

16

1990/91

The forest changed with the seasons and with Helen's moods, although her love for it did not diminish. In spring and summer it clothed itself, greedy for the space and the light after winter. In autumn, the dry gold and brown leaves crackled beneath her boots, but not the oak leaves, for they soon rotted to rich mulch, supporting the life of the forest, including the fungi, the well-named death cap mushroom, and the edible cep. She loved best the winter after the leaves had fallen, the bones of the trees on show, waiting for spring when the broad and spreading crowns would drink in the light. Sometimes a flurry of snow settled on the bare wood, throwing on a gauzy gown, forcing the trees to bow down.

Autumn announced itself with high winds that rattled the windows and the radiator did little to beat off the bitter cold in the studio. Helen carefully picked up the blank canvas that had leant against the wall for some time, until, two days ago, she had primed it. She carried it over to the easel then stood, her hands trembling.

A large mirror sat on one side of the easel, turned slightly so she could see herself and the other. With her back to the windows, a limpid light settled on the canvas, and she drew an outline, laid out her palette, took up her brush and diluted one of the hillocks of paint, thinning it a little, then, with deft strokes, painted over the pencilled outline of the two, both in loose-fitting, long-sleeved, wide-shouldered green dresses, bodies touching, feet clad in fawn, skimpy sandals and legs crossed at the ankles. She laughed at the sandals, her own feet just then clad in thick socks and sturdy shoes.

Helen was on the left, that curious little kiss on her right shoulder peeping out from the neck of her dress, as did Clemmy's on her left shoulder. They were turned slightly towards each other.

The sunlight, warming her back, told her it was hot for the time of year, as did the blackbird's song from the chimney pot. She tried to sing back to him but did not have the skill. Still, he enticed. She stretched and walked to the windows, to the forest. The uppermost branches of the nearest trees saluted.

'Too soon.'

The canvas was big and her first strokes tentative. Then she forgot about everything except the colours, the flat brush, thick with paint, moving almost of its own volition. She used her palette knife to scrape off a mistake. And again, not much later.

It was not working. She chose another brush, mixed different colours. It was slow, would never work. The past told her this happened but, she pleaded with herself, not now. She cleaned the whole canvas, lay on the sofa and tried to calm herself. She gulped down her cold tea and dropped her open bag of crisps on the floor, scooping them up and shoving them in, one small fist at a time.

The two were outlined again. Back to the faces: their slightly snub noses, cheeks, the almost-smile rounding the cheeks a little, full lips, eyebrows reddish brown, eyes green, copper hair bound in a plait, one on the right shoulder, the other on the left. She had to find Clemmy's expression, the cheekiness in her eyes. And something else. She touched Clemmy's mouth with her brush, turning it up just a little at the corners.

She put down the brush and ran her hands over her own breast, her hips; she posed slightly sideways, one way then the other. She worked for seven hours that first day, studying herself in the mirror then on the canvas.

The eyes took the longest. She added a hint of uncertainty to Clemmy's. The sunshine outside was lighting up the hair, their chins lifted, exposing unusually long necks. And she gave more life to the background with strong brushstrokes of cerulean and white, thus highlighting the copper hair.

Four days later she was finished, unsure why she had ever started. She had hovered over the place where the signature would be, and finally, copying her father, signed it. The 'Helen' was decipherable, not much else.

Winter snow dumped itself across the track, falling in ever heavier flakes, each still too fragile to arrive undamaged on its long journey down, to spread itself against the windows. The wind picked up and the snow banished the forest, enfolding the world in silence.

Clemmy's footsteps thumped up the stairs. Trouble. Helen was content, did not want one of Clemmy's tantrums just then, was messing about, painting mice at the foot of her oak: playing, running over the roots, up the mountainside of the trunk, a couple wearing witches' hats.

Clemmy slammed through the door, making the floor tremble. 'You drive me nuts. Up here.' She waved a hand in all directions. 'In his studio, pretending to be him; it's him you want now, not me. What is there to do all day?' And she stormed over to stand in front of the painting of the two, now resting on the back of the sofa. She stood, silent, clenching and unclenching her fists, then screwed her eyes tight shut.

Helen's face turned white and she put down her brushes and clasped Clemmy to her breast. 'Us, Clem, you and me. Always. Nothing can change that, I couldn't bear it. I'll try not to be up here so much.'

'You made your choice.' Clemmy pulled away, tears running. 'You're always saying that. You and me, it's always been that. Not anymore.'

'I'll stop,' Helen said.

'Don't bother,' Clemmy shouted, and ran out the door.

With the cold and the silence, the stillness inside Helen deepened and she wept for Clemmy's anger.

Clemmy beat her fists on her pillow, then on the wardrobe, then on the wall, then threw herself on her bed. The sides of her hands cracked and bled and might have been bloody tears from her eyes. And that painting, she wanted to take a knife to it, slice it down the middle.

The snow continued to fall. Downstairs was darkness and cold, only a meagre warmth from the wood stove in the kitchen. The electricity came on but not for long. The windows were shut against the wind and the air inside was thick and rank. When the wind and cold eased temporarily, Helen went into the forest and dragged back fallen branches, then took her small axe and chopped them up for firewood.

They huddled together in bed or on the settee. Clemmy clutched the unopened letters that had piled up behind the front door. In the dim light she sorted them, then held out several pieces of paper with a lot of red ink. 'I have to sort these, don't suppose you will. I'll get a job at Jack's, he'll have me. You can paint. You might be famous one day. Rich.' Clemmy smirked, love in her eyes.

The snow began to melt.

*

Clemmy dumped her bag in the basket attached to the front handlebars and rode towards the town, pedals swirling in tandem with her billowing skirt, the colour of the sky. She rode on the footpaths, past the mean houses, the parked cars and the outlying shops, not slowing for the pedestrians, ignoring the shouts.

She swung down a narrow alley, stopping at the rusty back door of the café; she locked her bike, put her shoulder against the stiff door and pushed, a surge of excitement, as always, running through her.

The door slammed back against the inside passage wall and she ran in, slinging off her jacket.

'Hiya, I'm here,' she called out.

Jack smiled to see her and so did the customers, and he helped her sort her bills, taking her to the bank to open an account. Each payday she walked along the street to pay in a chunk of her wage, and bought food to take home: cereal, jam and butter, and potatoes and milk and a few eggs. And leftovers from the café: quiche, lemon meringue pie, Battenberg cake or a cornet of chips to eat on the way home, or a slice of pizza. They were not fussy.

She took charge of the bills, paid them on time and left the cottage each day, for the café, just as her mother had, away from the forest, and her laughter rang out, so the punters were generous with their tips. No one mentioned her mother, not now. 'Say her name again,' Clemmy had said to Jack, 'and I'm out of here.'

'Come down,' Clemmy shouted, craning her head upwards to the studio windows. 'You gotta see this.' Her hands were fluttering, on her head a bright red helmet.

Helen peered out the studio window, put down her brush, and ran down the stairs.

On the gravel outside stood a new scooter, small-wheeled, compact, bright red, and with two red bows on the front handlebars.

'It's great,' Helen said. 'Where'd you get it? It must have cost...' What would she know?

'Come on, scaredy-cat.'

Helen scrambled onto the scooter and put her arms around Clemmy's waist, gripping her tightly. Clemmy started the engine and pushed off. They rode fast, swerving round the potholes, missing most of them. Laughter and fear mingled in them both and Clemmy's knuckles shone white. They would be out of the pulsating forest soon, away from the trees that threatened to swallow her in a final embrace. She breathed hard; Helen breathed in concert. Then they were off the track and onto the road and they shrieked, in unison.

*

A policeman turned up at the cottage.

Helen hovered on the stairs.

'Your father, mother here?' He stood at the front door, facing Clemmy.

'Not here.'

'When will they be back?'

'Later,' Clemmy gave him her best smile, one that no boy or man resisted.

'That yours?' He pointed to the scooter.

Clemmy nodded.

'Licence?' he asked in a voice already replete with surrender.

'It's here somewhere.'

The policeman smiled, leant a little towards her.

'I'll be back,' he promised.

He never did return.

*

'I need the big bed, just for me,' Clemmy said, standing in a dress, recently knocked off from a shop in town, hands on hips. She giggled.

Helen moved back to their old bedroom.

In her bedroom, once her mother's, no longer shared with Helen, Clemmy ran her hands over her body, feeling the full curves, and she danced a little to the radio, placing a hand on each breast, then between her legs.

The boy rapped softly on the door and stood waiting, sweat on his brow, his hands clasped tight in front of him. She led him up the stairs to the double bed. She had told Helen to go out, to that awful forest.

Clemmy enjoyed her game, stripping off her clothes slowly, panties last. She selected her lovers, the timid, and the beautiful, from among the ones she had known at school. With each boy she took a name for herself, preferably that of a famous actress and whispered it: Meryl, or Julianne, or Kate. And believed. She let them play with her, thrusting out her small breasts and placing their fingers inside her, which excited them more than it did her, so she laughed. She bent down, taking them in her mouth, waiting for their moans of pleasure, their need. They always wanted more and she refused.

And when it was done, Clemmy sent them away with a promise they could return if they told no one. Then she found Helen and held her tight.

'Just fun,' she whispered, and wiped away Helen's tears.

The days after the visits, Clemmy was her most loving. 'Just fun,' she would say, again.

The boys recognised the temporality of what she offered, took it and moved on if they weren't pushed.

One evening, Helen met a boy as she walked across the track.

'I'm here, gorgeous,' he said, and put out a hand to touch her breast, although he was a little surprised by her shabby clothes. 'Sorry I'm late.'

For a second Helen wanted to give in, be Clemmy. She had read about sex in books, seen a little through her fingers at the cinema. Clemmy claimed it was an act, surely she could do that.

Helen shrieked and shoved him away.

The front door opened. 'She's not for you.' Clemmy took a couple of steps and placed a hand on his crotch, squeezed a little too hard, pulled his mouth down to hers, and led him into the house. He didn't look back.

Helen lay late in bed the next morning, the sound of slamming plates downstairs.

'What's up?' Clemmy said, a few minutes later, standing in the doorway, hands on her hips.

'What do they do?' She sometimes believed Clemmy brought them home to taunt her.

'My fucks,' Clemmy said. 'That's all they are, I don't care about them. I should have been an actress, perhaps I will be.' She placed her hand between her thighs and giggled. She didn't care, was indifferent to most she met. They wanted her, and she knew she would send them packing as soon as it suited her. Helen shared her painting with Shorty so Clemmy shared herself elsewhere. She had amused herself with swathes of boys without a hint of disloyalty to Helen in her heart. She enjoyed the acting, the gifts they brought.

'You've seen it at the cinema.' She wore a broad smile. 'Tongues.' Clemmy enjoyed that part, driving them crazy, feeling them get hard, making them wait.

'I hear you laugh.'

'At them.' Clemmy's laugh then was a different sound to the ones Helen heard through the wall.

'Do you still love me, Clem?'

'Of course, Hel, always.' Clemmy took Helen's hand and looked at her troubled face. 'It's not about love. Let's not fight.'

'We'll always be together, won't we, Clem? Promise.'

'Promise. We came into the world together. That's our life.'

Clemmy brought home a cat, a small fluffy white thing not unlike the earlier one.

'Mine.' Helen laughed and hugged Clemmy, squashing the kitten between them.

Mine followed Helen upstairs, leapt onto the full sun of the windowsill, stretched and slept and when the sun went in, then curved himself around Helen's legs, making her smile, distracting her.

She let him out to do his business and he thanked her by bringing back live mice, once a frog. He must have been to the pond so for a moment she hated him, but still she scratched his head, between the ears and on the side of his neck. He bit her if she tried to rub his tummy. And when her painting was not working she held him tight to her chest, and in the evenings she cuddled him while in bed as she listened to the sounds from her mother's old bedroom.

She put a lead on him, attaching it to the handlebars of her bike, sat him in the basket, and took him into the town. He sat up, peering at the passing track underneath, then the footpath. In town, she carried him in her arms. The shopkeepers grew accustomed to him, called him Mine and rubbed his head between the ears.

Passers-by laughed and pointed at first, then they too, wanted to be friends with him.

Clemmy ignored Mine and Mine ignored her.

Some evenings Clemmy failed to return home and Helen ate alone, except for Mine, who sat on the stool next to her, or on her lap. On these nights she went to bed to listen to Mine's purring – bed was his favourite place – and to wait for the roar and squeal of the scooter and the bang of the front door. She wanted to tell Clemmy that she dreamt of being like Father, that Eleanor said her paintings were good; the word she used was 'brilliant'.

It was eight months since Mother had left.

Helen sat at the base of her oak in the early morning, nibbling her breakfast of a small cake. She had started baking, enjoying the eating of it, was becoming a little podgy, didn't care. Clemmy liked the cakes too so they both comfortably put on a few inches in the same places, mostly the belly.

Clemmy bought or shoplifted new clothes, shared some but now they rarely wore the same. Helen felt odd dressed in different clothes, so she stopped bothering about what she wore, not that she had ever bothered much, dressing in her beige trousers and top, a sweater, and her fawn fur-lined coat in the winter. Her dresses languished on their hangers in her bedroom.

When her painting stalled, Helen and Mine cycled into town to the café. Sometimes Clemmy was not there but Jack welcomed her, placing a saucer of milk on the floor for Mine and telling Helen to have whatever took her fancy. She indulged and he would not let her pay. She rarely had money on her, though Clemmy made sure that the kitchen drawer was never empty of notes.

Jack was content when either was there and enjoyed the surprise on his customers' faces, although Helen always sat at a table in the back corner.

17

April 1991

Helen turned the envelope over, hesitated. The gallery name and address were in bold letters. Eleanor had talked her into it, had insisted that only the one painting would do, had wrapped it carefully and taken it away in her car. 'You'll not regret it, you'll be the young star, the youngest ever, not yet seventeen.'

Helen ran her finger across the name of the gallery and checked over her shoulder, although Clemmy had left for the café. She inserted the tip of one finger into the corner of the envelope and eased it open, taking great care. Feeling a little sick, she pulled out a single sheet of paper, unfolded it, then slowly sank to the floor and wept.

And he came to her smiling, 'I knew you could do it.'

'I want you to come with me,' Helen said. She could not do it alone, had never been far from the forest. She'd heard about that city: millions of people, strange people she was certain, ones she might not like. Dangerous, surely. They'd get lost for sure, never find their way back here, the only place she ever wanted to be. And the train. She couldn't do it. She had to.

Clemmy was sprawled on the sofa, her head in Helen's lap, fiddling with the radio, and describing the customers in the café: the boring and predictable and the exciting and novel. Few of her favourites had been in. Most of her days at the café were passed endeavouring to be the Clemmy the customers wanted: smiling, cheerful, her laughter filling all the corners. It was becoming harder.

'Where?'

'A surprise.'

Clemmy swung around to sit up. 'A surprise, Hel. What have you been up to?' And she hugged her.

Helen flushed. 'Please. I can't do it on my own.' She bit her lip.

'OK. Don't look so worried, I'll come.' Clemmy reached up and hugged her again. 'A surprise, Hel, that's not like you. When?'

'Next Saturday. Can you get off work?'

'Oh that's easy.' Clemmy tossed her hair. Jack refused her little, but they would miss her on a Saturday.

It was the end of summer and the blackbird had ceased singing, so Helen's triumph went unheralded.

She ran upstairs and took the painting of the goldfinch, her talisman, her father's, out of her treasure box and slipped it into her bag. She dressed in light blue trousers and a blue and green floral blouse. Clemmy came downstairs, also in blue. Before leaving, they brushed each other's hair.

'A surprise,' Clemmy murmured to Helen, her voice replete with her excitement.

Eleanor had written down instructions on how to get there, had offered to drive them, but Clemmy would never agree even though she secretly admired Eleanor's car.

They parked the scooter at the local station. Helen consulted her notes and bought train tickets for them both.

'What's this mystery? Fun, I hope.'

'You'll see,' and Helen tried to slow her breath.

Neither had been to the city. The train was crowded, and the platform and forecourt when they got there, even more so. Clemmy jiggled her feet on the journey, wriggled in her seat, and Helen spent most of the time studying a piece of paper, moving it away if Clemmy tried to read it.

'Hope this is worth it.' Clemmy giggled. 'We could always go shopping. There must be some great dress shops.'

Helen looked away from the people they passed on the street, most of them in a hurry. She held tight to Clemmy while wishing she might flee back home to the forest. She couldn't imagine her painting hanging on a wall; it did not belong in this place which she already hated. And the people.

She felt Clemmy's excitement, saw it in her eyes as she swung her head from side to side. She scrabbled, for the umpteenth time, for the directions, then she saw the gallery sign up ahead and almost stopped and turned back.

'What's this? Why do we want to go in there? Boring.'

Helen pushed open the heavy doors and walked through them down a long corridor and into a large room. People were scattered around, standing in front of paintings, but a small crowd gathered at the far end, holding glasses of something.

Clemmy stopped. 'No, Hel.'

Helen took her hand. 'Please, Clem, do this for me.'

Paintings lined the walls. Helen scanned both sides. Was she in the right place?

Clemmy sighed, her serious Clemmy sigh.

The people at the far end were talking loudly, drinking.

Helen's heart beat fast, everything inside her thumped, some weird dance, and she flushed, yet didn't falter, hastening on toward the crowd, pulling Clemmy after her.

At the sound of their footsteps on the polished wooden floor, a man turned, said something, and the rest swung round to face them, the volume ratcheting up, full of laughter, admiration and amazement as they parted to allow the two through. The strangers gazed from Helen and Clemmy to the identical two hanging on the wall, and back again, some laughing, others silent, astonishment and admiration on their faces. Then the sound of clapping.

Helen heard words: beautiful, so young, amazing, talented, remarkable.

Helen tightened her grip on Clemmy's hand. The hand pulled away and Helen turned. Clemmy was running down the length of the room to the door, and Helen's own bravery fled with her.

Helen paused a moment. She could not talk to these strangers without Clem so she hurried down the gallery after her, hearing voices call out, 'Don't go'.

Clemmy ran through the street, her hair flowing behind, the applause a hammer inside her head, applause for Hel, and her painting.

She dragged one hand over the stones beside the tree she was sitting under in the park. People walked by, stared at her.

Some hesitated, none stopped. She punished her hand again until the blood ran.

You have betrayed us, Hel, stuck up there on the wall like two whores. I hate it, want to tear it down, burn it. What am I? Nothing. It's not fair. I have looked out for you all these years, loved you, and this is your thanks. Now I am truly alone, can pretend no longer. I will go, somewhere, anywhere, away from you.

She shoved her bleeding thumb into her mouth. She was suffocating.

I have to go. Yet I am afraid of life without you. Where can I run to?

I've failed at everything.

Helen ran towards the station, searching as she did so, in all directions, nearly falling. She pulled out her train ticket and Clemmy's, and waited. Clemmy would come soon.

At her local station she found Clemmy's scooter and sat on it until the sun began to slide behind the distant hills, then caught the bus and walked back along the track.

I have lost you, Clem. Will you ever come back to me?

Yet some of the words back there still echoed: 'amazing', 'remarkable'. And the painting, the sandalled feet, the two of them, on the wall of the gallery in pride of place, and for a short second back there she had believed in herself.

I had to do it, Clem. Was I wrong? I had to know. I was so proud, believed you would be, despite everything. The two of us on the wall. Now I wish I hadn't done it. I cannot lose you.

Helen dropped her head into her hands, all joy and pride vanished. 'I love you and I wanted to share it. It meant nothing without you.' It was nothing now.

Clemmy hopped off the chair. It screamed across the stone floor and crashed onto its back.

'Us,' she shouted. 'There on that wall. That's all I am, a circus act.'

'It was my best.'

'I suppose Shorty put you up to it.'

'Yes. Oh Clem, why aren't you proud of me?'

18

'Let's go down the cellar.' Clemmy tugged at Helen's upper arm.

'No, I hate it, there's nothing down there.' Helen was flooded with that other time, with the cellar's darkness, the locked door, her screams. Her lunch savaged her throat.

'Come on, scaredy-cat.' Clemmy dragged open the brown door.

Tears ran down Helen's face as she tried to loosen Clemmy's grip.

Clemmy switched on a light just inside the door and dragged Helen down a dozen steps, then several more into a small room with dark grey walls and one bare bulb hanging from the ceiling. She released Helen, took a notebook and a few coloured pencils from her pockets and threw them onto a solitary chair. 'There, you can draw. I'll bring you some paints if you want.'

Before Helen could move, Clemmy was gone, her footsteps fast, up the stairs and the door slammed shut, then locked. The light went out and blackness swallowed Helen, her screams giving life to the dead bulb so that it swung idly, performing.

She stumbled a few steps to a wall, dirty, rough, ran her hands over it, and, step by step, followed it to a corner, then on. She knelt and crawled up the first stair, then another. Her arms were weak, her head filled with the darkness. After four steps she stopped, her breaths short and sharp. She crawled onto a small landing, then dragged herself up more steps, rough concrete gouging into her knees, gashing open the skin.

She raised her head and screamed, pounding on the door. 'Clemmy, I hate you, I hate you. Let me out.' She dropped her head, sobbing, as her forehead hit the ground. 'Why are you doing this?' Her cries drowned out the sound of the lock being drawn back, the grinding of the door's rusty hinges.

Helen fell forward onto the floor, into the light of the open doorway.

There was light but darkness bound her heart. Was it her fault? Had she been careless? She put two fingers to her forehead, blood.

'Why did you do it, Clem, just like her? Are you a copy of her after all?' Helen sobbed, pulled herself up and sat, cross-legged, leaning back against the wall, picking at the blood on her knees, and, taking out a handkerchief, licked it and dabbed her forehead.

Clemmy dropped to her knees and pulled Helen into her arms, her crying shaking them both.

Helen pulled herself away. 'I trusted you; I have been too quick to follow.' She did not shout, for something was telling her that any life without Clemmy was darkness, like that room down there. She tried a smile, a mere stretching of the lips, nothing in the eyes and then she was back in time, lying in bed with Clemmy who was whispering, 'The cockroach's back,' and they were giggling, fitting one body into the other. And further back, those early school days as they ran along the track, hand in hand, satchels bouncing, plaits flying, dressed the same, eyes shining. Their own safe world.

Had the cellar been a nightmare?

Clemmy's face was white, drawn, wet. She dropped her head onto Helen's shoulder.

'I'm sorry, I'm sorry, Hel. That wasn't me that did that to you, some evil creature. Perhaps that is who I have become. I don't know what to do with myself now. You are all I have. The rest of me is a pretence.' Her words, a torrent, and caught up in her weeping. 'I love you, Hel, and I have lost you. Forgive me.'

The horror was fading. Helen took Clemmy's wet face between her hands. 'You will never lose me but it will take time for me to forgive you. I hated you down there, just as I hated her, but you will never lose me.'

They stood. 'Come on, let's dress up and go out,' Helen said, her voice still trembling.

19

Late May 1991

Clemmy stared down the track and at her scooter. That had been a waste of money. She hadn't driven any further than the town and the fun of it had faded. London it had to be. Would she manage, a country girl like her? She took one long, deep breath. She would go and carry forever the guilt of Helen.

She nursed a mug of tea between both hands and sat at a table at the back of the café.

Jack, carrying his coffee, sat down with her. 'No lipstick, a first.'

'I'm not me,' the words almost a shout. 'I'm just part of us, of her and me. People never see anything else.' She shoved her mug of tea away and it slopped onto the table.

'Yes, I can understand that's not always good.'

'There's more, there's got to be. Everyone knows us here. She saw to that as soon as we were born.'

'She was a good woman, your mother, but it didn't work out. She did her best.'

Clemmy snorted. 'Her best?'

Jack pushed the plate of cakes towards Clemmy. 'Where will you go?'

'London. I'll find something to do there. It will be fun; I can be me.'

Her voice trembled and Jack put his hand out to touch her arm.

'I have to give it a try.'

Jack lit a cigarette. 'I understand that Helen's quite a success.'

Clemmy's face clouded and she drank her tea for a minute or two, staring at nothing.

Jack stubbed out his cigarette. 'Mary,' he said, the word struggling to get out. 'My Mary was like you: impulsive, determined and lovely.' He paused and placed both hands around his mug of coffee. 'She was trying to find someone, something.' He looked up, at Clemmy. 'Perhaps herself.' He caressed his cup. 'She was a little older than you when she left.'

'Why did she leave?'

'That's one of the many things I'll never know. Every day I expected to hear her bang through the door and shout, "I'm home, Dad." There was only her and me.' His face grew more drawn and older with each word.

'Your wife?'

He placed his hands flat on the table. 'That's another story. But Mary, that was twenty years ago. That's why I've stayed here, kept this going so she can find me if...'

Clemmy took his hand. 'Perhaps.'

Jack shook his head. 'It's a long time. She's found another life without me. Maybe she's in London. I didn't know where to begin or what made her run.'

They both sat silent for a time.

'What about Helen?,

'What about her?' Clemmy's voice rose, sharpened. 'I'm not her keeper.' She pushed her mug away, half stood, then sat again. 'She doesn't need me. I'll come back sometime, or she can come to me.'

'It will be hard. You're not a city girl. London's big, perhaps dangerous.'

Clemmy sat up straight. 'I'm going. Soon. Before I go mad, and…' Helen kneeling on the floor at the foot of the door leading to the cellar, screaming, stopped her words. She took a deep breath. 'Will you look out for her?'

'Of course.'

'I'll send money. I've set up an account for her but she won't have a clue. You'll have to teach her, just like you taught me.'

Jack took out a pen and wrote his telephone number on a piece of paper. 'In case you need me. I'll always help you. I'll miss you.' He waved his hand around. 'You liven up the place.'

20

June 20th 1991

Clemmy loved the boy/man, as far as she was able. Helen would not understand the sacrifice, the weight of her gift, and she cursed the day they had unlocked the door at the top of the cottage. She had wanted him when she was at school, wanted to touch him, to have him touch her, perhaps even love her. She hadn't wanted the other boys in that way; they were conquests, nothing more.

He had not mixed with the other boys, or girls, and his stillness made Clemmy crave him the more. He was different. She liked that. The girls called him 'Beautiful Boy', loved his blonde hair and blue eyes, lean, long body and face. They teased him and he quietly ignored them but Clemmy caught him watching her. She was puzzled by him and what she wanted.

After the summer when she did not return to school, she waited for him. He would come to her.

And he did, almost a year later.

Clemmy opened the front door. The knocking had been soft, timid. Beautiful Boy stood there. 'Clemmy'.

'You took your time,' and she resisted throwing herself into his arms. 'Thought you'd fled the country.'

'I'm about to,' he said. 'The United States, the family.'

Then Clemmy had an idea that was so shocking that she stood stock still, the half open door in her hand, regret meandering its painful way through her.

Finally, she opened the door wide and lead him down the hall. Helen stepped out from the kitchen and whispered to Clemmy, 'He's beautiful.'

'Helen,' he said, and looked from one to the other, wonder and a smile in his eyes.

Clemmy led the boy into the sitting room. 'Wait a little while,' and she turned away before she could change her mind.

Helen hovered a minute or two in the doorway, observing him, then smiled at him and ran away.

Back in the kitchen Clemmy put her arm around Helen. 'You shall have him.'

Helen shook her head, bit her lips, yet there was a wistful expression in her face and her eyes, soft, touched with shy longing.

'I'm frightened, I don't...'

'I will be there with you. I wanted him more than any boy ever, but he's yours, Hel.'

Helen pulled away, her hands trembling.

'Come upstairs, we must dress.'

Clemmy found two identical blue/gold dresses in the wardrobe and flung one to Helen. 'Put this on.' Clemmy whispered into Helen's hair, hair that might be her own. 'He is my gift to you,' and walked down to the sitting room. The dress rippled over her body, reaching close to her ankles, sleeveless. Her feet were bare.

The boy stood, with a wide smile.

'You want me and I want you but I am giving you to Helen. I will be there, with you both; she has not had a boy before. I am leaving tomorrow.'

Beautiful Boy shuffled his feet and looked down.

'Run if you want.' There was scorn in Clemmy's voice.

He followed her upstairs.

Clemmy took his hand and Helen's and led them both to her bedroom, where she pulled back the cover, blankets and sheet.

'Your lover, Beautiful Boy,' she said to Helen, kissed her on the lips and unbuttoned her dress. Helen stood still, while Clemmy undid her bra and slipped down her panties, picked them up and threw them to one side, then motioned to her to lie down.

'Come,' Clemmy said to the boy/man. 'Love her, be gentle.'

Naked, he lay down beside Helen, on her left.

And Clemmy undressed and found her place on Helen's right side. She held Helen's hand and whispered, 'I love you. Always.'

Helen's eyes opened wide when she saw his erection, and she swallowed a giggle. It must be an uncomfortable thing to carry around. She examined his face; he would be kind to her, and would kiss her. She breathed deep and slow.

The boy/man did not kiss Helen but ran his hands over her body, his eyes not moving from hers. Clemmy's grip on her hand was tight. The three breathed, breath for breath.

Helen put her free arm around him, over his strong back, his trunk, his hairiness, his bark. She closed her eyes as a tremor travelled through her face and arms and hands, her stomach and to her thighs. She bit her lip and squeezed Clemmy's hand.

He pushed her legs apart. Something thrust into her, thrust hard and fast, tore her. He was breaking her apart, his moans the same as those she'd listened to through the bedroom wall.

She escaped, into a painting, one like she had never done before. Her brush dipped into crimson alizarin, then black, then yellow and back to crimson. No white. The shapes were jagged tears, overlapping, rubbing against each other, and, in the middle, this thing, much larger than the one she had seen. And as his moans muted then ceased, the crimson alizarin dribbled down from the top edge of the canvas, falling, falling.

Clemmy's hand moved between her own legs, a small smile turning up the corners of her mouth.

'Clemmy.'

Helen heard the whisper as he turned over.

She pulled her legs together, vowing never to open them again like that, and put her hands between them, protecting, comforting.

He lay still beside Helen until she opened her eyes. They looked at each other through tears, both. She turned to Clemmy and her wet eyes held her fast.

The boy/man had his instructions. He gathered up his breath, his beauty, his bewilderment and his clothes, and left the cottage.

Clemmy lay quietly, not sleeping. Almost seventeen years she had slept beside Helen. It had always been thus. Their room next door was the same, the carpet worn, their beds old, but they had only noticed one thing all these years, each other.

Until Helen found him. He had come between them, brushstroke by brushstroke.

Jack's was fun, but if she stayed here, she would never leave.

She gazed at Helen's naked body, a facsimile of her own. Her smell was hers too. Not her voice, Helen's was gentle and quiet.

Time passed, perhaps not much, and Helen left the bed, letting the blood run down the inside of her thighs. She clambered into her gold dress and, barefoot, fled into the forest. There she sat by the pond in the June evening, still warm, dusk far off. She wept, for the invasion of her soul rather than her body, for his beauty. She might have been able to love him, love his eyes and the gentleness of his hands, until the pain. And she wept for Clemmy's love.

Her goldfinch fluttered by, with his red face, black and white head and yellow bars on his wings. He was too wild, his beauty too unique, to be truly captured by her brush. It made her love him the more.

A snake lay on the other side of the water, still, its eyes on her.

She brushed her hands across her eyes. She would go back, to Clemmy. A slight breeze made her dress rustle and wrinkled the surface of the pond.

Much later, as dawn offered tentative light, Helen crept out of their bed, yet again, and tiptoed upstairs. There she sketched the beautiful boy with his kind eyes. And another, the tumult of bright, varied colours, mixing fear and excitement and love, and in its centre, a long stick-like thing.

21

June 21st 1991

It was their seventeenth birthday. A cake sat, preening, in the middle of the kitchen table. Helen had baked it that morning.

Clemmy came back from town with her hair cropped, barely covering her ears, darker now so her seven freckles stood out more, and her eyes seemed larger, more beautiful, in her porcelain-white skin. She had sat in the chair while Sue cut her hair, tentatively, regretfully, at first. Just like the other hairdresser had done. The locks fell, Helen's tears. Her first betrayal, her first independence.

Helen held out her hands as if to receive the severed locks. Then fingered her own hair, asking herself, could she do it?

Clemmy grinned and shook her head, forgetting that her plaits would no longer fly. Her eyes shone, challenged, or perhaps it was that the long copper waves no longer distracted.

'Why are you doing this, Clem? You swore we would always be together.' Helen's voice was loud.

Clemmy swung round. 'I have to go, Hel. There is a world out there that we know nothing about. You're a success now, you don't need me. One day you'll make plenty of money but for now I'll see you are all right. It's all sorted.' She took Helen's hand and pulled her close. 'And there's plenty in the drawer. Take the bills to Jack, he will show you how to pay them and the stuff at the bank. There's money in an account I opened for you.'

'Why now, Clem?' Helen's voice had lost its usual soft cadence, was harsh. 'That's right, run, just like her.'

'And him, your idol,' Clemmy threw back at her.

They both breathed heavily.

'Where are you going? Can I...'

'No, Hel, you belong here, I don't. I have to go, sort myself out. I won't do that as long as I am with you.' Her voice faltered.

At the café, someone had left behind a magazine full of London: pictures, articles, famous people, shows, and photographs of buildings like nothing Clemmy imagined could possibly exist. She would get a job, somewhere to live. London was big, exciting.

She had flipped through to the back. There were no jobs for her, only secretaries, marketing assistants, managers. Had she wasted her life? She had time. That was now.

Then she found the accommodation section and ran her finger down the columns: a cheap hotel. She might manage there until she found work.

'But where, Clem? You've never been to London. Will you be safe? We've lived here all our lives.' Helen waved at the surrounding forest, sullen, unmoving.

'I'll write, but not till I'm settled. Wherever I go, you will be with me.'

'Promise,' Helen said. 'Promise you'll write.'

'Promise.' Clemmy's hands were still. 'You could work at Jack's. Try it, you need to get out of this place.'

'When will you be back?'

'Dunno. I want adventure, life.' Then Clemmy's voice softened, 'You'll have to come to London. When I'm settled, you can visit.'

They laughed, the same small, uncertain sound.

Clemmy stalked the rooms of the cottage, noticing their contents as if for the first time, perhaps trying to imprint them despite their shabbiness, or chuck them away.

Mother's room had held them and Beautiful Boy.

It was their bedroom where she belonged, the shabby covers and carpet and the beds they had always shared. Wherever she ended up in London, there would be no one else beside her. She backed out of the room, trembling.

That night, a long one, they spent in each other's arms.

'I don't want to leave you, Hel. I will be stupid, get into trouble. I always do without you to keep me straight. I will be back. Will you forgive me?'

Helen held her close, shivering, silent.

Early the next morning, they sat opposite each other at the kitchen table, saying little, eating little.

Then the purr of a car's engine outside.

'Wait,' Helen said and ran upstairs, returning with a book, held it out. *The Little Prince*. 'Here, take it.' Clemmy was the prince, she the rose. The prince had loved the rose and been loved in return but he had to leave his planet for he was restless.

Clemmy slipped it under her arm.

She put down her case, opened the front door and threw her cigarette into the lane, deciding that she did not like them. Perhaps not all Londoners smoked. Her new life was a mystery, she was not sure she could do it, told herself she had to.

She turned back as Helen's tears fell, and her own.

She stumbled to the car, slung her case onto the back seat, a small thing for a new life, then slipped into the passenger seat beside Jack.

They drove along the track, and, as Clemmy clutched the door handle as if to step out, she heard Helen's voice, 'Don't go, Clem. You can't go,' and her head dropped into her hands.

Jack stopped the car and put his arm around her shoulder. 'We'll all miss you, Clemmy. I'll look out for her.'

Clemmy nodded and sat up straight.

Jack started the car. 'Bit different,' he said, nodding towards her hair. 'Got somewhere to stay?'

22

London 1991

Clemmy, with seven freckles on her right cheek, stood among a forest of buildings stretching into the London sky, her hands clenched into small fists at her sides, standing utterly still, outside King's Cross station. No one had waved her off at her station, no cheering, no admiring crowds.

'Where are you, Clemmy?'

Clemmy bent over, clutched her stomach. Her case settled on the pavement at her feet, like an obedient dog. She didn't much like dogs. Or cats. The streets were replete with cars, and she shook her head, trying to toss away her old life. Her hair didn't move. She had fled and was lost. 'Helen, I will be with you always.'

Time spooled back. Arms around each other, and she had tossed that aside. Always too hasty, believing London would hold its breath when she stepped off the train. It had not noticed her.

She closed her eyes, to keep private her fear, blinked away

the tears and gazed upwards at a red-brick building stretching so high up her neck hurt, awe in her heart. Around her, red buses the size of houses, and black taxis. The London air was closing in on her, sultry, suffocating. She had fled from the clear, cold air of the north to air that had passed through many lungs before she drew it in, and the dull skies; the clamour of people, cars, and buildings that threw themselves far up into the sky. She had wanted to be amongst people but hated them right then.

She was wearing the new clothes she had bought, more expensive than any ever before. They were wrong, utterly wrong.

She tried to read the words on the crushed piece of paper in her hand and took a deep breath.

She walked. A warm summer evening but the sky was different. A couple of men passed her, one body brushing hers. Laughter. She changed direction, walked more, then stood in front of the hotel. She stepped inside, spoke to the man on the reception desk, turned, and left through the double glass doors, chucking the piece of paper into the gutter.

It was getting dark. She turned back towards the station, then turned again.

The air thickened.

A noisy bright red car, missing its roof, screeched to a halt beside her. A man with swept-back blonde hair leant across and opened the passenger door.

'Hi, gorgeous,' he said. 'Want a ride? Hop in. A bit of fun.' He pointed to a small space behind the two front seats. 'Sling your case there.'

Clemmy giggled, slung her case and got in.

They roared off. The car was so low Clemmy listened for it to scrape the road. She glanced sideways at him, at his smile. He passed her a small bottle.

She gulped down a mouthful or two or three, and giggled again, flung her head back to gaze at the London sky. London was fun.

She took a deep breath and endeavoured to breathe Helen out.

Her head swung all around. Houses, so many, tied together like a never-ending parcel. Tower blocks reaching skywards. She tried to count the brightly lit windows, the floors, imagine the people inside, crushed together. And shops, shops, shops, many still lit and open.

He placed a hand on her thigh, driving fast, tyres protesting as they swung round corners.

Everything began to blur.

Someone was dragging her, she couldn't fight, didn't want to. She clung on to her handbag.

She woke, curled up on the grass beneath a tree. Perhaps she was back in the forest and Helen would find her. She closed her eyes.

Her tongue was thick, filling her mouth, her body sore.

She sat up, searched for the red car. Her case was beside her, the handbag on top. She tore open the handbag. Nothing was missing. She ran her hands down over her dress, her best dress.

The sun was up. Mown grass stretched far, only a few trees interrupting its flow.

Clemmy pulled down her dress and dragged herself over to lean against a tree. His wild blonde hair, his fancy accent and the small bottle of liquid, and she cursed herself for a fool. Perhaps she did not belong here after all. She put her head in her hands, had forgotten it was shorn so took them quickly away. She stood, a little unsteadily, her mouth dry, a sickness in her stomach. She had no idea where she was. She leant back against the tree. Where was Helen?

She remained there a long time.

There was a path about twenty yards away to the right, on it a runner and a few people. She straightened, picked up her handbag and her case, and struggled across the grass to the toilets, where she cleaned her face and hands with paper towels and gently wiped between her legs.

She left the park and walked along the street jammed with traffic, uncertain about everything. The next street was quieter, the houses, two-storey, each with small well-kept gardens. She swung round to retrace her steps and there it was, a small sign outside the house across the road. No. 13 Bishop Street. She didn't care where she was. London somewhere. The house was the same as the one next door, on both sides, and on and on.

She dragged her case to the gate and up the three steps.

A thin, old, bespectacled woman opened the door. 'A bit early.'

'The room.'

'Leave your case here.' She pointed inside the hall and walked up the stairs, and pushed open a door on the first floor. She switched on the light, then stood back to allow Clemmy past.

'A nice, quiet room.'

Clemmy swallowed a snigger. The room was small and lit by a single lamp hanging from the ceiling with one large window that looked onto a brick wall. A bed, a curtained wardrobe wide enough for a dozen hangers and a small chest of drawers took up most of the space. A kettle and plate, cup and saucer stood on a tray on the chest of drawers and, crouching beside it, a very small refrigerator.

'There's some tea and coffee to get you started. Plenty of shops nearby. I'll bring fresh milk later. The bathroom's through there.' The woman pointed to a door at the end of the right-hand wall.

Clemmy walked across the room and opened the door to find a shower and washbasin and small bathroom cupboard. It would do for now.

The woman's face softened and she named a sum that made Clemmy think she had misheard. Clemmy took a deep breath. 'I'll take it.' She had to lie down.

'Gwendolyn Mason,' the woman said, then listed the rules, although no sharing, no boyfriends and no noise after 11pm were the only ones Clemmy heard.

Clemmy showered. 'Stupid, stupid, stupid,' she spat out at the hot water, but wanted to bawl, confess all to Helen.

She threw herself on top of the bed and woke mid-afternoon. Where was Helen? Why had she ever left her? The punishment had begun. A pigeon perched on the windowsill, its back to her, but when she sat up it turned and inspected her with one eye. She chased it off but it came back. It was likely the same one but how would she know, and it watched, perhaps guarded, her. She staggered to the door and found the milk, made herself tea, and fell asleep again. She awoke when it was dark. She was hungry but could not force herself to go out.

The next morning, she unpacked what little she had

brought with her but the room remained stark and bare. She did not go out that day or the next, drinking all the milk and the little coffee in the bottom of the jar, asking herself why she had come to this awful place.

'I've been a fool,' she told Helen while waiting for sleep, waiting to shut off the dark.

Her sleep was dark and long.

A tap on the door roused her. She slung on a shift.

The old woman stood in the doorway, holding a bottle of milk and a large piece of cake. 'I thought you might be hungry.'

Clemmy stepped back. Nosey old cow, then she saw the concern in her grey eyes and longed to throw herself into her arms, tell her all. She could be her granny. She had never had one, never even imagined one.

'Thank you.'

She ate the cake quickly, dressed and went out while it was daylight to find food. She waved to the woman as she passed the door to her sitting room where she saw her, sitting, knitting, and watching the television, a cat resting on her feet.

She brought back a bottle of alcohol, some clear liquid. She hadn't bothered looking closely, just gave the money he asked for. She poured a full glass, took a large mouthful and spat it out.

She began to leave the house in the mornings, not early, returning to her room before dark. She turned away from men, all men, especially those with fair hair. Her room was a mess. It didn't matter. No one saw it. Her very best clothes – they were few – were in the wardrobe, others piled on the chair and over its back, shoved to the floor if she needed the chair, not often, for she mostly just flung herself on the bed.

She washed her undies in the basin or shower and spread them on the windowsill where the pigeon occasionally pecked at them. There was a launderette around the corner where she took the rest of her clothes.

She stayed out as much as possible, wandering the streets, sometimes marvelling, often wishing she had never come. The Queen lived here but Clemmy didn't bother much about her. She hurried after girls with copper hair, believing, then calling herself a fool. She took some comfort in the memories, the two, keeping the world out while not knowing what that was. Then the regret.

The pigeon was her only friend. She reached out for him, any touch. He flew out the window.

She put hands between her legs, imagined Beautiful Boy there, heard his groans.

Her money would not last long. She bought a book called an *A to Z of London* to stop getting lost.

Granny, as Clemmy called her in her head, sometimes invited her in, always with freshly made cake and biscuits, and Clemmy wolfed them down while the old lady sat, not eating, smiling at her.

'Where are you from?'

It was a few weeks after Clemmy had arrived. 'The North.'

The old lady nodded. 'Me, London born and bred, but it can be a lonely place. It's the theatre I stay for. Wonderful actors, plays. You must go.'

The theatre. Excitement rippled through Clemmy, and a flush rose up her neck, blanketing her face.

The cat sometimes made its way upstairs to lie outside

her door. Clemmy cursed it at first, then took it inside her room to hold in her arms. Helen would be doing the same with Mine.

People in the street hurried past, never smiling or saying hello like everyone back home. (She gave herself a little slap to be rid of that word.) She sometimes saw old ones peering out through barely opened curtains to check that the outside world hadn't vanished.

'What am I going to do?' she asked the pigeon.

She found a dingy café where everyone sat around all day, smoking, drinking coffee and talking about things she didn't understand, reminding her of school and the taunts about the TV programmes she couldn't watch. She didn't go back. They were laughing, they belonged.

She bought a newspaper full of Princess Diana. She was a little envious so didn't buy another.

She came to a cinema, stopped, hesitated, then walked on.

At night, when it rained, the street lamps threw back their light from the wet pavements. The lights and the cars and the chatter of passing strangers kept her awake for long hours, until Helen took her in her arms.

I'm here, Clem, let's sleep.

She found the water, a river running between stone walls, paths alongside it, the water wide, inviting, with strange long boats. And a burger joint, bigger and more exciting than anything back home. She wrinkled her nose and stuffed herself on a hamburger and lingered.

Most often she perched on the canal's edge. Men stopped to chat. She was civil, no more. She considered being a lesbian. Sapphic sounded more exotic, but it didn't excite her.

Sometimes there was another warm body beside her, hips and thighs touching. She turned to say something, point something out. No one. Or, walking along a London street, she was grabbed from behind, arms flung round her, laughter in her ear. Touched with fingers the same as her own. And the giggles. No one else giggled like her. Or she woke in the night to hear someone whisper, 'You are impossible but I love you,' and was unmoored.

23

The vixen screamed in the middle of the night, frightening Helen. Perhaps it was her, the wild thing screaming.

Only birdsong cracked open the silence, yet it no longer filled Helen with joy. The forest had changed. In its deep heart, the trees grew close, intertwined, and the brambles defied any to pass, offering up stories of slaying and ill deeds. It would haul her deep into its darkest self, strangle her, eat her whole, and her friends in the trees would cheer it on. She locked the doors, closed the blinds and the sun never rose.

She ate little, with no sense of what it was, choking often. She found her favourite knife and the sharpener, turned it over in her hand, round and round.

Was death stillness? She could bear that but would miss the birds, although they were silent right now.

The wind taunted her, whispered that her life was over.

Then she left the house to spread herself over her fallen oak and mourn. One day, half asleep, she heard someone move in the nearby trees and sprang up, called out, 'Clemmy'.

The figure was tall, blonde-haired: Beautiful Boy. She opened her lips to call to him. He had vanished. She had not forgotten him, perhaps never would.

One late afternoon at the pond, she stepped off the rocks and sank deep into the water, lying back as her skirt floated above her. She welcomed the water, dark and cold, willed herself to sink lower into the silt at its bed, her bed. She failed to hear the alarm of the birds or see the ducks paddling beside her sinking body, too small to aid her. She put out her hand for Clemmy, heard her calling, the sound blurred by the deepening water round her ears.

'Where are you, Helen? I will be back. Wait for me.'

She bent her knees, letting her feet sink a little into the silt, then pushed upwards bursting through the surface.

Her painting was dead. The gallery had sold her painting to an anonymous buyer. Helen cursed herself, regretting the whole thing, blaming. She needed it here, with her.

She locked the front door and hid when Eleanor called.

When the weather was clement, she went outside and sat on Clemmy's motorbike with its red ribbons, her mouth trembling the way it had when she was a kid. She reached out her arms to place them round Clemmy's waist. Hours could pass like this. She tried to tell herself to be brave, like Clemmy, and failed. She blamed her, and she blamed her painting, so did not climb the narrow staircase.

She listened for Clemmy's music: the banging of pans and dishes, the sound of running feet, the laughter. She longed to be that child again, perhaps she was one still, hand in hand with Clemmy, the world out there untrammelled, seen through eyes of all-encompassing curiosity and innocence;

the untarnished hope and dreams of the young, living only in the present. 'Look behind you,' little ones screamed at the world, warning of the ghost in *Snow White*. No one had warned her.

She walked to the far end of the pond, up the hill a little, to sit beside the fast-flowing water, and her heart beat in tandem with the stream, which no longer tinkled, had abandoned its gentle self, its song becoming hoarse, fed by heavy rain, as it hurried over the stones. A bird was singing something: be still, listen. She breathed hard and watched the clear water tumble into the pond and take on its brown hue, become one with it.

She showered four or five times a day until the water ran cold, then stood naked, shivering, forgetting what it was she had to do next. She stood in front of the mirror, put her hand out to her, wrinkled her nose slightly, for that was Clemmy's special signal to her, and Clemmy wrinkled her nose back.

She missed Clemmy's perfume filling the air, missed the reassurance of her footsteps, the whine of her complaints; her tales, tall and short; her laughter; her pig-headedness and her certainty that she was always right.

She climbed the narrow stairs, picked up her brush, dropped it; her hands were numb.

The rain washed the windows, washed everything. She ran outside and stood still as it coursed through her hair, over her cheeks and down her body, and the clothing of her life fell away.

A bird crashed into the window, and flew on, leaving three feathers attached to the glass. They made a letter C.

She opened the window and pulled off the feathers, screaming, 'Where are you, Clem?' The crows cawed and her forest friends fled, having known only gentle, soft love from her, not this shouting, which caused the surface of the pond in the distance to ripple and the branches of the surrounding trees to sway in protest.

Mine prowled. He was hungry, so he went outside to hunt and brought back his prey.

At dusk, as she was moving among the silvery trees beside the pond, the water flickering with fading uncertain light, Helen heard her voice, not in her ears but in her organs, her bones, her spirit.

She sat, long evenings in front of the open fire, putting out a slender white hand towards the flames, asking herself if it would burn brightly, like the log. She stretched further, gasped, pulled back, and shoved her fingers into her mouth. The ash in her mouth was loss, of her and of her painting. Frightened, she ran upstairs and crouched under the shower until the hot water ran cold again.

She stayed away from high open windows.

She stayed in bed until the postman made his noisy arrival known. Not often. She ran to him and was disappointed.

Mine lay, in his neat way, front paws curled in towards each other, his eyes solemn, purring. She did not notice him.

She no longer obsessed over her father, turning his portrait to the wall.

The forest started to smell rotten although still green, then mist came and light rain. At night, blackness and the screech of owls.

The butterflies lingered, overlong. A red admiral landed on her knee, trusting. She slammed her hands together, opened them to its crushed beauty, and sobbed.

She shut her eyes. Clemmy barged into her dreams.

She counted her own freckles, expecting some to be missing. Seven.

At night she left all the lights on, played loud music, the first record her fingers touched, putting it on repeat. Some nights were peaceful, when she dreamt Clemmy was beside her or in her arms. Some days her eyes failed her and she could not go into the forest. She dressed in whatever her hands touched.

She would give everything up just to hold her hand.

Mine followed her everywhere, sometimes stopping, arching his back to show his displeasure.

She stood long in Mother's room, recalling that once she had gone to her, stood at her knee. 'What do you want? Not me,' and Mother had pushed her away.

She had left her too.

And she did not answer the door when Jack knocked, a brisk tap, then again after a few seconds. There had been the same knocks over the past couple of weeks and she had hidden inside the dark corners of the cottage and heard the sound of things being put through the door. An envelope with money in it lay on the mat, and a note asking her if she needed anything. And parcels of ham, cheese and slices of bread. Her body was changing, something inside her was moving. She put that to one side and stayed all day in her pyjamas, pulling on her winter coat over them.

She hurried into town a few times, in the early mornings.

Her belly swelled with the passing of each day, while her face grew thinner. She did not eat enough for two.

Eleanor called many times. Helen recognised the knock, which became ever more urgent. She had lost words, yet longed to run to Eleanor. Could not.

Then, one morning, Helen swung her legs out of bed and moved across the room surprisingly quickly. She dressed, ran downstairs and back up to the studio, carrying a bowl of cereal and a cup of strong tea.

She needed strength so ate quickly.

She searched for the paints and brushes she had bought months back when the idea was a mere glimmer.

Hastily, she painted a slab of the wall white. She was not one for large scale, her work being more on the small side, careful, planned. The brushes she used felt unfamiliar, alien.

She waited until the paint was sufficiently dry, well almost, for it merged at times into her next wild sweeps of the brush. She found some paint that would do. The brush was overlarge in her small hand and she was clumsy at first. She had to stretch to reach the top of the wall but that was not where she started.

A goldfinch in the bottom left corner with its bright red face and yellow wing patch. She worked on, carefully, with her strokes, her selection of colours. Excitement drove her hand, and her imagination. In the other bottom corner, a pair of clasped hands and, above them both, the bloodied blue/gold dress. There, her hand trembled.

The sun lit the dress, played with it.

Clemmy had thrown her away like some broken doll that she had grown out of.

The next day she started on another.

A knock at the front door. Helen hovered. Jack's knock.

'It's me,' Jack called.

Helen opened the door a few inches and blurted out. 'She's not here.'

'I know,' and he reached forward to prise her hand from the handle and push the door open. 'I miss her too.'

'Where is she?'

'I don't know. Come to the café. I promised her.'

Helen was silent.

'I have your favourite cakes, the little white iced ones, and I won't leave unless you promise.' He put his hand out to touch her shoulder and soften the words.

The next day Helen exchanged her pyjamas for a bright dress and brushed her hair. She climbed onto her bicycle, and cycled into town, leaving Mine behind.

At the café she made one coffee last an hour or two. Some customers expected her to wait on them, others came over to chat and were puzzled; many called her Clemmy. Jack watched and listened and brought her cake. He tried to persuade her to work there, offered her good money. She shook her head, her plait swinging.

She took up baking seriously, bought a recipe book in town, thumbed through it.

Cakes, small cherry cakes. She made dozens. There was magic in turning plain ingredients into something that had her longing to eat it all at once, stuff it into her gob; something that satisfied her greed.

She took a dozen or more into town and gave them to Jack to sell to his customers. He slipped her some notes.

Then, several mornings later, seated at her back table in the café, she had to run to the toilet, retching.

'Are you OK, love?' Jack asked when she returned yet once again.

She returned to the toilet twice more, running again. Not understanding.

'Are you pregnant?' Jack's voice was soft, as they stood, well away from other customers.

Helen put her hand to her mouth and fled.

*

The lightning flashed through her open bedroom window, lighting up all the corners and secret places. She curled up, pulling the bedspread over her head. Thunder, dancing across the sky, followed. Then the scream of breaking trees.

The wind persecuted her, rattling the windows, or lightning knifed the sky, slicing the thick dark.

Next morning, the storm had passed and she ran along the forest path. Her oak lay fallen across it, slain. It had snapped off at head height, at the cut into which she had so often inserted a finger. Bushes were crushed by its branches, and far off, among the brambles, was its crown. The remaining trunk stood jagged, broken, revealing.

She threw herself onto the fallen tree and held it fast.

24

October 1991

'It was only a chocolate bar.' Clemmy suppressed the shrug.

'That's how thieving starts,' Don said. He was middle-aged, kind, but stern with his staff. 'Think it's a one-off, get away with it and then it gets serious. I like you, Clemmy, but you've got lessons to learn. You're out. A pity, you're a good worker.'

Clemmy collected her bag from her locker and left the store without saying goodbye to anyone. They'd had some good times together, her and the staff at the small food shop, but that was done. Three months was long enough, she was ready for something else, and she had enjoyed that chocolate bar, and the others.

She strolled through the store and out the front door. No sneaking out the staff entrance. Some customers waved to her, and John, on the checkout, looked away.

She spent the last of her pay in a bar, drinking whatever the men offered. They were generous. At first, she shook her head but nothing much happened so she accepted. She left with one, the most presentable of the bunch, and they wandered along the street. He pulled her into a dark alleyway and fucked her, pressed against a stone wall.

She pulled up her knickers and shoved him away.

He laughed, 'You seemed to like it.'

She had, in the way she had enjoyed the boys in Mother's bed. They made her feel special, but five minutes later she couldn't recall what they looked like.

She wandered around the nearby park. Granny would be out at one of her theatres and the house would be drear and lonely. London was no longer special. The excitement of the new had soon died and she'd made no real friends. The girls at the store had been willing but there was something missing. She did not feel special here. She should go home. Helen would throw her arms around her and forgive her. She bowled that idea away, far away, to the other side of the park. She had promised to write.

She pulled out Jack's phone number from her purse. Yet again. And put it back.

One evening, she heard loud music bouncing out through a solid-looking door that was not all that far from her room. She opened it and walked down the steep narrow steps. The entry was more than she could afford but she shrugged that off. It was a small room with a bar on one side. Half a dozen people sat on stools, chatting or just drinking. The rest was filled with people dancing, wildly, unselfconsciously. No one noticed her so she flung herself onto the dance floor and danced like never before. She threw her head back, wishing, as she did so often, for the long hair to match the wild flinging of her arms and hands. She hadn't been able to send Helen money. She was broke.

Then she came across a café not too far from her room,

wondering how she had missed it all this time. She pushed open the door.

It was twice the size of Jack's, with shiny grey tables and chairs and red floor, and tiled walls with a red stripe running round at chest height. Most of the tables were occupied, the air hummed and smelt of coffee. It was early afternoon and customers were eating sandwiches and cakes, or sitting with coffee or tea and smoking.

Some of the customers, men and women, stopped what they were doing to watch her as she strode past the tables and towards the back. She walked quickly, with purpose, certainty in her heart. A man, wearing a blue apron, and with small eyes that smiled, approached her. He reminded her a little of Jack with his apron straining to cover his belly.

'I'd like a job,' she said, giving him her best smile, one few men had refused.

He stopped and looked at her. 'Would you?' he grinned.

'I've worked in a café back home. Jack, he'll tell you.'

'Up north,' he said, that grin again. 'Good. Let's have his number and we'll see. Call in tomorrow.'

He lingered, standing close. 'We open at ten.'

Clemmy left and walked to the canal where she sat on the bench, her legs beneath her, pulling her skirt down to cover her knees. The sun was not too hot and the water gently rippled by, speaking its own language. She half closed her eyes and Helen's warm body was beside her.

Who am I, Hel? Have you forgotten me? I can't believe that. You know me better than I know myself. What are my secrets? What are yours?

London is strange, too many people, but I'm used to that now, like it. What did I expect? I don't know. Fairyland, if I believed in fairies. That will make you laugh. I can hear you saying, 'My Clem.' The canal is the best. I walk there most evenings and talk to you. You won't have seen a canal. It's a sort of river with boats on it that people live in. Looks fun.

Are you OK? Jack promised to come and see you. He will sell my scooter for you if you need money. I'll send you some soon. I expect you are up there painting all the time.

I've bought a new wardrobe. You won't want to hear about clothes but I'm telling you anyway. And make-up and a handbag. No longer the country girl. Well, in truth, I'm a bit lost here. Yes, that's me speaking, Hel, the super-confident Clem. Do you still love me, Hel? It's too many months. Have you changed? I expect not. Still wearing the same old clothes, not bothering how you look. Up there in a world I couldn't share. I look carefully at the girls in the street, just in case you have come to find me, search for copper hair, wide green eyes, freckles on a cheek, and a smile that is mine. My hair is growing. It feels odd to look in the mirror, you are not there. Are we real, Hel?

She stretched out on the bench and fell asleep.

Clemmy dressed carefully: flat smart black shoes, a tight-fitting black skirt and green blouse that almost matched her eyes. And her brightest red lipstick.

She was at the café at 10am exactly.

'Keen,' said the girl in a black dress and white apron. 'Hi, I'm Fiona. He's expecting you.'

She would get on with this Fiona with the chubby face and smiling eyes, and fringe that almost covered them.

'You made an impression. He didn't bother chasing up that reference you gave him. I could tell what would happen by the grin on his face. He told me to show you the ropes. It's a fun place to work. He's in the kitchen but he'll be out soon enough.' Fiona smirked and stopped to catch breath. 'To see you. Let's get you your uniform. Mike's a good bloke, two kids at home, his wife comes in often to check on him.' She turned towards the back of the café. 'Come on, uniform, then I'll show you the ropes.' Fiona pointed to the floor and giggled. 'Try not to drop anything, it won't bounce. I dropped tons when I started. It's the best café for miles. We have a lot of regulars, some sit for hours, others rush in and out. You'll get to know them. The food's good: sandwiches, burgers, doughnuts, prawn cocktails. And cakes.' She paused for breath and patted her tummy. 'I like it. We're famous for our gnocchi. You can try some at break.'

Clemmy took in little except not to drop anything and ran through most of that first day until her feet ached. After five or six hours, she had no more to give. Too often she didn't understand what the customers wanted and too many times she heard the words, 'You're new here,' or 'Not from around here then. Where from?' So Clemmy replied, 'The North,' and the tone of their 'Aah' response told her she'd come from a foreign country.

And yet, when she had the time, she felt their friendliness.

Fiona took her to the pub after work. There was a painting of a dangerous-looking black bull swinging outside. 'Come and get me,' Clemmy whispered under her breath, and didn't admit to Fiona that it was her first time in a pub.

They strolled into a large, dingy room with a bar running down one side, men and a few women sitting on tall stools. Behind the bar were four shelves of brightly coloured bottles of all different shapes and sizes. Chairs with small tables were scattered round the rest of the room, many with girls sitting round them, glasses in hand. Some waved to Fiona.

Clemmy's eyes widened and she shivered with excitement. She pulled back her shoulders and pushed her small breasts forward. This was London.

There were a couple of whistles as they walked through the noisy bar to a table.

'What you drinking?' Fiona asked.

'Same as you.'

Fiona returned with two drinks. 'Vodka and cranberry. Vitamin C, it's good for you but take it easy.' She giggled.

Clemmy took a mouthful and struggled not to spit it out.

Fiona laughed. 'Told you. Bit of a country girl, aren't you?'

Clemmy turned her head away. Perhaps it was kindness but she didn't like it.

'Sorry. Want to come shopping with me on Monday? Me and my bloke split up so you...' Fiona took another large mouthful. 'I threw him out.' There was satisfaction in her voice. 'You got family up north?'

Clemmy shook her head. 'Nope.' How easily she had erased the other.

The café was hard work. At Jack's she had swanned about, but here whole cakes disappeared in less than an hour, and gallons of tea. And the coffee machine never ceased its noisy toil. Clemmy liked being among so many people, mostly young, and soon she found the same customers at her tables, many young men. She made all of them feel special but committing to none. The tips were good. Londoners were a generous lot. Over the next weeks it got easier. She liked Mike and Fiona and life slipped into a pattern: the café Tuesdays to Saturday, 9am to 6pm. It was closed evenings and Sundays. 'No need,' Mike said. 'It's quiet round here then.'

She spent much of her first month's pay, except for the chunk she paid into the bank for Helen, at Selfridges, over several shopping expeditions. At first, under Fiona's willing guidance, she bought a pair of high heels, black leather pants and red flared pants, and a clutch of brightly coloured blouses and baby doll dresses, with nowhere to go in them. She bought a slim gold watch and threw her other away with its ugly, scratched-leather band and overlarge, plain face.

She was introduced to credit cards.

She took leftovers home. The gnocchi was good, but she was not a fussy eater. She explored the streets and found pizzas, Chinese takeaways and fish and chips. Terry's All Gold chocolates were stuffed in her mouth by the fistful but her hectic days saw to it that she didn't put on weight.

When she was off work and the sun shone in the meagre way it did in London, she dressed up and went out, exploring the nearby streets. The buildings – tall, squat, modern or old – and the people were her forest.

25

December 1991

Helen recognised the firm knocking, peered out of the window, and was relieved that she had dressed that morning in trousers and a sweater, both somewhat clean. She opened the door, one hand resting on her stomach, Mine wrapped around her ankles, forever her defender.

Eleanor stood, smiling, cakes in a basket over her arm.

'It's too cold upstairs,' Helen murmured, the mural filling her head, and led Eleanor into the kitchen.

Eleanor seated herself on a chair while Helen busied herself with the small, exquisitely iced cakes and the kettle.

'My mother,' Eleanor pointed to the cakes. 'She loves baking.'

Helen placed a plate with four cakes on the table, keeping the rest for later, and sat opposite Eleanor.

'I have called many times. You must have been out. I even called at the café, spoke to Jack. He told me Clemmy has left. For London.' She paused, waited.

It was six months and Helen's body would have told her if Clemmy was dead. She would be back soon, she had to be.

'How is your painting?'

Eleanor selected a cake, twisting it around in her fingers before biting into it. 'You should not be here on your own. I could move in with you for a while, until...'

Helen stared at her. 'What about your mother?'

'That would be difficult,' and Eleanor wiped her hands on her handkerchief. 'Have you seen a doctor?'

'Yes,' Helen lied. The words had just slipped out so she embellished them a little. 'You don't have to worry, all is sorted.'

Eleanor gazed at Helen, 'Won't you tell me, when is it due?'

Helen counted on her fingers, and offered, 'March.' She bent down, picked up Mine and held him close to her overfull breasts.

'The father,' Eleanor spoke so quietly that Helen almost missed it.

That lie would not come so Helen shook her head.

'You must come and see my mother; she will help you.' Eleanor took out pencil and paper and wrote down a number. 'Phone me any time.'

Helen had seen Eleanor's mother around school, at the special events – a plump, grey-haired old woman who often held Eleanor's hand, which made the children laugh; dressed in ill-fitting skirt and sweater and constantly pushing her glasses back up her nose. She asked them their names and sometimes remembered them, saying, 'Eleanor has told me all about you.'

'You must not give up the painting. You are too good. The gallery will want more.'

'I'll take you to the pond,' Helen's words slipped out, they had a way of doing that. One day she would take that small creature inside her there. Faint dreams of a miniature of Beautiful Boy long, thin, blue-eyed and fair-haired.

She had set off for the library, for books that would tell her everything, and had turned back before getting on the bus, staying away from the librarian with her kind eyes, endeavouring to dismiss her expanding belly.

Outside, the sun was niggardly in its warmth and Helen led the way, breathing in the scents. The ground was thick with leaf mould and the acorns had fallen. Her pace quickened a little until she came to the oak. It was now becoming difficult for her to climb over it. She still mourned it a little.

'Here, let me help you.' Eleanor put her hand out but Helen shrugged it away, sitting sideways on the oak and swinging her legs over, now her regretting her rash offer.

At the pond they sat on the bank, a mist hovering. One of her favourite trees, Bare, she called it, stood proud, some small distance away, its trunk and lower branches strong, broad and grey. It was bare of any growth whatever the season. Its top had disappeared in the mist, giving it a strange, ghostly appearance, imposing a silence, a sombreness, and the few shards of sunlight flickered and fled, only to return, like stars in a cloudy night sky.

Helen relaxed; she could count on the pond for that. Her fingers moved, her thumb and forefinger holding a brush.

Eleanor turned to Helen. 'You must be lonely.' Her voice was soft, loving. 'I will look after you.'

Lonely. Helen massaged the word, disembowelled it. She had been abandoned, however childish that might sound.

Eleanor took Helen's face between her hands, held it a time, then leant forward and placed a kiss on her lips. Helen started. No one had held her like that, except Clemmy. Trembling, she stood and stumbled along the path back to the cottage.

*

Eleanor drove many miles, far away from the forest and Helen. And her mother.

It was late, after midnight and several hours after her mother's bedtime, when she arrived home to her soft, kind face, its wrinkles deepened. Eleanor dumped herself into a chair opposite her.

When Eleanor had told her she was going to the cottage, Mrs Wood had said, 'She's a lovely girl. She is young, be very careful.'

'You should be in bed,' Eleanor said, a little sternly.

'I was waiting up for you.' Her mother put out her arms.

Eleanor stood and started up the stairs.

'Eleanor,' her mother called. 'Sit with me just a moment.'

Eleanor paused, stood a few moments before walking back down to sit on the sofa next to her mother.

'It's late,' her mother said. She took Eleanor's hand. 'Thirty-two years I have loved you. It is sad that you have no one else but me. Others think you are a closed book, not to me, I can turn the pages. She is young, naive, don't hurt her.'

26

1992

Clemmy was restless. Christmas had passed, barely noticed, spent in her room with the pigeon, Granny away somewhere.

The wonder and fear of London had vanished. Sundays and Mondays, she wandered the streets, describing everything to Helen, chattering to her in her head. Yet she had begun to ask herself what she was doing here. Perhaps she should be in New York, the other great city in her imagination ,although she knew little about it: The Big Apple. She'd seen photographs: Liberty Island, the Empire State Building. It was far across the sea.

She came across theatres – the National, the Aldwych, and the Theatre Royal, and she peered into their foyers but had not heard of the plays or most of the actors. Granny had mentioned some of them, just names. She wandered on, to the South Bank, to the Globe. Shakespeare, she knew little about him. She looked up at the three tiers of galleries, at the sky and wondered about the rain, and the large empty space around the stage where Granny said people stood to watch performances. She tried to imagine herself on that stage, heard Mrs Thompson's words, 'You could make a good actress', and asked herself what it would be like to be up there, on stage, all heads turned towards her, waiting. And then the applause. She might be famous even. And a tremor ran through her, starting at her cheeks and finishing at her restless feet.

The next Monday afternoon, Clemmy stood, gazing into the window of one of London's most expensive shopping districts, fingering her purse, knowing she did not have the money, yet loving to dream. There was no law against that, was there? The clothes were stunning, different to the ripped jeans and Doc Martens she was wearing. Her bright red blouse was too skimpy for the February weather, even under her jacket, so she pulled her scarf tight around her neck. She was embarrassed to go in; she'd done so many times and walked out empty-handed. She would have to find herself a rich boyfriend.

A woman stopped beside Clemmy, close, very close.

'Too expensive for you,' the woman said and threw back her head, and laughed.

Clemmy stared at her, her eyes open wide, that voice running through her, causing her heart to thump. It was her, a different her, in expensive, smart clothes, good make-up. Clemmy took a couple of steps back.

'Look good, don't I?' Mother said and started up the street. 'Come on, we can't stand here all day. There's a place up here, I'll treat you.' And she strode ahead, her heels clicking on the pavement, her slightly plump hips swaying in her tight skirt, above it a smart short jacket.

Clemmy followed, some distance behind.

Not much further on, Mother turned into a doorway. A man in a suit smiled and said, 'Your usual table, Madam?'

Mother nodded, a small thing.

They were seated in a large restaurant with thinly spread tables and more waiters than customers, although most of the tables were occupied. Their table was covered with a pristine white cloth, set for two, with equally pristine white napkins.

A waiter offered each a menu.

'Have whatever you want,' and she looked around while Clemmy examined the large and strange menu. Mother waved to a couple a few tables away.

After a time, she beckoned to the waiter. 'Scones for two, please, jam and cream, lots of both. And tea.' She crossed her legs and leant back in her chair, her skirt just reaching to her knees, her slender legs on display.

He smiled. 'Your usual, ma'am,' and scurried away.

Clemmy shifted in her seat, picked up her bag and put it back down.

'So, what are you doing here? Thought you'd never leave that dump. Is she here too?' Her eyes were hard.

Clemmy shook her head.

'Well, that's a surprise. Thought you two were inseparable.'

Clemmy spat back, 'You loved it, all that parading us down the street like animals in a zoo.'

Mother laughed as she recrossed her legs and carefully adjusted her skirt. 'Sometimes you fought like animals in a zoo. At each other's throats. I had to tear you apart, then you both fought me. Sometimes it was war.'

She sat back. 'Sixteen years, lonely years, of being ignored. Sometimes I wished I'd given you away at birth.'

'Wish you had,' Clemmy countered as she leant her elbows on the table.

'Me, I didn't count. I wanted you both to love me, someone at last. I loved you, but you beat it out of me, the two of you.' Mother spoke softly. 'I didn't have much love as a kid, and I believed I could make your lives better than mine had been. I never expected your father to bolt, believed he would hide away up there in that pigsty of a room, but not run.'

The waiter placed a pot of tea in front of each of them, milk, sugar and a plate of four large scones with a bowl of whipped cream and a smaller one of jam.

Mother undid her napkin, shook it, placed it on her lap and put a scone on the small plate. Then she put a very large spoon of red jam on its side and a larger pile of cream beside it. She cut the scone and covered it with jam, then cream, and raised it to her mouth.

Clemmy watched and copied her, action by action, almost giggling.

They both ate in silence, Clemmy constantly wiping her mouth with the large napkin perched on her lap.

'I hated that place, the best he could do. And that forest.' Mother pushed her plate away a few inches.

'So why did we stay?'

'Money. It was his. I couldn't afford to rent anything. He hasn't thrown you out then?' She ate her scone slowly.

Clemmy had almost finished one scone and was fingering the second. Her fingers stilled and she stared at the other woman, her eyes wide. 'He wouldn't, would he?'

'He could, but I don't suppose he will after all this time. He doesn't need the money and I think you hated it too. Not like her. So you've run, to the big smoke.'

Clemmy said nothing.

'Why did you hate me?'

Clemmy did not answer for some moments. She picked up a scone and placed it on her plate. 'You weren't part of our world. We didn't want you.'

'So you didn't really hate me. That's what it felt like, you were little fiends. That silly language you two made up, to shut me out. You believed I couldn't tell you apart. After a while it was easy, you with fury in your eyes, even as a baby, and Helen dreamy, unsure. But you still played your tricks on me. I never laid a finger on you, not that I didn't want to.' Mother stopped talking, drew breath, and tightened her hands into fists.

Clemmy shrugged and slowly covered another scone with thick layers of jam and cream 'What about him?'

Mother's laugh was loud and bitter. 'Your father, he never wanted you, he didn't much want me either but it took time for me to see that. His painting, that was all he lived for. Like your sister.'

Clemmy gagged, almost spitting out a mouthful onto the pristine cloth.

'And you, I never knew where you were, trouble wherever that was. That's what the school said, trouble.' She stared around the room, then at Clemmy, and said in a wet, full voice, 'Could you not have loved me, just a little?'

Clemmy fingered her cup, poured some more tea and shivered in the overheated room, and said nothing.

'My new man, he wouldn't have you.' That laugh again. 'Why should I inflict that on him, risk losing him because of you two? I'd given up all those years of my life, for what?'

Clemmy picked up the last piece of her scone, not looking up.

'For what?'

Clemmy stood.

Mother put out a hand. 'Sit down. You haven't told me about you and your sister. Where is she?'

'Where do you think? The cottage? She'll never leave there.'

'So, what are you doing here? Please sit a minute or two.'

Clemmy sat, crossing her legs just like Mother.

'You can grin.' Mother waited a few seconds, closing her fists again, feeling the nails bite into the flesh. 'I bought you things, everything I could think of. The dolls. I spent a fortune on toys, clothes for you and if they weren't the same, you chucked them. I loved you, but I couldn't stand it, your indifference, perhaps hate, it was destroying me. You could be little devils.' She paused. 'What did I do wrong?'

Clemmy shook her head and muttered, 'It was just her and me.'

'You were beautiful as young children. Everyone admired you, and you appear to have survived but you could do with some better clothes. Don't suppose you have the money.' She half smiled. 'Sorry.'

'Are you going to buy them for me, from that shop?' Clemmy threw back her head and laughed, so loudly that many turned around to stare at them.

'Hush,' Mother murmured.

Clemmy chewed her thumb, the smile gone. 'I left the forest, that dump.' She looked straight into her mother's eyes. 'I left her.' She stood.

'Poor Helen.' Mother had lied a little to her man about the girls, but she had done her duty. No one could deny that. They were old enough back then to take care of themselves.

157

He had no children. She'd had enough of the twins competing with her.

'Well, I know where to find her.' She opened her handbag, took out a notebook and wrote in it, then stood, and held out the piece of paper. She wanted to hug the girl.

'My man died. Here is my address and telephone number should you want to find me.' She almost said, 'I hope you do,' but she had her pride. 'Please tell Helen.'

Clemmy took the piece of paper from the outstretched hand and strode out.

Mother sat and put her slightly trembling hands firmly into her lap.

Back at her bedsit, Clemmy flung herself on her bed, breathing heavily. Mother had looked good, better than she remembered, not the old witch they had laughed at. Some rich bloke, but so what? Clemmy wanted to tell Hel. She sat up and put the piece of paper in a safe place.

She had achieved nothing except leaving Helen and the forest. Everything was supposed to happen here. She was scraping a living but there was a glimmer of a dream. Somehow she would make it real.

27

The first flakes fell, unhurried, feather-like, then in flurries, draping the trees, smothering everything, changing the light. Other years Helen had greeted the snow with joy, the transformation of the forest, the blue-white light. Now the trees, muffled, groaned under the weight; branches snapped and the wounded trunks bled. She staggered to the pond, a swimming motion through snow that reached close to her knees. Her friends, who might have offered solace, hid from her (she did not blame them): the fox, the pheasant, the birds. Her goldfinch had flown south to warmer climes long ago.

She didn't sit on her favourite stone, would have struggled to get up from that, so sat higher up the bank. Small branches stuck to her hair, antlers. Perhaps she was a deer. A fox or a rabbit had recently dug into the soil and the snow had not quite covered the mounds and the hole. She leant forward and put a gloved hand down it. She would have liked to be the burrower, to escape down into the earth. There would be cold stillness there.

Then the creatures began to emerge, to stop and watch her or tiptoe across the untouched surface, and the clouds took up their cudgels and fought, war between sky giants.

A deer trotted, sedate and carefree, through the trees. 'Stay with me,' she murmured. She had always seen herself as a slim silver birch, now she was bovine, ungainly, the thing inside her all-consuming.

The people in the town smiled when they saw her belly. Generous-hearted people but they loved to talk. Only the women smiled at her, at her belly. She did not smile back. Sometimes she felt movement in there. That creature.

The windows rattled, the bitter wind poured in and letters with windows in the envelopes slipped through the door. She took them to Jack. He had explained several times about the account Clemmy had set up and the money he gave her. The letter she longed for did not come.

She'd forgotten it existed, the small room at the back of the cottage. It was filled with boxes, her mother's junk. Tying back her hair, she opened a few, then did not bother with the rest but carried them down, one by one, to the shed, stretching her arms over her belly.

She tried to open a window but it was stuck tight. 'Damn,' she shouted and picked up the broom, and swept the room in a desultory fashion. Mine prowled, wanting out, demanding the forest.

She looked in the mirror. Clemmy was not there, smiling at her, love and laughter in her eyes.

She carried her belly up to the studio, picked up her favourite brush and painted the forest as an island of green, surrounded by giant waves, both keeper and protector. On the highest wave in the distance, she picked out with the tip of her smallest brush a small copper-haired girl, running away.

When her head was drained of stories, she carried the paintings to the small room and stuck them to walls, stood and smiled at her painted world.

Perhaps her blossoming belly might also be magic.

Back in the studio, two birds, kestrels, drifted on a thermal in the clear sky, right there above her. Wings barely moving and when they did it was a dance, the two in unison. They flew closer together and descended a little, their wing tips surely touching, circling, dancing. A sudden movement by the one as it slowly turned away from the other, flew some distance, turned back one more time and then sped away gracefully, with seemingly little effort until it was a dot in the sky, then gone.

The other was still buoyed by the thermal.

She opened the window. The bitter cold caused her to tremble. Helen smiled and rested her hands on her strange belly.

Clemmy was not lost to her.

'Be still,' the wind murmured. 'This is not a day for storms.'

March 2nd 1992

Helen's waters broke as she lay on the sofa, half reading, half dreaming. She panted, felt the wet beneath her and opened her mouth wide. It was happening, what should not, what could not. She longed for it to be over, to abandon whatever monstrous growth filled her belly, run into the forest and hide. Forever.

The pain changed that. She wanted to die.

No one was out there. She screamed and her terror increased. 'Clemmy, Clemmy,' she shouted. 'Where are you?'

Her screams flew through the window into the forest, and the birds rose from their perches and joined in.

She bent double, then leant on the table, placing one hand on her belly. A sharp pain.

In the hall, she grabbed a coat and her bag and carried her belly out the front door and along the track, stopping frequently with each stab of pain.

Her friends, the trees, taunted her, rain splattered her head and the sky closed over.

She counted her steps, beginning again when she reached twenty but stopping at any number, gasping when the pain hit. She reached the bus stop, staggered, the pain sharper, more frequent. She knocked at the door of the first house, looked up, as she fell onto the front step, and the limpid sun edged out from behind the cloud.

Many hours later, Helen gazed down at the baby. She would find Clemmy, take him to her. He was theirs. Relief poured through her.

Then she carefully removed the towel and laid him, naked, on her bare breast, his skin against hers, and wanted him never to leave her arms. 'Samuel,' Helen said aloud, wondering at the name. 'You are safe. It is a strange, bewildering world but I will love you and keep you safe always.'

She held Samuel in her arms, gazing at his plump mouth, his nose, cheeks, eyes and sparse hair. She gave his chubby hand her forefinger. He grasped it. What was he saying? And then she placed his mouth on her nipple and she wept a little for the beauty of it.

No one visited her in the busy ward. The nurses were kind, the other mothers too, but the one she wanted was there only in her dreams.

The sister asked her who was at home to help her. Helen was puzzled by the question and the sister was puzzled by her youth, the absence of medical information on this mother and baby. The address appeared odd and Helen was an independent creature, but far too innocent. She would make arrangements for health visitors when mother and baby returned home.

The whispers, the concern, the hints of adoption reached Helen, so she scrabbled in her bag for a telephone number, paused a moment or two then handed it to the nurse.

28

March 1992

Clemmy woke to a dull, clouded sky. Something was wrong. Helen needed her.

She stayed in bed long after she should have left for work, trying to decide, a pain in her stomach. Should she go back to Helen?

She could not go back, not yet.

Late afternoon, as she came through the door, Granny got up from her armchair, her light feet hurrying, knitting in her hand. Her face alight.

'I have something for you.'

Clemmy tried to smile, the shadow over her day diminished a little.

'Judi Dench, you'll love her.' She dug in her pocket and then held out a ticket. 'The National, Anton Chekhov, Judi Dench.' The words rushed out, competing with her excitement.

Clemmy had seen the posters at the National Theatre but

had not tarried. She took the ticket, saw the price and held it back out to Granny.

'Don't worry about the price, I have to go out of town, family. I want you to have it, dear.'

Granny had never mentioned family in their teatime chats.

'She's in *The Seagull*, a wonderful play, pity to waste it.' And her smile broadened.

Clemmy laughed and briefly touched Granny's arm. She would play her game, had never heard of Chekhov except when she'd glanced at the posters at the theatre and thought it an odd name.

The next afternoon, Clemmy pulled out everything from her wardrobe, slinging it on her bed. Her first night at the theatre, she trembled a little. It sounded foreign, the play. She finally selected a red silk sheath dress that ended just above her knees, showing off her long legs. On her feet, red patent-leather high heels and over the dress, a plain black, short jacket. Her hair was tied back with a red ribbon, high on the back of her head.

She left the quiet house early and walked to the bus stop.

She stood outside the theatre long minutes, clutching her ticket, moving from foot to foot and watching people stream in, young and old. In the foyer she stopped abruptly, almost making the couple behind bump into her. They all laughed.

Inside the theatre she stared around, filled with wonder at the number of people, the seemingly hundreds of rows curving around the stage, the seats already almost full, the pulsating excitement and expectation and lights everywhere. She had never been in a place so exciting, so different and beautiful. She craned her head upwards, to the tiers high up, filled with young people, eager faces. That was where she wanted to be.

She had found London.

She didn't move from her seat during the interval, sat trying to imagine who the actors really were, how they became someone else who she believed in utterly. Judi Dench, in costumes and hats the like of which she had not seen before, as Arkadina, a beautiful middle-aged woman, aristocratic, selfish, hypocritical, speculating about her life. She wished she could meet Judi, but Nina was the one that fascinated her most, her need for fame and fortune as an actress, the need to find happiness and self-love.

For the first time she hailed a London cab, giggling and excited as she slid into the capacious back. The sense of magic, of love, that she'd had as she took her seat had evaporated, and something else was replacing it. Through the night, almost until dawn, she relived the play. 'That is who I must be,' she told herself, thinking of Judi Dench as Arkadina, betrayed by her ageing lover, playing cards while her son lay dead in another room, or Nina, a whirlwind across the stage. Words, phrases came back to her. She cried for the son, blamed the mother. 'What will come in life will come,' Irina had said. Clemmy did not believe that. You were the one, it was you who had to decide.

Could she do it, become someone else? Did she understand herself well enough to leave that self?

The next morning, Clemmy skittered down the stairs to peer into Granny's sitting room. She was back, perhaps had never gone anywhere. The knitting was on her chair, and a book. She heard movement above then her footsteps downwards, and Granny, with a smile that made her seem as if she was dancing.

'Tell me,' she said, standing in front of Clemmy, then, bending to place the book on the floor beside her chair, she picked up her knitting and sat down.

Clemmy sat cross-legged in her chair opposite. 'Wonderful, thank you. I haven't slept all night.' Clemmy waved her arms about, then stilled them. They had laughed together, mostly about Clemmy's stories of the café, but this was different. 'Granny...' Clemmy placed a hand across her mouth, but a smile lingered in her eyes.

'Granny,' the old woman said. 'Granny.' Her voice sparkled.

'Sorry,' Clemmy held her arm. 'It's what I call you.'

'That's lovely, but what about your real grannies?'

'I have none.' The words hurt her a little.

'Then Granny I shall be. I'll get tea and biscuits, breakfast can wait.' She stood a little stiffly and walked, humming, towards the kitchen door.

Clemmy blurted out after her, 'I want to be an actress.'

Granny swung round, then back. 'Just wait a minute, dear, that's exciting. Two minutes.'

Clemmy tried to sit still when Granny returned, with the tea and biscuits, but grabbed a biscuit, shoving it whole into her mouth, from the plate that Granny set down on the small table beside her.

Granny sat, her hands around her tea and her smile still bathing them both in warmth and unspoken love. 'I have seen it, *The Seagull*, knew you would love it, you are a bit like Nina.' She picked up a biscuit and ate it, small bites and long spaces between, her brow furrowed. 'It's a hard life, being an actress.' She sipped her tea and added so softly that Clemmy had to lean forward to hear. 'I wasn't always an old lady.' She leant back in her chair and laughed.

Clemmy leant forward, eyes wide, struggling for her words. 'What did you play?'

'Oh, lots of different things, some small, some big. You have to start small, walk-on parts, then a few lines, make yourself useful off stage.' Her voice faded a little.

She was elsewhere and Clemmy, slumped back in her chair, uncrossed her legs. That was not her dream.

'It's like anything else, you have to learn the job, learn to really listen, work out what's behind the words, even in everyday life.'

Clemmy wished that this fragile old lady, always dressed in ankle-length flowing flowery dresses, with plain round glasses and a thin angular body, really was her granny.

'Practise, practise, practise,' Granny said, again as if speaking to herself, 'getting into someone else's head, learning the lines. I expect you are dreaming of being a star. You're young, you should, but there's a lot more I could tell you. Perhaps another time.'

Clemmy shoved away her memories of the school play.

'How Granny, how?'

Granny's voice softened. 'It's a tough profession, being someone else.' She stopped. 'Enough, you will learn, like I did. There's a playhouse near here, small and a very local audience. A good place to start. I still know a couple of people there. You have energy, enthusiasm.' She looked across the room to the bookshelves. 'Do you read a lot? I think not.'

Clemmy stayed silent.

'You should,' she smiled. 'Here's Granny talking. You

need to get into the heads of others, work them out. Novels are a good start. I'll pick some out for you.' She looked at her watch. 'You'll be late for work.'

When Clemmy got home, downstairs was in darkness, and on the stairs a pile of books. Donna Tartt, *The Secret History*. She ran her fingers over the cover, weighed the book in both hands. It was big. She flipped through the pages, liked the look of Donna. She might get round to that. Toni Morrison, *Beloved* – a black woman – so she was curious but perhaps not enough. And others by writers with foreign-sounding names: Salmon Rushdie, Haruki Murakami. She'd heard of Stephen King and John Le Carré. She sighed. They looked like hard work.

29

Eleanor stood in the kitchen doorway and looked around. The large table was clear but the rest was a mess, dirty dishes littered the surfaces. She could find little food. She sighed, made a cup of tea and took it upstairs, then drove to the town and bought nappies and food, and went home to pack a bag and tell her mother she would be gone a few days.

She had picked Helen and the baby up from the hospital. Helen had said little on the way home, saving her words for the infant she called Sam.

Winter was hanging on.

Helen walked, a little unsteadily, into the kitchen, smiling, 'You've cleaned up my mess. And the flowers are beautiful. Thank you.'

Eleanor had reorganised much and bought pretty baby clothes, and everything her mother said Helen might need.

In those first few days, Eleanor left only briefly, to drive to the shops. She had never expected this, not in her life plan, but was learning fast.

She had to return to school, half term was over, but came back to Helen and Sam most evenings, after checking on her mother. She observed Helen's love for the child grow. As did her own. In time Eleanor took Sam into her arms, trembling a little, and drowning in his smile.

When the health visitor came, the surprise on her face as she looked around, and watched Helen feeding Sam, was evident.

Eleanor, carrying Sam, followed Helen up to the studio. 'Mummy's pictures, Sam,' she said and kissed the top of his head.

Eleanor stepped forward, close to the mural then turned to Helen. 'It's good, new for you but...'

'Let's sit,' Helen said and walked to the sofa.

'I don't understand.'

Helen bit her lip. No one would understand the meaning of that dress.

'The hands?'

'Clemmy and me.' Eleanor had lost her school teacher shadow. She was her friend – one she could rely on. Perhaps a first.

Eleanor sat beside Helen, still nursing Sam in her arms. 'Will you tell me who the father is?'

'A gift from Clemmy. I will have no other lovers.'

'Rape then.'

'No, her gift, Beautiful Boy, that's what I call him.' Helen's lips closed tight. Sam's birth certificate would be like hers and Clemmy's, which they'd found among Mother's things: fatherless. He had no need of a father. Her love and Clemmy's, for she would love him totally when she came back, would carry him through life until he found love elsewhere.

Eleanor continued to stare at the bloodied dress. Then took a few steps along to stand in front of the second mural. 'And the other?'

Helen said nothing.

'I will come back soon and take you to Mother's.' Eleanor hovered on the doorstep. 'She is longing to see you both, I have told her so much.' Eleanor flushed a little.

*

Mrs Wood's house was in the middle of a row and abutted the pavement. She loved the closeness of the street and sat in the window where she could watch her world stroll by. Most were strangers but a few friends stopped to wave, knowing she would be there, and many others had grown accustomed to her, had ceased thinking of her as nosey, so they too waved.

The room had an old but comfy-looking sofa and two similar armchairs. A large worn Persian carpet covered most of the wooden floor, and a couple of small tables lazed, somewhat randomly. Two china dogs guarded the room from the mantlepiece, and a china cabinet sat in the corner, with exquisite delicate crockery and on its top a large photograph of Eleanor.

Mrs Wood found the stairs difficult, had done so for a few years, but cleaned her own bedroom and the front room with a duster, and a heavy old-fashioned Hoover when she felt like it, which was not often. 'I'm old,' she told herself, 'I can do what I want.'

Helen knocked, Sam in her arms. Eleanor stood back a little.

'Come in, dear, I've been waiting for you. Lovely. And this is Sam.'

Sam gave her his best smile.

Mrs Wood was small and stout, wearing a check skirt and a heavy sweater. A pair of glasses attached to a cord bounced on her large breasts. She led Helen down the hall and into the front room. She pointed to the chair in the window. 'I saw you both outside. Sit there, dear.' She motioned to an easy chair. 'Eleanor will get us something to drink and some biscuits.'

It was not long before she said, 'Could I hold him? It is so long since Eleanor was his age.'

As Eleanor emerged from a door on the opposite side of the room carrying a tray, Sam was in Mrs Wood's arms, gurgling his contentment.

'Didn't think it would take long, Mum.'

Helen was startled to hear the love in Eleanor's voice when she said Mum. Perhaps it had been there for her and Clem and they had refused it. Mother must have held them in her arms like that, once.

'He must be the joy of your mother's life, her grandchild.'

Helen took a deep breath. 'She left us a few years ago. We haven't heard from her.' Helen gave a small laugh, 'And are not likely to. She does not know she has a grandchild.'

'That's a shame. Two beautiful girls like you, she must have loved you. And Sam, his granny.'

There was puzzlement in her eyes.

Granny. Helen bit her bottom lip, wanting Sam back in her arms. His father was far away, but he would have two mothers, of that she was certain.

'Mum,' Eleanor said, sounding a little like she had done at school.

Helen picked up a biscuit while looking around the room for a wedding photograph and found none. Eleanor had never mentioned her father. Later, leaving a contented Sam on Mrs Wood's knee, gazing up at her as she told him stories, laughing with him and kissing his soft cheeks, Helen wandered into the small back garden with its borders of rose bushes and a small patch of grass in the middle.

'Mother's,' Eleanor said, as she followed her out. 'If she can tear herself away from the window and it's sunny, this is where she is,' and she pointed to a large wooden seat. 'I do a bit of weeding.'

*

That night Helen lay in bed, Sam in her arms, and travelled back to her own childhood, her arms around Clemmy, giggling with her, plotting, running away. They had turned to each other, not Mother. Would Sam refuse to run to her arms? There was no one else to run to. Surely all children were not as cruel as she and Clem had been. Her eyes searched his, his fist in his mouth, his small feet dancing in the air. Her hair was tied back and the necks of her dressing gown and nightie pulled down, to allow Sam to reach her breast. The first time he'd closed his gums on her nipple she had gasped, then relaxed. She held him close now, placing her own lips on his head. His small hands clasped her breast, his mouth on her nipple and he sucked, eyes closed, a frown wrinkling his forehead, as her life flowed into him.

There were the good times, and some days she wept, telling herself, 'I can't do this, I can't. I'm a bad mother.' It wasn't his bawling or the screaming; it was the helplessness and the fear. She had known nothing of babies, a total omission from her sense of the world. Little foreigners. The hospital had instructed her in essentials: feeds, nappies, and much more to which she barely listened. Not indifference, for she had entered a world of dream.

His nappy was full. He didn't seem to care. Why should she? Sometimes pain in his eyes. Could it be pain, the unknown, terrorising him? He didn't understand love yet. She was just there, his.

Slowly the bad days decreased, replaced by the music of wonder and joy. However much love she drowned him with, he would, after a time, survive without her, become somewhat unknowable. He would always love her, she was certain of that. Love others, perhaps more than her. For now, she was his world.

When the sun offered more warmth, she carried him into the forest where he gazed upward at the trees, his eyes wide, a small hand waving. The hazel bowed to him, as if to a king, with its long hairy leaves and clusters of nuts, and the horse chestnut, with its saw-like leaves and tall arching branches.

'Conkers. We will have a game with them one day. I'll teach you.' Clemmy had hated that game.

They stopped. 'My oak. It was the king of the forest, once. Now it's resting.' She laughed and kissed his small, fat lips.

He opened his eyes wide. She had read him many stories about kings. Sometimes he seemed to be practising his words, odd sounds from his lips, a serious look in his eyes. They scrambled over the oak, passing the swathes of white, the wild garlic, its smell greeting them and the drooping heads of the bluebells, on the slopes leading to the pond. They sat on the grass on the pond's edge, Sam on Helen's lap, water gently lapping. Small ducklings, brown, fluffy, each little more than a man's finger length, swam their own paths through the water, creating individual V-waves behind them, turning in circles. Paddling, paddling.

Sam made soft noises and Helen bent her head to place a kiss on his forehead. His eyes didn't move from the ducklings.

Males and females foraged on the nearby bank. They had bright orange feet, and the males had green iridescent head plumage and white banded necks. They moved closer, over the firm mud, quacking softly. The young followed, scrambling and pecking Helen's feet, trusting. Sam wriggled.

At the far end, the heron, tall and elegant, waited. Many years he had feasted – one duckling, one mouthful.

She would teach Sam everything about the birds, the trees. Everything.

She snatched brief hours' painting; she had a story to tell. She would paint or go mad, and she had been there before. She carried Sam up to her studio, dragging his basket behind her. He slept some of the time, Mine curled up beside him. Or on her knee at the window, where she showed him the tops of the trees, told him tales of the animals in the forest.

She no longer trembled to see the bloodied gold dress on the wall with its red stain, sparrow hawk and goldfinch. And the second mural. When some of her anger and despair had subsided, she tried to imagine Clemmy in London, doing what, she did not know. She understood that Clemmy had needed the drama of London, whatever that was, and that one day she would astonish the world at something. She was not like the other girls at school, and they had scorned her for it. Her time would come.

And there was the anger, for the desertion of the one who

had sworn throughout their lives together that she would never leave her. Yet she too had changed, her determination had grown. Any free time from her studio was used with visits to the library for her and for Sam. He loved his picture books.

She was his mother.

She painted the rest of the wall white, then drew the outlines of more pictures. She might never finish them but that didn't matter. She relived the stories that her brushstrokes were creating. Her hand, unhesitating, did the thinking and the painting, although sometimes it ran riot and she had to paint over much of it.

30

Clemmy found the books disappointing at first, a load of rubbish, she muttered, to her friend, the pigeon. Helen was the reader, not her. There, she was doing it again. Perhaps she should have tried harder at school, but there had been little point. She persevered with Donna Tartt and *The Secret History*. Like its narrator, she believed in fate. But it was too clever for her so she gave up. She tried John Le Carré and got into his ways.

And she waited for Granny to return so she could talk to her about them. They invited her into a world she had never even imagined. That excited her. Granny had told her, 'Watch and observe what they are they doing and why. The little things, not the obvious. The café is perfect for you, but hardest of all you have to know yourself if you are to understand your character.'

One night when Clemmy got home from work she found Granny sitting in her chair. She did not say where she had been for the past days, was away more frequently nowadays, although usually only a few days at a time. On those evenings, Clemmy sat in Granny's chair in the sitting room and turned on her much larger television.

'Clemmy,' Granny called out as Clemmy opened the front door.

Clemmy ran in and hugged her, 'Granny,' then stepped back, feeling her face redden.

'Sit a while, dear. I've had a long journey but I stayed up to see you.'

'I've read some.' Clemmy picked at her thumb. 'I didn't like all of them.'

'That's all right, dear, I didn't expect you to love them all. I have some news for you. My friend Will at the playhouse wants to meet you. You'll have to start small. Backstage theatre is tough but it will be a start.'

'Who? What?' Clemmy blurted out.

'I don't know.' She smiled. 'Might be just a walk-on part, no lines. Don't expect too much.' She stood. 'I need my bed. It's lovely to see you again, here's his name and telephone,' and she held out a piece of paper then climbed the stairs very slowly.

*

Clemmy put on a bright yellow blouse, tight black trousers and new sandals, ran her hands through her hair, now just reaching her shoulders. She bent quickly to the mirror to give Helen her special face, wrinkling her nose. 'I'm going to be an actress.'

She pushed open the double doors that led into the small

theatre's foyer. Laughter and chatter catapulted out. She stepped back, then pushed through the doors. People were clustered in groups. Some swung towards her, expectant, smiling, then turned away.

Clemmy paused.

A man with a huge smile walked up to her. 'You must be Clemmy. Welcome. I'm Will, Gwen told me to expect you.' He stepped away a little and his eyes took a long, slow journey from her feet to her face. 'Gwen said you were keen, said she'd told you you'd have to start small. Any experience?'

Clemmy shook her head.

'So why do you want to act? It's not easy.'

Clemmy opened her handbag and dragged out all the tickets for the shows she'd been to. She held them out.

'Impressive,' he said. 'You are serious. Who's your favourite?'

'Judi Dench.'

'Me too. You could help with the teas and backstage. It's on for a week and we'll see after that.' He pointed towards a door. 'Have a look around, they could do with some help backstage; we're about to start our last rehearsal. It starts tomorrow.'

Clemmy stared at him. The teas. She would leave. She stopped herself.

She glanced into the auditorium, a sliver of fear and excitement coursing through her. It was much smaller than she had expected. Then she slipped through the door to backstage.

She stood totally still. It appeared to be chaos, bits of furniture and people everywhere in such a small space. No one noticed her. A woman hurried by with a dozen dresses slung over her arm and men and girls were pushing furniture about. A few, in costume, were scattered about on their own, reading or just sitting silent. She was lost, unnoticed, thought she might not come back.

From outside came laughter and the sound of banging seats. Here there was noise and constant calls for quiet. She heard a voice say, 'Give us a hand, love,' and she continued to stare around.

'I mean you, love,' and the voice sounded impatient.

Clemmy flushed and rushed over to help.

The play was a comedy but she had little time to laugh or even hear it clearly. Backstage she was a dogsbody, quick to help out when asked but often in the way or feeling excluded. She made few friends. She would not be backstage long, she swore to herself. She did the teas at interval, willingly and with a smile, a friend to everyone.

On the last night she stayed for the party, knew many of the names by then, mostly the stage hands. She carried her drink, which she didn't much like, to where Will was sitting and squeezed in beside him. She had tried and failed to get a moment to talk to him about Granny.

'Had fun, Clemmy, saw you running about, well done.'

'How do you know Gwen?' she kept her voice low.

He looked around the room, sipped his wine before answering. 'We haven't seen her for a long time. She doesn't even come to the performances now.' He twisted the stem of his glass. 'She was our star for nearly ten years, all the best roles were hers. We all loved her. And she went on to much greater things.'

'Why did she stop?'

'Her family, her lad. Got into trouble, serious trouble with the law. It was in the papers. She almost bankrupted herself helping him out, went up there for some years, then she returned but never came back here. A shame.'

He turned to Clemmy. 'She likes you, I think.'

'She goes away a lot,' Clemmy paused. 'And is a little sad.'

'It destroyed her. I'm happy we are back in touch. You did that.' He shifted in his seat. 'I need another drink. There might be something in the next play for you. Not sure what it is yet. Not a big role but it will get you started.'

Clemmy waited, for one thing only, and it came a few weeks later.

'A small part, a maid. I promised Gwen.'

Clemmy wondered if she heard reluctance in his voice.

Her silence told him all. He laughed. 'Perhaps you'll be a star one day. You'll have to prove yourself.'

She made mistake after mistake, wanting to cry walking home. She was a failure. In the dressing room, most had their special place, especially those who had been in the playhouse a long time. And the stars. She fell foul of one on the first night of rehearsal, had spread out her things on a bench and came back to find them placed, neatly enough, elsewhere.

A maid. That made her laugh. Well, she was already that, in a way, at the café, but she had to learn to be a different maid on stage, be unobtrusive, servile. She had never been those things, hated it, wanted to stamp her foot and run. Too often she found herself in the wrong place, her voice too loud. Not servile.

She had to light a cigar for one of the toffs, a tall, leering man. She lit the match and held it out. It burnt down to her fingers before she could blow it out and she put her fingers in her mouth. The audience cheered, but that moment, a serious one, far from comic, was trashed. Later, Jim, the cigar smoker, laughed his stage-loud, braying laugh, patted her on the shoulder and said, 'We'll have to practise.'

And a folding card table that she had to set up in the middle of Act Two nearly collapsed on her although she had practised endlessly.

'You'll get there,' Will said. 'Watch, listen, leave yourself behind, become a quiet, obedient maid.' He touched her arm lightly. 'Not easy.'

She saw sympathy in the eyes of the kind, and irritation in others.

*

Granny was waiting up for her after the first night.

'Success?'

'A dozen lines.' Clemmy slumped in her chair, legs crossed. 'I'll have to do better. You would have been ashamed of me, Granny, I was rubbish.'

'You will get better. Nobody steps straight into acting. It's the hardest thing.'

'Will you come?'

'I think not, I can't go back there, although I loved it.'

*

Clemmy slipped off her shoes and flung herself on the bed. It was too late for the pigeon. She missed him. She did not expect to hear from Will again.

She crawled into bed, fully clothed.

My first acting and I made a mess of it, Hel. Perhaps I should give up. I was a maid. Can you believe it? Me, a maid, and a pretty stupid one at that. Thank God you weren't there. Not sure I can go on trying. You know me, Hel, think I can conquer anything. Well, I can't. And I want this more than anything else. But I won't give up. I AM going to be an actress. You and I, we will both be famous.

I need you here to tell me that, every day.

31

Sam took his first steps, often landing with a bump on his bottom, giggling. His fist was much in his mouth while his eyes did the talking. His wispy hair had changed to copper curls. Helen knelt and held out her hands, 'Come to Mummy,' and heard an echo in those words from many years ago.

His eyes followed her everywhere, full of questions. She watched him grow in wonder at the world around him and did not regret too much abandoning her painting. She endeavoured to understand the world through his eyes, living in that moment alone. She failed, her own innocence long since gone. The daily new lessons of life had drowned the old.

She carried Sam to the pond, strapped to her breast, and told him stories of the forest. Little people and magic figured large, and evil not at all, wanting for him all that was good and generous.

At the pond, the mallards, their nerveless orange legs paddling fast, welcomed him and clambered out of the water to sit on the stone pier beside him. He stretched out his small hands to them and spoke back to them in his own language.

The birds in the trees joined in with trills of joy and welcome.

She painted Sam's room, a story on the wall of a forest for little people, and for the mice she loved, too shy, always disappearing. From the forest floor they would see the oak's roots transformed into insuperable hillocks, its trunk into a mountain reaching to the sky. They might climb the mountain and swing on the lichen. She imagined them in her lap, giggling as she tickled their tummies, and a squirrel, scampering up the trunk, along the branches, leaping from tree to tree, jumping high and wide. Trees whispered to each other, and on their branches, played elves with pointed caps, long skinny legs and pointed shoes. And a goldfinch and a kestrel. A strange, magical light. Badgers, foxes, rabbits, birds.

And in one corner, a small boy.

Helen told him a story, of the forest and a small boy.

A small creature ran along the forest paths, barely disturbing the calm, his copper hair overlong. Chaffinches and tits, and a robin flew close to his head, and rabbits, and foxes followed him.

Like all small things, he grew quickly, his green eyes darting every which way. He feared nothing, stumbling from time to time but picked himself up and carried on, his steps becoming firm, steady.

His tree, his sturdy oak, welcomed him and each branch waved its pleasure.

His nimble feet and his limbs carried him swiftly upwards, the squirrel leading the way, and he followed over the moss on the branches and through the curtains of lichen. Soon he could run up the trunk, springing lightly from branch to branch in his bare feet. The rabbits and foxes climbed after him, branch by branch.

The birds stayed close, their songs urging him on and up, except the goldfinch, which waited at the top.

The boy sat the day long on the topmost branches, his head on one side, listening to the birds and their songs, trying to sing with them, and listening to the wind's stories of the places it had travelled. He did not feel the cold so he was lightly clad. Some days he wore a cap made of green cloth but mostly he let his copper hair fall on his shoulders. The birds collected any hairs that he lost and carried them to their nests.

From the treetops, he saw Mummy at the window. His other mummy was many miles away but he saw her too. They had both come to him once and said, in one voice, 'You must love us both.' And he promised.

Then he grew lonely for others like him to play with, so he came down from the tree. It bowed its branches as he left for the last time, the birds sat on his shoulders and sang sweet, sad songs and the fox and rabbit returned to their homes.

The beloved boy ran back to where he belonged, bidding farewell to his friends.

Sam listened, gazing around at the trees and the water, perhaps searching for the little boy while gurgling noises of approval.

Not long after his second birthday, dressed in woollen beanie, yellow jacket, trousers, boots and a Sam-sized pack on his back, he stepped onto the pebbles at the edge of the pond, took another two steps and watched his feet sink into the water and rush up around his boots.

The mallards stopped to watch.

The blackbird applauded.

Sam then bent down and wet his fingertips in the water, gazing at the mark he'd made in its surface and chuckled.

He tottered from the shade of the trees onto the sunlit track, his shadow stepping out with him. He pointed to the shadow and danced. The creature danced with him.

'You, Sam,' Helen said. 'Sam.'

He was wearing his little backpack and the shadow was wearing his.

Sam danced back into shade.

'Where gone, Mummy?'

'Here, Sam.' Helen pointed to the sunny path.

Sam ran forward. 'Sam, Sam,' he shouted as he and his shadow danced, backward, forward and around. Then, 'Mummy, Mummy.'

The word Mummy coursed through her head, a river in flood. She had never used that word, had refused. Both of them had refused. Sometimes now when Sam came running to her, shouting 'Mummy,' she felt Mother beside her, heard her. 'Why would you and she not call me that?'

He sat at a small table, crayons enclosed in his fist, paper in front of him, his tongue out, moving across his lips in concert with his crayon. Mother would have adored him. And he would have loved her.

On the grass, outside the cottage, was a blanket spread

out on the ground, strewn with his toys, mostly bought by Eleanor. Sam fingered them all, for a short time, surprise on his face, or held Owlie in his arms or let him fall to reach for his paper and crayons. He refused to wear shoes, sometimes hurting his feet, but that did not change his determination to go barefoot.

When it snowed, Helen held his hand as they staggered along the path, and he reached out to touch the white jewels on the trees. A mantle of snow crystals clung to him, to his hair and eyelids.

And sometimes she pushed him along the track to the bus into town and Woodie, as Sam called her. There Helen lay on the couch, daydreaming about her painting, getting up occasionally to make tea and find the cakes Mrs Wood always had tucked away ready.

Eleanor continued to call most weekends and Helen left the two of them to play and wandered up to her studio.

One weekend, Eleanor arrived with a large parcel. 'A seat for Sam, for your bike. The two of you can go together.'

Helen cycled into town with Sam in front of her, laughing and shouting. And they explored the shops and surprised Woodie.

32

1994

On a late spring day, a tall, slim man carrying a black bag loped into the café. Clemmy turned away at first, from his long hair, like him in the portrait. Not many Londoners had big smiles but this man did and after a time she giggled to see his shoulder-length wavy hair, and his clothes tatty and worn. He sat at a corner table, placing his elbows on it before opening his bag.

His tanned, strong hands unpacked a camera and held it carefully. It was large and very expensive-looking. The only camera she had really seen was the one under the bed.

'Thomas, a photographer. He's always off on some adventure with that camera. He's quiet but good, takes pictures of street people. A bit weird.' Fiona pulled a face. 'I keep trying it on with him. No luck.'

He came in the following four days, always sitting at the same table, ignoring Clemmy.

Then, on the fifth day, he bent to place his camera on the table on the other side of the café, Clemmy's territory, and his fair hair tripped around his neck and partly across his face.

Clemmy walked over, trying to dampen her excitement, pencil and pad in her hands, although he ordered the same thing every day: tea and two doughnuts.

'You're new,' his voice soft yet strong. He put down his cigarette, raked his hair roughly back, reached into a pocket and pulled out a band and tied it back. Some locks escaped and Clemmy's fingers moved as if to tuck them back. He had a broad, tanned face and was wearing a buttoned-down blue shirt, his sleeves rolled up, revealing tanned arms covered in fair hair.

'Clemmy.' She wanted to sit down and talk to this man and didn't understand why.

'Gorgeous, isn't he?' Fiona murmured. 'He can't take his eyes off you. You lucky devil.'

Then he disappeared.

'Off on one of his trips,' Fiona said. 'He'll be back.'

He returned a long week later and sat at the same window table. Sometimes Clemmy stood and chatted or listened. He showed her his camera, the clever things it could do, his eyes shining, and she found it hard to follow. That didn't matter, she just let his soft voice wrap around her.

Each day, at work, she waited the slow minutes, until she saw him pass the window, then through the door, and when not at work she couldn't stay in, forgot the books, wandered the streets, but still spent much of her pay on theatre tickets, hearing Granny's words, trying to understand the characters, and at other times restless, waiting for him.

'I won't see you for a time, a job to do, a week or two, me and my camera.' He put his camera down.

Clemmy endeavoured to keep smiling.

The day Thomas was back, it was Clemmy's twentieth birthday, something she shared with no one but Helen.

'I could cook you dinner.' His eyes were serious.

Clemmy's eyes opened wide, her shoulders shook.

'Wait and see, I'm good. Tonight, I'll pick you up. What's your address?'

She wrote on her order pad.

'Six-thirty, OK?' His voice contained its usual smile.

*

Thomas was thirty-two, and past girlfriends, possibly a misnomer, had refused to compete with his photography and his absences, so had faded. Sometimes he came back from his trips wrecked, exhausted from sleeping in hostels, cheap hotels, or in his car in a sleeping bag he always had at the ready. And bad food. People and places in well-off areas did not interest him. When he couldn't get the shot he was searching for, the soul of the person or of the building or whatever, through the camera lens, he lost faith in himself and that was all he had.

That first day, Thomas had tried to work her out, his fingers straying toward his camera. Mike had told him about the copper-haired beauty. The streets had taught him to look for the little things that everyday eyes missed. He couldn't help himself, he was a watcher, always searching for that unique expression. He ignored the obvious, her beauty, difficult as that was, caught the confidence and exuberance. She wanted to tame the world. There was a flicker of something else. Perhaps loneliness? He should recognise that, had seen it often enough in his own eyes. He wanted to photograph her but he would have to be clever to really find her. And he wanted to hold those slender white hands with their brightly coloured nails. So, he'd come back to the café day after day. He'd had no one in his arms for a long time.

*

A large, red-brick house with windows the size of doors confronted her. She followed him down a short path running between paved brick squares with pot plants dotted about on them.

'The kitchen,' Thomas pointed to an open door in the hall.

She was itching to run upstairs and explore but strolled into the kitchen. It was like something she'd only seen in magazines – white cupboards lined one wall with a giant fridge at one end. On the opposite wall, more cupboards and a cooker. In the middle was an enormous smooth, white table. She ran a finger across it, smooth as silk. Lights hung low.

She perched on a stool, swinging her legs, leaning her elbows on the table, wondering. To have a man cook, just for her. She wanted to laugh while watching his long legs move quickly across the kitchen. She waited for him to look at her, so she could wander into his hazel eyes.

'We'll eat in here. No fuss.' He stubbed out his cigarette, opened a drawer and put on an apron.

Clemmy's eyes opened wide and she placed a hand over her mouth.

He grinned. 'Never seen a man in an apron? Chefs wear them.' And he rolled up his shirt sleeves, then reached up and took a book from a high shelf. 'Elizabeth David, a bit old-fashioned but my mother swore by her. I've got half a dozen of her books, this is her best, *French Provincial Cooking.* Mum taught me when I was a kid. I eat a lot of rubbish when I'm away so like to cook when I'm home. The French, you can't beat them – not their cooking anyway.'

He grinned and it made Clemmy want to eat him. His mother sounded fun, but the French – she knew nothing about them or their cooking. Or Elizabeth David. What sort of mother taught a boy to cook? She was a little jealous. And she remembered the bread Helen cooked; Mother had taught her. Clemmy wondered why Mother hadn't bothered to teach her anything much. She wriggled on the stool.

'Boeuf en Daube.' That grin again. 'Don't be too impressed, beef stew. You like beef?'

Clemmy nodded, although she didn't much like it.

'Best beef you can get, bacon, carrots, onions, tomatoes, garlic and some herbs. Perfection. And some red wine, of course.'

Clemmy swallowed. It sounded awful.

'I made it last night, have to heat it and cook some pasta. Won't take long. You'll have to entertain me while I cook.'

She didn't offer to help. How could she? She sat and watched him, his smiling face, wanting to throw her arms around him, hold his face between her hands and make him kiss her, to have those strong hands on her breasts.

'What's this bedsit of yours like?' he said, over his shoulder.

'A cupboard. Doesn't bother me, a place to sleep.' She didn't mention Granny.

'You got family?' he asked, straining the pasta into a bowl. 'Other beauties like you?'

'None,' she said, too quickly, so he turned around, almost spilling the pasta.

'Ah, like me.'

Clemmy examined her fingernails.

'So why London?'

'Sounded exciting, didn't know where else.' She tossed her hair. 'Except New York. I expect you go everywhere.'

'Sometimes, but mostly this country. I'll show you some pictures.' Joy was in his voice.

He opened a bottle of red wine. 'French,' and he poured it into two long-stemmed glasses, then twirled the wine around in the glass, before sniffing it and drinking. Clemmy copied him until some slipped over the rim.

He sipped and she sipped. Hated it.

She enjoyed the pasta and liked the stew with the crazy French name. 'Great,' she said in response to his question. She giggled, 'Never had anything like it.'

'Tell me, where in the north?'

'The middle of a forest, no father, stupid mother.' She paused, some time. 'No TV so the other kids thought I was an idiot.' She stumbled a little on the word 'I'. 'Didn't see the point of school.'

He looked puzzled. 'I loved my mother.'

Clemmy needed to get away so slipped from the stool and ran upstairs to the bathroom. She hadn't been able to get Mother out of her head since that meeting and the tea. Needed to talk to Helen, really talk.

'First on the left,' he called after her.

The shower was so big she might have danced in it. And she wanted to wrap herself in the large, fluffy towels and curl up in the bath.

She walked slowly back down the stairs then stumbled and stopped in front of a large black-and-white picture of a building, its front only.

'The clouds,' Thomas said, from the foot of the stairs. 'In a night sky. It's all about the light.' He stopped, laughed softly. 'Sorry, you're barely in the door and I'm already lecturing you about photography.'

Further down hung half a dozen more pictures on the left-hand wall: a couple of buildings and people, ordinary people, a man sleeping in the street and above that a woman and two kids.

'Weird,' she said and put her hand over her mouth.

He laughed. 'I do weird. Well, it's street photography, black and white. It's my life. One day I'll tell you the story.' And he led her back to the table.

*

The girl had come to him again. It was usually Doug.

Not far from his patch was a young girl with hair down to her waist, streaked in red and tattoos on her arms. She was a few years older than him, cheeky to the passers-by, calling out to the young men in suits, 'Hello Wonder Boy, you look as if you could spare a bob or two.' And mostly they stopped and gave her plenty. In her hair, she wore brightly coloured ribbons and put on a smile to match.

One night she had crawled into his sleeping bag and run her hands down to his crotch.

'Soft boy, you,' she said.

Then the sex was over and his head was in a mist, a bright, gleaming mist. 'Your first time.' She lit a cigarette, passed it to him. 'Stay away from the hard stuff, and watch yourself, the old fags will be after yous.'

She packed up her things in the morning, softness in her eyes. 'Take care, you. Streets are tough. Yous gotta learn.'

Only sixteen, he was beaten up by a gang of boys, chanting, 'Pretty boy, want a fuck, pretty boy.' They stole his money and dragged his sleeping bag and pack through the water in the gutter. They didn't fuck him, left that to the older men. Before Thomas ran from the older men, he found their wallets and took their cash. And laughed.

He lay awake through the night often, loved the stars, the night sky. They were his friends. He wanted to go home, find his mother, told himself he would go soon but time passed and the money he got from begging was barely enough to keep him alive.

*

'What do you want to do with your life?' Thomas picked up his glass.

Clemmy was startled. He had seemed far away.

'I don't know. That's what I came to London to find out.' Her eyes met his, like making a vow. 'But I will.' Not so long ago, before the maid, she would have answered, 'Actress,' with shining eyes and loud voice.

'I believe you.' He lifted the bottle.

Clemmy shook her head.

Not much later, he said, 'An early start tomorrow. We'll do this again as soon as I'm back. I'm off before it's light in the morning.'

Where had she gone wrong? She picked up her handbag. He might think her a fool but he appeared to enjoy her chatter, although seemed a little shy.

He pulled up outside No. 13. 'I'll pick you up in two weeks, 7pm.'

Clemmy smiled. 'Of course.'

'I know a little restaurant when I get sick of my own cooking. Not posh but good.' He opened the door and walked around to hers.

She got out quickly.

He reached down and briefly touched her lips with his, his hair swinging down to enfold them both, and he stepped back just as she was raising both arms.

'Be good.' He smiled and watched her walk up the steps.

She didn't look back.

She lay in bed, Helen and Thomas with her, and smiled at the memory of Beautiful Boy. She would not share Thomas.

I've met someone, Hel. You would like him. Will you mind? This is real. Perhaps he's a little like you, obsessive. Photography. I am beginning to understand. Not the photography but obsession. You changed, I didn't. I abandoned you. Do you understand? I was nothing...

I wanted him and all he gave me was a brief kiss on the lips. I clung to him but he smiled then drove away. That will make you laugh.

Is he the one?

33

The weeks passed slowly.

'You miss him,' Fiona put an arm around Clemmy's shoulders.

Clemmy shook her head and tried to believe he would be back when promised. Work at the café was easy now. She smiled and chatted her way through each day, and sometimes went to the pub with Fiona after work but never grew to like it much. Fiona helped the days pass quickly. There was more laughter in the café since Clemmy had started and business increased. So too did the tips.

She went shopping, brought a dress and cardigan.

She was outside waiting at 7pm, shivering slightly in her new clothes and a heavy coat. Bad tactics, but so what? She had spent a fortune on her make-up and had great hopes for the restaurant: white tablecloth – posh waiters and customers.

Thomas got out to open her door. He was dressed in the

same old clothes. Once seated in the car, she turned to him and no words came.

Neither acknowledged the two long weeks that had passed.

He parked outside his house. 'It's only around the corner so we can walk.' He examined the sky. 'No rain.'

Clemmy pulled her scarf tight around her.

They didn't hurry, their bodies occasionally touching as they walked. People passed them on the well-lit streets, many carrying shopping bags. Some shops were still open, not ones that interested Clemmy.

Thomas stopped outside a café.

It looked nothing special. Inside, were only about a dozen tables covered with red check cloths, all with people sitting at them except for a table tucked in a quiet corner at the back. A man with an apron, just like Jack, and a big grin walked up to them.

'Hello, Thomas. And who is this this exquisite creature you've been keeping from me?'

'Clemmy.' He turned to her. 'This is Derek, the chef.' He grinned and Derek punched him lightly on the arm.

'You don't deserve it but it's your favourite tonight – Cassoulet. It's a beauty. And Tarte Tatin. That should make you happy. Look after her, Thomas.'

His grin made Clemmy want to hug him but he was too far away so she gave him her best smile.

'I promise you you'll like it. French.'

Clemmy didn't care what it was. Under their table, her feet jiggled with joy.

'They love you at the café,' Thomas pushed back the errant locks of hair.

'I have my admirers.'

'So I hear.'

Thomas ate slowly and she tried to. The pieces of duck were OK, but she hated the white beans and struggled to eat any. The tastes were strange. The Tarte Tatin was great, a posh apple pie, and she ate that quickly.

'So, tell me, where have you been?'

He intertwined his fingers and his voice became a little dreamy. When he smiled, she wanted to run a finger over his perfect white teeth. 'Beach huts, on the sand, bright yellows, blues, reds.'

Clemmy drew in her breath. She would love a place like that.

'And a whole street of tall houses.' He stopped, took out a cigarette and lit it. 'Painted pastel colours: pinks, pale blues, yellows.' He looked shyly at her. 'Black and white usually my thing, until now.'

She waved her hands, 'The sea?'

'Not much, mostly the people and the streets.'

'I've never seen the sea.'

'We can fix that. How's the café?'

'A bit boring.'

Both had questions and both waited, uncertain.

They left the café with promises to come back soon and hurried down the street, hand in hand.

He opened the front door, leading Clemmy into the hall, then up the stairs, hips touching, step by step, a dance of love.

The bedroom was huge with a double-doored wardrobe and a dressing table with eight drawers. The walls were painted white and the rust carpet was thick.

Clemmy sat on the edge of a large brass bed, her feet not quite touching the floor, making her feel like a kid. She had the delicate wrists and ankles of a smaller person. Her breasts were good, she considered. She cupped one in each hand then stroked the silky softness of the bedcover before turning her head to gaze out of the large windows, at the high wall of the back garden and, some distance away, sky-high buildings.

He pulled back the covers.

They stood, back to back, clothes falling to the floor into two separate piles.

The heat of her body matched his, and he ran his hands over her soft skin, marvelling. He loved her small feet; he was size eleven.

He'd been alone since he was sixteen, giving most of those years to his photography. He didn't regret that, yet he could not live through other people's lives forever. He wanted her more than he'd ever wanted anyone. No one had really loved him since his mother. He did not expect Clemmy to love him, she was too wild, too different; she was adventure. Driven. That stopped him. Driven, they shared that. He wanted to hold her in his arms, always.

He held her, her soft, exquisite body, and lowered his lips to kiss her. He paused, less than an inch away, feeling her warm breath, her lips slightly open. They breathed together, each wanting to keep that aching certainty forever. Their lips met, softly at first and then…

He kissed her: her mouth, her breasts and between her legs. His hands were gentle, tender. He hesitated to enter her until she had whispered, 'It's safe.' And still he did not, but ran his hands down her long legs, sat back on his heels and admired her. 'I've wanted you ever since that day I first saw you.'

They were two snowflakes, slowly dropping down, melting together.

She let her head fall onto his chest, taking some of his hair between her fingers, tugging, nuzzling into him as he stroked her. She nibbled her way along one collarbone, then the other. She was not in a hurry, wanted to delay the minute. He laughed. She loved that soft, deep sound.

'You've taken your time,' she said, holding Thomas's face between her hands, then kissed him, gently.

She hadn't really bothered to understand boys or men, anyone except Helen, and her love for him puzzled her a little. Life was for living. Her love for Helen had always been there, in them both, but this was utterly different. Sex had been a game, but this time she was vulnerable, powerless. When they made love, there was nothing else, no past, no future, just love and she became something ethereal, slipping softly into the unknown, of solely Thomas and her.

She wanted to tell him everything. That would be hard.

*

It was the first time she had stayed out the entire night, and Granny was at the door of No. 13. when she came back to change the next morning.

'You are safe,' Granny said and soft tears welled. 'Perhaps you have found someone.' And she hugged Clemmy for the first time. 'I won't worry now.'

'He's beautiful, Granny, and I think I love him.' And Clemmy put her arms out for another hug.

Granny was away more and Clemmy spent nights with Thomas.

One evening, Granny called Clemmy in to sit with her.

'Sit, my dear. I have missed you.'

Clemmy sat, her legs tucked under her.

Granny smiled to see it. 'I think it's time we parted, me to the north and you to your Thomas. He sounds a lovely man.'

Clemmy opened her eyes wide.

'Promise me you'll not give up the acting. You will be good, very good. Please believe me,' and she made a sound that was almost a giggle. 'You need to know what your character has for breakfast.'

Clemmy gasped.

'No, dear, what I really mean, is you have to turn yourself inside out and be someone different. I've been there, the failures. It's a struggle. You will win. I count on you.' She stood and walked over to Clemmy, bent down, and hugged her again, holding her longer, and did not hide her tears. 'I should have gone sooner. They need me, up north. It was only you that kept me here. You have a presence and an energy that will help you succeed. And beauty. You have brought joy to me so late in my life. I thank you.' She walked back to her seat.

Clemmy leapt up and sat on the floor at Granny's feet, placed her head in her lap and held her hands tight.

34

They sat downstairs on the sofa, in the dim light of one small lamp, Thomas's arm around her, her head on his shoulder. Clemmy had showered and put on a clean nightdress and her dressing gown. She sipped her tea and he, his malt whisky.

The sitting room was big with two large leather chairs and a sofa. A bookcase took up much of one wall.

She had run her hands over some of the books, reading the titles, mostly about photography. And the magazines, also photography. She was missing Granny's books.

Clemmy lifted her head from his shoulder. She had to get rid of that thing gnawing at her stomach. She swallowed. 'I have a twin, Helen,' she murmured, her tongue lingering, enfolding the syllables with love. 'We did everything together, we believed we always would.' She flushed. 'We each had our own things we were good at, didn't bother about the rest. There were loads of things I was better at.' Clemmy stopped, hesitating, asking herself what those things were. 'Between us we were one.' She paused. 'Can you understand that?'

He nodded, although he didn't really understand. He had been an only one, always.

'She was the careful one, stopped us getting into trouble.' Clemmy stopped; she'd never spoken like this, to anyone.

'She loved you.' Thomas leant forward, lifting his arm from her shoulders and taking her hand.

Clemmy shifted, tucking her legs under her. 'We shared everything, until…' She leant forward and stirred her tea, although she was drinking it black, no sugar.

Thomas sipped his malt.

'We found him and his painting.'

'Him?'

'Our father. He didn't hang about after we were born but when we were fourteen, we found the key to this locked room at the top of the cottage. He was a painter, had left us a self-portrait and stuff. She fell in love with him and with painting.' She hesitated. 'She is really good, but spends day after day up there, painting. We weren't together anymore. I didn't know what I wanted and I hated living in the middle of that dark, gloomy forest, miles from anywhere, from anyone.' She sat up. 'I had to leave.'

She put her fingers in Thomas's hair and tugged gently. 'He had hair like you except dark. He left us a portrait. Famous, I think.' She was startled to feel a hint of pride in the last sentence.

Thomas kissed her. 'I hated my father, think I always did, from the time I could understand things like that. Kids learn emotions early. He was a lawyer and I was told to study law, promised gold at the end. That was the last thing I wanted to be and I didn't have the grades. He and Mum were separated, he bullied her too. "You be what you want to be," she told me, often. So I bunked off and went with her on her expeditions to the streets, with my own small camera. She told me I had to notice things no one else did, a strange face or a look that tells you something is about to happen. You can't learn that from books.'

Clemmy started. That sounded a bit like Granny. She held his hand tight, felt a flash of envy. 'Perhaps I was lucky mine ran. I hated him for leaving us with her.'

'Her?'

'Our mother, she didn't really exist for us.'

'A bit cruel.'

Clemmy put her head in her hands. 'I only wanted to be with Helen, could not imagine anything else. We were kids, identicals, the two of us were one. Lot of kids at school didn't even bother working out which was which. She did but we still played tricks on her.'

'And you've never heard from her?'

The dress shop and the tea, and the woman who no longer somehow was entirely the enemy. 'Perhaps we were cruel to her. We ignored her so she gave up on us, did a runner when we were sixteen. Good riddance, that's what we thought then. She was on her own, didn't have much money and hated the forest like me. She's here in London. I met her once and she took me to tea, said we were little fiends. I suppose we were. There were only the three of us, no neighbours, no friends for her. She seems happy now, got money from a new bloke who died. Convenient.' She smiled.

'Will you see her again?'

'I don't know. She gave me her address.'

'So why did you leave Helen?'

Clemmy took a deep breath. Then spoke quickly, the

words surprising her. 'She was a success, exhibited her painting. I was not. Jealousy, I suppose, but more than that. Her painting was more important to her than me, that's what I believed. She was upstairs all day, painting. What was I to do? I still loved her but who was I?' She dropped her head into her hands. 'It is the worst thing I have done. I have not been back, not even written. I would know if something was badly wrong, but that is all. We always looked out for each other, yet I still ran, left her there, alone.'

They were both silent a time.

'I will take you back there. I'd like to meet her.'

Clemmy kissed his hand. 'Thank you, but not yet. Perhaps soon. She is still with me, I talk to her, even though she is far away. That will never change.'

'I would like to have had a brother. There was only me. I lived with my mother. Until my father came and threatened to take me back, so I ran, to London to live in the streets. I loved her.'

*

As the banging on the door reverberated, Thomas saw the photos slip from Mother's fingers. His father never bothered with the bell; his fists were so much more powerful. They could read the level of conflict to come by the music of the banging.

Mother stood, tugging at her long, loose hair when he burst through the kitchen door. He reached forward to the table and, with his large hands, shoved the camera off, shouting, 'That's not what I give you all that money for. Cameras.' It crashed to the tiled floor, splitting apart.

Thomas gasped and stepped back, his broken dreams scattered across the floor.

'And precious little that is,' Mother said, in a soft voice, refusing to look down.

He raised his fist, paused, then lowered it.

'I'm taking Thomas back with me. This can't go on. He needs discipline.'

*

Thomas rubbed one side of his face. 'That's her,' he said, pointing to a framed photograph set well back on the sideboard.

Clemmy walked over and picked it up, hesitated. 'She looks lovely.'

'Bit weird, you mean,' Thomas said, smiling. 'She always dressed like that: long skirt, blouse and old cardigan, boots on her feet and hair pretty unkempt, like mine. She didn't cut it often. Didn't bother about things like that.' He laughed, 'Perhaps I learnt that from her. I'd like her here right now, critiquing my photos. I always wanted her to be proud of me, but most of all I would like her to meet you.'

Clemmy put down the photograph and held him tight.

'I went back to look for her. Too late, she'd died. She left me a note. It said, *Take good care of yourself, son, look for the ordinary and make it remarkable. Love, Mum.* So that's what I've tried to do.'

He stood, took her hand and led her to another photograph. 'Doug and Charlie.'

'Which is which?' Clemmy giggled.

'The alert one is Charlie.' He put his arm around her. The

dog's ears were pricked, his eyes wide and he was leaning in towards the camera. 'Doug was the only real friend I made on the streets. Thugs killed him. He was kind, Doug, looked out for me, a stupid, naive kid. That's him again.' He pointed to a picture of an older man with a kind face, curled around a dog, and wrapped in a stained, torn sleeping bag. Something like mother and child.

'And what do you mean – the streets?'

'I lived on the streets. With others like me, in doorways, wherever we could.'

The streets. There were words, inadequate words: fear, loneliness, bewilderment, cold beyond all imagining and hunger. And sometimes time had simply stopped. He did not know how to restart the clock. He should go back to his mother but his father would find him so the streets took him and held him fast.

London. He walked head down, rarely looking upwards or around, until he found people sleeping and begging in the streets. He unpacked his sleeping bag in a doorway, lay down and slept, trying to forget. He watched and learnt. Some of the old hands helped, showing him the best waste bins for scraps of food and how to avoid the cops and thugs. It was dangerous to gab too much on the streets. He found public toilets to wash in, and scraps of food in the bins but was mostly hungry, sleeping in archways, under railways bridges, by canals and in graveyards and doorways. His nickname was Posh Boy.

He sat, with downcast eyes, camera hidden, his box at his feet, with its few coins. Many stopped, pity in their eyes at one so young, a young boy who might have been their own, so they dug deep. He flushed and they dug even deeper. Others offered advice, told him to go home or chastised him.

The rain fell without ceasing and cars sprinted by sending showers of dirty water over him. He kept this head down.

Tarnished with fear and guilt, he lived off the money strangers threw at him. He would go back, but not yet. In the quiet of the bitterly cold nights, he dreamt of her and wept.

He blended in with the shadows, perhaps he was a shadow. Strangers smelt him before they saw him. Sounds carried in the darkness: laughter, squeals, screams, car tyres, police and ambulance sirens. The cops were decent mostly, the good ones not making up for the mean buggers.

Sometimes he saw a long-haired woman with a camera bag over her shoulder and he scrambled to his feet, then sank back down, head in hands.

Clemmy turned to the photograph on the nearest wall. A ragged sleeping bag bundled on a sheet of cardboard and a pack beside it.

'Your life,' she said and took his hand.

'Yes, my life back then. A woman rescued me, took me home, helped me get my photography published, although she didn't know much about it. I stayed with her on and off until she died. A sort of mother, I suppose. She left me this house. She was lovely.'

*

Shortly after his third Christmas, when few were about, Thomas heard a woman say, 'Come home with me. You could do with a good meal.' His head was down, Charlie was resting on his legs, gently snoring, and expensive black shoes were almost touching his bag. Perhaps it was his mother. Or was he dreaming? She would not wear shoes like that.

He struggled to lift his eyes to a thin, gaunt face. His fingers itched to take a photograph.

*

'Helen's painting. I'm like that with my photographs.' He gazed at Clemmy in the soft light. 'I'd like to meet her.'

'Helen and Clytemnestra.'

'Clytemnestra,' his eyes widened, filled with laughter. 'She took a lover while her husband was away in the Trojan War.' He could see Clemmy didn't have a clue what he was talking about. 'A determined, strong woman,' his grin broadened. 'She killed her husband when he returned from the war.'

'Dangerous,' Clemmy murmured, running her fingers over his face.

'I was pretty hopeless at school but I loved those stories. The Greek myths, gods, heroes and adventures. I'll tell you them one day. Odd name for your mother to choose.'

'She didn't, he did. He liked them because Helen was supposed to be the most beautiful woman in the world. That's what she told us.'

Thomas kissed her. 'I love you, Clemmy, I always will. Can you love me?'

She punched him lightly, 'Of course, you idiot. I love you, Thomas, I always will. I may be difficult sometimes but that won't mean I don't love you.'

35

Summer 1995

In the far north, a man sat on the cliff edge, a pad on his knees, pencils beside him. The waves far below were gentle, with the occasional cat's paw, and the sand shell white. He had feared wild seas, crashing, changeable, to match his mood. He searched the sky and found only blue.

He'd temporarily abandoned his blue/purple hills, his inspiration, his soul, fearing he might be done with his painting. He had changed over the past twenty-one years, once proud of his black hair, so thick and luxurious, now thinning and grey. He didn't like old women and young ones no longer offered themselves.

He had his house at the foot of his mountain, his paintings sold for good sums, if not in the Picasso realm and he loved his glass-walled studio from where he could commune with his giants. He had his routine, immutable, up before first light, paintbrush in hand, and stopping work only to eat and when the light faded, which meant he got little sleep in summer and too much in winter. His body had learnt to be tolerant.

He gave himself one day a week off, and if the weather was agreeable, he climbed one of his loves. In bad weather he cooked himself a feast. In another life he might have been a chef, but now even food had lost its magic.

He had counted the years since he'd fled the forest and mourned a little for what he had left behind, what he had thrown away.

He had been moderately content until that letter from his interfering agent, telling him of a new star, her first painting, identicals, two beauties. Surely them. He had written back in haste to instruct his agent to buy it, regardless of cost and had hung it on the wall of his studio. Many mornings he flung himself out of bed and hurried (not something he usually did) into the studio to stand before them.

He did not like people. In truth it was stronger than that, starting with his father, not that he had seen him for decades. His mother was little different and he realised, as he grew older, that he was unwanted, had always been. Love, that was for his giants, not people.

She had been an aberration. He had enjoyed the sex for a time, that was all.

None of this had bothered him much until the painting of the two. He could read paintings better than photographs. Helen was the painter. She had something of his style. She was good but he could improve her skill, teach her techniques. Did she think of him? Surely, she painted the forest as he had done, from up there, above the treetops, in his studio.

He tried and failed to banish a whisper of regret.

The winter had been hard, so the papers said, not for him a problem, the blocked roads, snow dumped indiscriminately.

He had run, again, to the sea, was wearing an old pair

of warm trousers, a shirt and sweater. There was a coat and a scarf on the sand beside him. He held a small stone in his hands, rubbing his thumbs over its pattern, its life story, caressed and fashioned by the sea over how many millions of years? He had selected it from the thousands nearby and now held it gently in the soft flesh of his palm, his fingers lightly curled.

He had never held a baby, not even the two she had held out to him. It had not bothered him for he had nurtured his painting as tenderly as any child. Or so he imagined.

And yet, he had, from the photographs, watched them grow into young girls, until a few years back.

The seaweed lay not far from his feet, scattered around like strands of young girls' hair. Drawings in the sand, feathers, radiating thin lines revealing a grey sand below the white. He would paint those when he got back to his cottage, if he could master the delicacy. He was careful where he walked. Further along the sand, black slabs of rock the size of one of his rooms, draped with brown seaweed like discarded knitting. The sea, deep blue out beyond the turquoise shallows, soft susurrations of the waves, reciting their stories of time past, of aeons-long memories and promises to return.

His mind rambled backwards as he sat on the sand, his bum cushioned, his eyes following the changing colours. He shivered in the wind and wrapped his arms around himself. Clouds had kidnapped the sun. He came to this spot when troubled, when the muse fled his hands and his brushes, and he walked the long, empty white sand, speculating on how many trillions of shells of creatures had been in their making, or retreating to the rocks in the storms and wind. The rocks, washed over millennia, thrown around in tumult, their lines angular, demanding, each unique, something humans swore belonged to them alone. Always wind. Not far away, oyster catchers shrieked at him to go away. He understood for he was an alien here, had painted these beaches with their grey striations in the sand, and these tumbled rocks, many times.

Would he have loved the two had he stayed? Would they have wanted his love? So many questions. A pain in his stomach, or was it his chest, a heart attack perhaps? Too soon. He would like to talk to someone about the two, perhaps boast a little, but he had no friends and until now it hadn't much bothered him. He didn't usually want to share, except through his painting. His colours and his brush were conversations, many he often did not understand.

He asked himself the question again: was it worth it?

He picked up his pad and pencil, planning to draw the seaweed, and the paintings of the retreating sea at low tide. He put them down, listened to the gentle waves. He examined the small stone in his hand again, with its surprising pink striations. 'I am coming to see you,' he murmured as he fingered the stone. One of them would understand its beauty.

He brushed the sand from his trousers.

He stood, quickly, and his pencils tumbled over the edge, a rainbow leaping from rock to rock before finally spreading across the sand.

Back home, he found paper, pen and an envelope. His hands trembled, and he struggled to write.

My Beauties,

Surely, they were still that.

I am hoping you are still there in the forest. I have bought the painting of the two of you. It is the first thing I look at every day. One of you has my talent. That pleases me.

Would you meet me at the train station? A bit of a journey for you.

There, he'd come straight out, no shilly-shallying, before he could change his mind.

My train arrives at 2.45 Thursday of next week. Please be there.

Your father

He'd never been a daddy. He folded the piece of paper badly, and shoved it in the envelope, as a tremor of excitement ran through him, such that not even his best paintings had provoked.

36

It had been a bad week: mistakes at the café, loud complaints. She tried to look at the customers closely, listen to their chat, imagine their lives. Sometimes it worked. But she lost her concentration when Thomas was away and life felt pointless. And she was frightened in that big house on her own, as it creaked and rumbled in the darkness.

Slowly she worked her way through some of the novels she'd dismissed at first, and began to look forward to entering others' worlds, their pain, their love. Had she wasted those years in the forest? Except for Helen.

She pushed her away.

She found *The Little Prince* in the bottom of her wardrobe where she'd chucked it, sat on the bed and read it from cover to cover and smiled to think of the rose and of Helen, but a planet of two was not for her.

She binged on TV, on *Coronation Street*. The programme the kids at school had raved about it, but she didn't much enjoy it. Her trophy went to Jane Austen's *Pride and Prejudice*.

She'd expected to hate it and switched it on in a moment of desperation. She'd heard about the book at school, had been supposed to read it. Now she fell in love with Colin Firth as Mr Darcy and longed to play Elizabeth.

When Thomas returned, she shouted at him. 'You should be here. You say you love me but where are you when I need you?' They were seated opposite each other at the kitchen table. She'd turned her face away from his kiss as he walked in, camera still on his back.

'I'm sorry, I stayed away too long. You know how it is.'

'I don't.'

Her fury was reflected in her thinned lips, her furrowed brows, her half-closed eyes.

He took a packet of cigarettes from his pocket, tapping one out, lighting it then staring into the light of the match before blowing it out. Perhaps he would sell his camera and his gear. He stifled that in fear and disbelief.

'That's all I know, Clemmy, photography. Do you want me to give it up? I will.' Part of him died when he said those last words.

Clemmy didn't answer immediately, picking at her thumb.

'Who would you be then? Not my Thomas.'

He tried to spend less time away, hurrying back to her, but his darkroom called, for he had buyers for his photographs, if they were any good. Could not bear the idea of leaving her again.

Almost a year had passed since that first meeting in the café. 'I've got something for you. Just a minute.' He jumped up and ran from the room, returning shortly. 'Come on, let's go.'

Clemmy, a little bewildered, walked with him, holding his hand, out the front door, into the muted London sunshine and down the street to the canal and the bench they considered exclusively theirs.

Thomas reached into his pocket and handed her a small camera. 'A simpler one than mine but a good start.'

She held it in her hand, turned it over.

'Got some good pictures this week, perhaps you could come out with me sometime.'

Clemmy stared at him, letting her astonishment show.

'I'll do the research, we'll explore new places, it will be fun.' He added, 'And hard work, in rough areas sometimes. You'll have to hide that hair, wear some old clothes, we don't want to draw attention to ourselves.'

He studied the water, then said, 'It's not what you see, but how you see it. You have to make the complex look simple, distil the complicated and try to get its essence, give yourself to the thing, building or person, and it will open itself to you. You have to be patient.' His grin spread.

Clemmy wasn't sure she could be bothered. It sounded a bit like acting but she didn't really understand what he was talking about.

'Take the camera, and when I've shown you how to work it, you can explore. If you are still interested when I'm back, we can do a shoot together.'

She kissed him and took the camera. She would try, but she wasn't sure.

She picked up the camera many times during the week, after he had left, urging her to go out with it, and promising to return within a week. She held it in her hands, held it up to her eye. At first it shook in her hands and she tried different ways of holding it, until she finally worked out that if she gripped the side of it hard with her right hand and supported it from underneath with her left, it stayed still. She pulled it close. Thomas had talked about exposure, focus, light and shutter speed – a foreign language to Clemmy – his eyes full of joy, the words tumbling out. Composition was the word he used most, showing her buildings, then reducing the view so that the picture was entirely different and sometimes she understood what he was trying to show her.

One Sunday she was hanging about the canal, camera around her neck, studying the reflections on the water, searching for something to photograph. She swung round and looked at the tall buildings through the lens; they were just buildings. She was about to give up when a boat, with half a dozen lads about her age, laughing and shouting, moved slowly by. She had her picture. Leaning far over the side was a fair-haired boy, gripping the boat's edge, staring straight at her. Clemmy focused on the group, then the boy, his mouth already open, a silent scream.

Thomas had said to look deep into the shadow of the thing, not at the thing itself. The boy's terror was there, between his open lips. Before he fell.

'An excellent start,' Thomas said. 'It has promise. What did you see?'

'Terror,' she said. 'And loneliness.'

Thomas took her hand.

'Why do you love me, Thomas?'

'You make me laugh; you are fun. And beautiful. Why do you love me?'

'I believe in you and you believe in yourself. I want to learn that from you. You are like her, obsessed.'

So Thomas stayed home for the next week and their nights and days were spent together, although the first few nights Clemmy lay awake. She was safe at Thomas's side, but that was not the purpose of her life, to be safe.

They took out their cameras and Clemmy began to understand a little.

'You have to be brave, get close, there is uniqueness in everything but you have to search for it,' his voice was soft, his eyes alight.

'My Thomas.'

'I hoped you might grow to love it too, but I think not.'

She heard his disappointment. That picture she had taken of the boy on the boat turned out to be a one-off.

'Sorry,' she murmured and was taken aback by her own regret, longing to share Thomas's passion. As a child, she could pretend to be anyone she wanted to be. Something gnawed at her, was eating her from the inside out.

The pattern of their lives changed little. When Thomas was away, Clemmy's fingers ached to touch him, to hold his broad face in her small hands, to feel the roughness of his skin, to look into his eyes and be safe.

And she ached for the other, starting to believe it would never happen. She was beginning to understand something of what Thomas was talking about, to ponder others' lives, their dreams and disasters, but not through the camera lens.

She sat across the kitchen table from Thomas. 'I need some money, Thomas.' It was months since she'd first seen Judi Dench.

'Of course,' and he took out his wallet, shoving it across

the table. 'Take what you want.' He carried on eating his steak.

Carelessness, her comfort blanket, had fled and instead she was consumed with a dread of time escaping, taking with it her dreams.

'Don't you want to know why?'

'You'll tell me if you want to.'

Clemmy reached into her bag and pulled out theatre stubs and shoved them across the table. She took a deep breath. 'The theatre. While you've been away, there's almost no play in London I haven't seen, it's cost a fortune.' She'd sat high up in the gods, where her heart beat fast. She'd been to see Judi Dench in *A Little Night Music*, waited for her outside the stage door with many others, and came home singing 'Send in the Clowns'. Even when Thomas was home, she was distracted.

She had simply existed between the plays, living each over and over in the following days, selecting which character she might have been. Never a minor part.

'I've been wondering,' Thomas said. 'You've been preoccupied. I guessed you were churning something about in that lovely head of yours.' He took her hands. 'I love you, Clemmy, you know that. I'll help you, whatever you want.'

Clemmy wanted to stamp her foot. She might have done had she been standing. 'Oh Thomas, you drive me nuts sometimes.'

'Me too.' He pushed his plate away.

'It's what I have to do. Why didn't you ask?'

'Acting. It's a hard life and a long road, you have to be sure.'

Clemmy didn't believe any of that.

'Come here, my dragonfly.'

Clemmy walked round the table. He pushed his chair back. She snuggled into his chest.

'You will be a brilliant actress.' He chuckled. 'They will be falling at your feet.'

She held him tight. 'I tried, last year, a small part, a maid.' Her voice so soft.

Clemmy noted the twitch in his mouth and slapped his back. 'Stop it. I failed, I didn't understand what I was doing.' Her voice rose, 'I don't think they want me back. I've been waiting.'

Thomas held her tight.

'It was at the local playhouse.'

'I believe they put on some good stuff.'

'It's what I have to do, Thomas, nothing else will do.'

'It's tougher than this.' He pointed to his camera.

'I know.' She didn't, but that didn't matter.

'Patience, not your thing,' he murmured and kissed her.

Her fingers tingled. And her feet.

'What about drama school?'

Clemmy sat up, put her hand up, shook her head. School of any sort was not for her.

'There are other amateur theatres around.'

Clemmy hated the word amateur.

Thomas didn't go away for the next few weeks. He cooked for them or they ate the food that Clemmy brought back from the café. Summer evenings, they spent on the seat by the canal.

One evening as they sat, hand in hand, quiet, content, in the last of the sun, he reached into a pocket and took out a small box.

Perplexity and dismay filled her eyes.

'No, it's not a ring, you're saved. Marriage isn't for me, nor, I think, for you. Our love does not need that.'

She smiled and took his hand. 'I love you, Thomas, but we don't have to marry and be like other people.'

'It will be perfect. I was going to give it to you later but it wants to be with you.' He held out the box.

'So, what is it?' Clemmy struggled with the box a moment or two. Inside was a long, thin, exquisite creature with four wings, its body a bright red, thin stick.

'It's beautiful,' she breathed. 'My Thomas.'

'A dragonfly, they symbolise change and transformation, discovery of oneself.' He paused. 'One landed on my sleeping bag when I was living on the streets. I wept for its beauty then, have looked out for one ever since I met you.'

When he returned from his next trip, she woke in the morning to find him fast asleep beside her, his face relaxed, almost smiling. Perhaps he was dreaming of her, or of a photograph more likely. His shaggy hair lay loose on the pillow, relishing its escape from the band. She stopped herself lifting a strand to her lips and when he woke, she clung to him, no longer reproaching him for his absences. She didn't ask him not to go again, that could not be, for she would lose him if she did or she would find herself with a simulacrum of the real Thomas.

37

Helen stared at the letter, wept a little and tucked the note away in her box of precious things, with her father's other letters, and the key to her studio, which she no longer locked.

She would go, Sam would meet his grandfather. His third birthday had been five months back, and Woodie had made him a magnificent chocolate cake. 'Woodie, Woodie,' he cried out to her as he used both hands to stuff the cake into his small mouth.

Her father was now rarely with her. It had become her studio. The word no longer stumbled out of her mouth.

Sam had no Daddy, she had had no Daddy, hadn't missed one, she had Clemmy. Now she asked herself how different their lives might have been. And they'd had a mother. They had found most adults annoying, outside their world.

When she had Sam in her arms, her hand in his, heard his high-pitched laughter, she began to understand that his love was special, different, and unbearable would be the pain if he refused her his love. Impossible.

She dressed carefully, raiding her wardrobe for clothes she hadn't worn for years, for a mid-length dress, strong shoes and a coat. She pulled her hair back and covered much of it with a scarf. She never bothered with make-up, would not do so even on this day.

Sam, as always, ran ahead, darting into the trees alongside the track to hide and then peep out with that high-pitched giggle of his. His eyebrows were faint below his bright orange woolly cap, copper-coloured hair poking out over his ears, mouth open in a wide grin showing perfect small teeth, and his flushed cheeks.

In town they caught another bus, getting out at a small railway station. Sam ran down the platform, ignoring her shouts. Waiting passengers swung round to smile and some to cheer him on. They ate buns in the waiting room and drank Coca-Cola, and Sam ran out to watch the trains as they pulled into the opposite platform.

Their train was coming from the north. Helen had read about the north with its high mountains, far, far taller than the hills around here, high, purple and often snow-capped. And the beaches with white sand.

A few seconds before 2.45, a rumble and toot announced the train. Helen watched it approach, slow, stop. Doors opened and adults and excited children stepped or tumbled out. She scanned them for the man in the portrait or an older version.

She had told Sam they had come to meet his grandfather, had shown him the portrait, so he pointed to each man alighting from the train, shouting, 'Grandfather, that him, Mummy, that him?' Some waved but walked on.

An older man stepped down onto the platform. Helen

stepped towards him, then hesitated, as a woman his age ran to him and placed her arms around him.

*

In one of the carriages (it was not a long train, five carriages in total), a couple of passengers watched as a man stood, took down a small bag from the rack and walked towards the door and bent to stare out the window, standing well back.

He was not usually given to impulses and certainly not ones like this. He didn't dare think it through. He could not, would not, change his life. He was too old, although that was not it.

One of his beauties was there, the colours of the painting. Were there flecks of paint on her hands? Perhaps. He half raised one hand, brought it back down to his side. They could talk about painting, he might even teach her some techniques, although he shuddered a little. Painting was solitary, that was how it had to be. She had a kind face. He'd seen the beauty for many years.

Then she turned away and shouted at someone further down the platform.

Perhaps it was the other. He could manage that.

A small boy ran towards her, his hair the colour of hers, sticking out from under his hat. She took his hand, knelt, while keeping her eyes on the alighting passengers, now few.

A child. She had her arms around him. His eyes filled, something almost unknown. He turned, hurried back to his seat, replaced his bag, murmuring to the man opposite, 'Wrong station.' He sat back down and waited, feet shuffling, endless minutes for the train to leave, not looking out the window again.

He pulled his handkerchief from his pocket. He had refused the babies held out to him. He had done it again.

Despite his best endeavours, they would not let him go, the girl crouching with her arms around the boy, disappointment in her eyes.

He was a fool; would he never learn?

It was only a few steps off the train to them, and he had not been able. A tsunami in his life. He had always rebutted change, love.

When he got home, he got out his cheque book.

*

Helen turned away, pulling Sam after her. She was sure the man at the window was him.

It was the trains that had excited Sam as he shouted, 'Train, Mummy, train,' and he had soon forgotten Grandfather, not really understanding the word.

Why had she bothered? Yet she had longed to meet him, touch him, talk to him about painting.

Clemmy would laugh and say, 'What did you expect?'

He had abandoned them already, why not once again?

She pulled Sam roughly to the other platform and he started to cry. She held him close so he could not see her tears. What had she done wrong? Where was Clemmy?

A few days later, a large cheque arrived and she tore it up.

38

The days in the café dragged. 'Hey, Clemmy, what's up?' her regulars joked. 'Give us a smile.' London had muted her northern accent a little.

One evening Will telephoned. 'It's a panto so some fun before Christmas. We're doing *Sleeping Beauty* this year, you might like to be in it. There's one role you might like, Maleficent, the wicked witch, although a shame to hide that beauty behind a mask. The girl who played it a few years ago has left, so you are in with a chance. Our pantos are different to our other productions, fun for us and the audience, but we have to be good.'

Clemmy jiggled from foot to foot, nearly whooping with joy. 'I did it at school once. "Jeer if you like – you can boo for hours! You can't hurt me – I've magic power."' Clemmy drew a breath, and she stamped out the last time she had almost played that role.

She was bursting to share it with Thomas. He was away.

It was not as easy as Clemmy had believed. She stood in the wrong place, exasperating the other actors and confusing them.

'Not there,' Will said.

Clemmy, hands on hips, did not move. The cast waited and smiled to themselves and to each other.

'The blocking, your position on the stage, is a bit like a game of chess. Everyone knows the moves. Think of the stage as a picture, a painting,' Will said to her, as they stood apart from the others. 'The artist is precise about where he places the figures and the painting must live, the actors must understand the space, the sight lines, the interactions.'

When she went back after the break, there was a chalked large letter C on the floor. She rubbed it out with her foot.

She began to use her hands only to enforce her words, to change her voice to harsh: 'The power of evil will always win the day. And I always do evil because it's my way.'

'You leave Clemmy, abandon her, as soon as you step onto the stage, find Maleficent and abandon Clemmy,' Will had told her at the first rehearsal.

Clemmy liked him; he was fun, kind and tough when he needed to be.

Granny had said she had to listen to what was being said, really listen and not just the words but the nuances of happiness, sadness, fun, anything locked away inside them. And the moving or still hands.

On stage, a slow process, she began to leave herself behind. Other actors helped her, told her it had been the same for them. 'It will work, give it time,' one girl said, 'you will be good.' And Clemmy understood that she was not that yet, and she had to do more than know the lines to become

Maleficent. And after many mistakes and struggles with herself, she became Maleficent, truly Maleficent.

Off stage, they all laughed and joked together.

Before going on stage each time, she pinned her dragonfly to her blouse and fingered her good luck charm in her pocket. Somehow, they calmed her, helped her believe she was Maleficent and would triumph.

Ruling from atop a mountain, dressed in a purple cloak, raven on her shoulder, Clemmy garnered boos and rapturous applause. Thomas's cheers were the loudest. And she hoped Granny would be proud of her.

As they all parted, late into the night or early morning, after the last night's party, Will clasped Clemmy's hand.

'I have another play in mind for next year. There's a possible part for you, the best. It will be hard work. You have the ability, but only when you give yourself totally to the character and to the other actors. I'll let you know.'

*

Sometimes Will had worried that he had made a bad mistake. She overplayed her role and she refused to listen when he tried to go over it with her. The other players were old hands, yet something about Clemmy made Will believe she would get there, if she didn't wreck his production in the process. And in the end, her performance as Maleficent, the wicked witch, was better than he believed possible.

39

The cottage changed little, except for Sam's room with its painted walls and Helen's pictures of the forest and its creatures, and the living room. Helen's bedroom with the two single beds was untouched, waiting, memories undisturbed.

Sam could name many of the trees, rolling the words around his mouth. She taught him a few letters. He demanded more, and more.

Many mornings he ran outside shouting, 'Pond, Mummy, pond.'

She still cycled into town with him in front of her and he stared at the small children they passed. So she found a park with swings, a slide and a wire climbing frame where he ran to join other children, laughing and shouting. And a local nursery school with less than forty children, and each morning he ran outside to the bike, often stumbling in his haste, shouting, 'School, Mummy, school.'

She was a little lost without him.

And he followed her upstairs with his crayons and paper

and pointed to the easel and to the brush in her hand. 'Me do, Mummy.'

'A picture, Sam,' and she spread a sheet of paper over the easel, stood Sam on a chair, and held him tight, although he wriggled to be free. She held out her jar of brushes.

'Choose one.'

He pointed to the largest.

'Which colour?' She expected him to choose the red.

'That, Mummy.' He pointed to green.

'Like the trees.'

He nodded and his copper curls nodded with him. 'Picture, Mummy.'

She placed the tip of the brush the in the mound of viridian green and put it in his hand. He curled his fingers tight around it and leant forward.

She had drawn pictures as far back as she could remember. Now she and Sam shared most things. Sam would have a box full of memories of their time together. She had none with Mother.

From time to time, Sam did shut her out, refusing when she pleaded, 'Come to Mummy.'

40

One evening, just as spring was waning, Clemmy answered a knock on the door.

'Hi.' Will stepped inside.

In the kitchen he placed a book on the kitchen table. He had refused tea or coffee. 'This is the play I mentioned. You'll have to audition for Nora, there's no guarantee. You did well as Maleficent but this is different, very different.' He sat. 'Couldn't be more so. It will be hard. See what you think.'

Clemmy picked up the book, ran her fingers over the title: *A Doll's House* by Henrik Ibsen. She looked inside, scanning a few pages. 'What's this Nora like?'

'You'll have to work that out. It was written late nineteenth century and society was different back then, men ruled.' He grinned.

Clemmy wanted to hug him. Or slap him.

'Only kidding.' He leant over and patted her arm. 'You don't judge her, you find out who the real Nora is and somehow you must work out how to reveal that. I can help but you must find that for yourself.'

He stood. 'Good luck.'

*

By the end of the evening, she had read the play.

'How's it going?' Thomas said as Clemmy closed the book with a bang.

'I hate her, Nora. The wicked witch was fun, but this is daft.' Will's words came back to her, over and over: *What does she come to understand about herself?*

'Come here.' Thomas held out his arms.

Clemmy settled herself on his lap.

'You can be anyone you want to be, my clever Clemmy.'

She kissed him and doubted.

'Let me have a read of it.'

*

'Nora. The way I see her is like a photograph,' he said the next evening, putting out his cigarette. 'At first it's just a snapshot, the obvious. Until she reveals herself, you have to search. You're no twittering lark, but you are brave like her.'

'That Torvald.' She opened the book and read, "'I'll sing for you, dance for you.'" She laughed. 'I would for you, Thomas.' She searched in the book again. 'But I'm no one's little doll, not even yours, Thomas.'

'Of course not. He was a control freak and she's not as silly as she seems at the beginning.'

*

As Clemmy climbed the stairs to the auditorium, Jane joined her. Jane had been Princess Aurora in *Sleeping Beauty*.

Jane was tall and slim, had a couple of inches on Clemmy, and was fair-haired with a strong, chiselled face. Her accent was clipped, which had once made Clemmy laugh.

'Hi, Clemmy. It was fun, the panto, you were good. This one's a bit different. There's a rumour that you want Nora. So do I.'

There was an absence of doubt in Jane's deep laugh. Clemmy shrugged, a tiny thing. She, not Jane, would be Nora. She had immersed herself in Nora, doing what Granny had told her, and did not know what she would do with herself if she wasn't Nora.

Players were scattered round the auditorium. It was small, not many more than a hundred seats wrapped around three sides of the stage. Clemmy found a seat on the back row. Others arrived at the top of the stairs and a few joined her. She looked around, trying to work out which of the men might be Torvald Helmer.

'Right, girls and boys.' Will stood on the stage. 'Time.' His voice was loud enough to cut through the chatter.

'It's set in Norway in 1879. Hopelessly sexist by today's standards.' He grinned. 'The men ruled.'

The girls jeered.

An hour passed. Other parts were read but not Torvald Helmer or Nora. She saw Will having quiet conversations with some of the actors.

Clemmy fiddled with her hair. Her bum was getting sore on the hard seat.

They stopped for coffee. Excitement was building in some, disappointment in others, although they would not know until next week, or perhaps the week after, who had got the parts. Everyone had nodded when Will reminded them; only Clemmy looked devastated.

In the second week, Jane read Nora. She was impressive, but Clemmy believed she did not have Nora in her soul, did not truly understand her.

'I'm Torvald Helmer,' the man waiting in the wings said to Clemmy. He was a few inches taller and a little podgy. He chuckled, 'Well, not really, but you know what I mean. I'm reading with you, my rebellious little squirrel.'

And I am your featherhead, your lark that gets through a lot of money. She'd hated that line and many others when she'd first read them and had doubted if she could say them, claim them as hers.

Clemmy stood tall. 'You've done this before?' she asked.

'Many times. It's tough, the first time.'

She heard the sympathy. 'I was in the panto, Maleficent.' Clemmy tossed her hair.

'Ah, I missed that one.'

The others were casually dressed: jeans and shirts. She had dressed carefully that evening: smart black trousers that showed off her slim legs and an eye-blasting red blouse. Her copper hair hung loose on her shoulders, but while waiting, she tied it back with a bright red bow.

Clemmy stepped onto the stage, feeling both sick and excited. She was Nora, the silly twittering lark. She took a few steps onto the stage.

Then stood unmoving, not speaking.

The bright stage lights fled. Darkness. She was in that other city, fleeing, away from Hel, away from her voice, begging her not to go.

She was nothing.

Yet Hel was there, in the auditorium, whispering to her. 'My Clem, you can do this. You will be a star.'

Stage lights and Torvald's puzzled face. Her lines washed through her, and she turned to Will and the others, her voice loud and clear.

'Hide the Christmas tree carefully, Ellen; the children must on no account see it before this evening.'

She was Nora.

'You were great,' and Torvald put his arm around her waist as they left the stage. 'We will be good together,' and his grin split his face.

Clemmy shook her head. She had wanted to be perfect, had not been.

Clemmy sat through another hour, taut and upright, trying to pay attention to the others' reading. She had learnt her lines. Many of them hadn't, just read their parts.

'Right, boys and girls,' Will said. It was just after nine when he read out the parts and names.

All Clemmy heard was her name. Jane swung round to stare at her.

'Well done,' Jane said, and held Clemmy's arm a moment. 'I knew when I heard you.'

'A nervous start,' Will smiled. 'Often happens, probably won't again. You did well but you aren't her yet and it shows. She leaves her young children, believing they will be better off without her. Women, not respectable ones, didn't do that back then.'

*

That night, she dreamt that she was back at the cottage with Helen, sitting on stools, side by side in the kitchen, gorging on cake.

She would find her way back to the forest and tell Helen she was going to be an actress.

Helen would laugh, love her, and tell her she'd always been one.

41

July 1996

It had been a drag, the overcrowded trains and the bus. Why had she come? There was a rehearsal tonight and she'd had to get up at the crack of dawn.

Clemmy caught a taxi at the station and asked the driver to stop some yards before the cottage where the forest had retreated, leaving a grassed-over space.

'Here?' he'd said. 'You sure?' He looked around.

Clemmy stared down the track. The cottage, with its dirty windows and peeling paint. When she was rich, she would spend money on it, a lot, and Helen would have whatever she wanted. The cloud moved across the treetops and threw its shadow across her, across the cottage and her London life.

She stood quite still, long after the taxi had finally managed to turn and drive back up the track.

It was five years, two months and one day since Jack had driven her to the station, Helen's voice following: 'Don't go, Clem. You can't go.'

She had run, had not written in all this time, yet no one else mattered as much as Hel. Why, why had she behaved like this? Helen would hate her, would not care about her acting. Why should she?

Would Helen forgive her? Love her still? Found another to love?

'Fool,' she spat at herself. Perhaps Hel had flourished, was famous, rich. Did not need her. Or she was no longer there. Clemmy almost laughed. Helen would never leave the forest. It was still, silent, not even birdsong.

Clemmy took a deep breath.

The sun returned directly overhead, so she was warm, hot even, joyful. They were in the bath together. There wasn't much hot water so they washed each other, the water occasionally lapping over the bath's edge to puddle on the worn linoleum. Mother was around somewhere, staying out of their way.

She and Helen would be together again, if only for a few hours, and she would tell her all about Thomas and Nora. She laughed aloud, imagining Helen's amazement. And her love.

By the track, tall grass. She waited, a few heartbeats, expecting Helen to come running out to her, instead, a high-pitched voice, and a small boy ran towards her, his bare legs, his hair the colour of her own, caught by the flickering sunlight and dancing along with him. He stumbled, fell, picked himself up and ran on, towards her.

He stopped suddenly. 'Mummy,' his voice uncertain, then he turned back towards the cottage.

'Other Mummy,' Clemmy said, wondering at her words and the child before her. Who was he? His copper curls, his green eyes, told her. She put her hand to her mouth, breathed hard. She could not be sure of his age, but… she gave a small sob.

She knelt and held out her arms.

He ran into them.

'I'm your other mummy,' and she held him tight. Had she gone mad? What was she saying?

'Other Mummy,' he repeated, puzzlement in his eyes.

'Two mummies, my lovely.'

'Other Mummy,' Sam repeated slowly, looking over his shoulder. He turned back to her. 'Owlie,' he pointed.

'Can I hold him?'

Sam shyly held him out.

'He's beautiful.'

Sam grinned and held out his hands for Owlie.

'Let's go and find Mummy.' Clemmy stood and took his small hand, then gripped it more tightly.

After a few yards, Sam pulled his hand loose and ran towards the cottage, Owlie hanging from one hand, and shouting, 'Mummy.'

Helen rushed out of the front door and turned towards his voice, then stood absolutely still, her hand to her mouth, breath coming in short gasps.

They ran to each other, love and stories filling both heads, held each other tight, Helen's tears soaking the small birthmark beneath the left shoulder of Clemmy's blouse, and Helen's tears on Clemmy's right shoulder's birthmark.

Sam endeavoured to make his small arms stretch around them both, failed and tried to squeeze between them.

When they finally separated and handkerchiefs had been taken from pockets and put back again, Helen put her fingers through Sam's curls, and he threw back his head and his eyes wandered from one to the other.

'This is Sam.'

'Other Mummy,' Sam whispered, his face grave.

Helen took Clemmy's hand 'Come, we have much to share,' and led her into the cottage.

Clemmy was startled at the confidence in Helen's voice. 'You must tell me about Sam.'

Helen laughed. 'There's no man lurking in a cupboard. Have you not guessed?'

'Tell me, tell me everything. I am a fool.' Clemmy ran into the sitting room and flung herself onto their old couch.

'Wait,' Helen said, 'I'll bring tea. And I'll get rid of him so we can talk.' Sam was trailing close after them, still gazing from one to the other.

Clemmy studied the room. It had been painted, looked almost smart. The furniture was the same, old and tatty.

Sam ran after Helen into the kitchen and then outside, clutching a fistful of biscuits and Owlie in the other hand.

Helen sat down beside Clemmy, bodies touching, and the tea was drunk quickly, during which time neither spoke; they held hands and sat, as they had always done.

Clemmy tightened her grip on Helen's hand. 'I abandoned you.' Her voice softened, her words slowed. 'I wanted to be me, be Clemmy. It didn't mean I didn't love you. After Mother left, we could do what we wanted but you found your painting. I wasn't anything anymore, not me, so I hurt you. I'll never forget that or forgive myself.'

Helen's head fell onto Clemmy's shoulder.

'Who was I, Hel? I was hiding somewhere and I had to find her. Find me.'

'I longed for just one word from you, Clem, anything.'

'I should have…' Clemmy stopped. She wasn't sure exactly what. They sat silent, some long minutes.

'I was your doll,' Helen laughed, then added, 'but I've had to change that. I'd always let you make the decisions. I went into some sort of dreamworld, or nightmare, when you left, I suppose I didn't really believe it, kept expecting to see you, to hear your laughter. I kept smelling my skin. It was you and it wasn't. I was angry, lost, so I didn't make anything of it when my periods stopped or when I started throwing up.'

Clemmy was silent, staring into nothing.

'I noticed nothing except you were not there, had gone, was somewhere else. Did you never think that might happen?'

Clemmy heard the undercurrent of anger. 'Oh, Hel. How stupid, stupid, I am. What did you do? How can I make it up to you? Will you ever forgive me?' She put her head in her hands and sobbed. 'I just didn't think, that's me, careless. What did you do?'

'I was spending a lot of time in the café and chucking up in the toilet there. It was Jack who asked me if I was pregnant.'

'Jack,' Clemmy said. 'He promised he would look after you. Tell me about him, about Sam.'

'Sam, heaven or hell?' A low giggle from Helen. 'Which do you want? I knew nothing about babies, probably imagined that motherhood was like painting, finding the right colours as I went. That's not kids.' The badly broken nights, the piles of unwashed coshes, bins full of dirty nappies, the mess everywhere, that was mostly gone. 'He's a bit like us with his toys. Loads: teddies, cuddly dogs, the lot. He threw them all away, except Owlie.'

'Good,' Clemmy grinned.

'He'll start school soon, doesn't like wearing shoes and runs naked down the track if he can.'

'Wild, love that. I've been a fool. Sam, he is exquisite and I've stayed away all this time.' Clemmy wrapped her in her arms. 'I'm so sorry, Hel, I will never hurt you again, I promise. He is ours.'

'Only you could see it like that but yes, I do forgive you, I would forgive you anything not to lose you. And I have Sam now, so I've changed, grown up. He is my life, always will be.'

Clemmy turned away a little from her words.

Helen sighed. 'As long as you loved me, nothing else mattered. It must have driven you mad at times. And now I have got you back.' She kissed Clemmy on the lips then murmured, 'You will come to us again soon, won't you?' Her anger was subsiding. 'Yes, he is ours.'

Clemmy words were soft and slow, 'I will come and go, you know me. And we will share him.'

She watched Helen's face change, her smile take over, give her back the old Hel. 'And your painting? You must have had other exhibitions.'

Helen hesitated. 'Yes, and I've sold quite a bit. I didn't understand back then, how much it shut you out.' She shifted, smiled. 'What about you? Got someone? Life in the big smoke!'

'Got used to the people, the cars. Oh, and the shops. They are great.'

'So I see. But you know me, never cared much about clothes.'

Clemmy giggled.

'And a man?'

'Of course,' Clemmy chucked back with a grin. 'It took

some time. He's odd, a bit like you. Obsessional, not painting, photography: people, dumps, awful places. But that's what he loves and he sells well.' She paused, 'Long hair, that will make you laugh, but blonde. He is gentle and strong, and clever. He understands me, lives for his photography.' Clemmy grinned, 'And me. Thomas and I are good together. Wait till you meet him, he's wonderful – I've never met anyone like him.'

She stopped speaking a moment, then said, her voice soft, 'I've never known life without love, your love for me, mine for you. Now I have learnt love like others do, and understand myself a little, but do not be afraid, my Hel, nothing can harm our love.' She leant closer and took Helen in her arms.

A moment later, Sam was there squeezing in between them. 'Come and play, Mummy.' And he looked from one to the other.

*

Clemmy barely noticed the trip back to London. Her head was crammed with pictures of Sam, his small running legs, his smile that pulled his face into a different shape, and the feel of Helen's arms around her. Perhaps most of all she heard his high, excited voice, a little puzzled: 'Other Mummy.'

'Always,' she murmured to herself.

Part of her had wanted to stay forever, but time had passed too quickly, she had to be back. And there was Thomas, but she would never let them go again.

She had forgotten Nora, forgotten to tell Helen.

42

Clemmy waited, impatient, she wanted to get on, to be Nora on that stage. She had rehearsed with Thomas until she knew every line but now accepted that was not the hard part.

'Time, boys and girls. Some reminders of what we are tackling. It's a tough one.' Will grinned. He was standing at the front of the stage and everyone else sprawled in the auditorium. Except Clemmy, who sat taut and upright, leaning forward a little.

'*A Doll's House*, hope you've all read it, lived it. A very different society, and the men determined everything.'

The men cheered and whistled.

'Sorry chaps, that all changed. Ibsen set out to highlight the negative treatment of women. And back then, marriage was holy. All the women in the play sacrifice themselves.'

Cheers and laughter.

'Torvald, the husband, and Nora, the wife, are both damaged by the lack of equality. Nora lies, big and small, to Torvald, who craves respect. She has to work in secret to pay off a loan and save her husband. At the beginning she is silly, childlike, and doesn't seem to mind, but appearances mislead and her dependency on her husband changes.'

More cheers, this time from the women.

Clemmy's feet jiggled. She knew all this. Why didn't he just let them get on with it?

'A doll-like wife who treats her children like dolls, tries to save her marriage, then all that changes and she sheds her doll's dress and steps out into the real world, leaving her husband and children behind. Revolutionary, especially back then, and Ibsen intended that. To find out who she is, a lifelong journey for Nora. She throws away everything she has been taught and has to take the audience with her. That's our job. The final stage direction is a slammed door. You have to make the audience believe.'

There was total quiet in the playhouse.

Clemmy closed her eyes and sank deep into her chair. Had she been a doll until now? Could she change everything? She was Nora.

It was another half-hour of tedious discussion of parts and Will's expectations before Nora, humming softly, walked onto the stage.

'*Hide the Christmas tree carefully, Ellen.*'

A few sentences later, Helmer spoke, '*Is that my lark twittering there?*'

Nora, '*Yes, it is.*'

Helmer, '*Is it the squirrel frisking around?*'

Clemmy breathed a little more slowly. Her voice had carried clearly, with the freshness of the prancing squirrel. She would keep it that way. A songbird. Until.

It didn't go as she had expected. Will kept stopping them

all, making them do the same lines over and over and she grew impatient, almost even began not to care. Perhaps she was not made for this acting business after all.

She had come to her first rehearsal convinced that she understood Nora, was Nora, could be Torvald Helmer's wife/child. It was hard work, as Will had predicted. Often, she struggled, breathing in the wrong places, stress on the wrong lines and many times wanted to stamp her foot and walk out. Stamp she might, but leave, never.

She argued, she'd had a lifetime of arguing, but learned to talk to Will in a quiet place, not in front of everyone, to offer her suggestions. Slowly, confrontation became friendship. She ceased crying in Thomas's arms afterwards.

She liked Torvald Helmer. Not his real name, of course, she forgot that. They worked well together, although she had wanted to hit him at times, for his patronising words.

*

Will accepted that the panto had taught Clemmy much, that she brought drama to the stage, sometimes the wrong sort, and had a lot to learn. Did he have the time or energy to teach her? Yet she could be brilliant, would be as the play progressed and Nora took her freedom. Will guessed that much of Clemmy's life was in the play. If they could work together, it might be his best. What he loved most about it was Nora's transformation. Clemmy was tough, but she had to learn how to use it and cease being a performing monkey. He would have to harness her energy.

'You are good enough, strong enough to stick it out. There will be tough times, doubts. I've been there.'

Clemmy's eyes opened wide, and her mouth.

His lips tightened. 'Move on, Clemmy, there's a whole world out there for you. You are a star here but you have barely begun. I know it's what you want. Drama school is what you need. It won't be like school, much tougher. It will help your actor mindset. Famous people have gone there. You'll love it.' That grin again. 'Eventually. It's tough to get in but I can help you. You'll meet people important for your career. As Nora, you are a winner. You must take that out into the world.'

After one of the early rehearsals, Torvald took her hand. 'Come on, my car is not far. I'll drop you off. Or you can come back to mine; we can rehearse, just us. It might help.'

It had been a difficult night. 'You're great,' he said, 'the play is you. The problem is, it's the way things are done, what we are used to.'

Clemmy hesitated. He was an attractive man and working together was good.

*

'What's this Torvald like?' They were on the canal bench, Clemmy's head in Thomas's lap.

'Not a bit like you.' Clemmy grinned. 'You don't have to worry.'

He touched the side of her face to feel her smile.

'Haven't worked him out yet.' There was a different, exciting world waiting for her and London was only the first stop. 'You've had tough times and they helped you. I shall not leave you, ever.' She took his hand. 'Only for brief times, for work, and you will do the same. Each time we will come together again and explore each other anew. What do you think, Thomas? Am I mad?'

She sat up, wriggled around and placed her lips on his, pressed her body into his.

Minutes later, Thomas stood and took his camera out of his bag. A wind stirred the water, a light ripple.

'Just ignore me, my Nora.' Small clouds were beginning to rush across the sun, diminishing the all-blue sky. The light would shortly be perfect. The wind was his assistant, gently lifting Clemmy's hair, rearranging it from time to time.

Clemmy placed her hands on her hips and threw back her head, relaxed and dropped her head a little. She crossed her legs, uncrossed them, then sat on them.

A couple walked by, stopped to watch. It did not bother him and he was not sure Clemmy even noticed.

He had watched her ever since they met: how she waved her hands with excitement, joy, sadness; how she picked at the skin below her left thumbnail, covertly; or opened her eyes widest when pretending; twisted a lock of her copper hair, and her green eyes reckless, laughing and loving, the emotion sometimes leaking from her eyes and taking over her face. Sometimes nervous, but rarely fearful.

After some minutes she looked at Thomas, at his camera pointing at her, 'Nora, she had to leave. That's what I have to convince the audience. They must understand she had no choice.'

Thomas nodded, but she had forgotten him. He moved to one side of her while she gazed into the water, her hands now clenched. 'You miss her, don't you, your other half?'

Thomas put down his camera. 'You will be a brilliant Nora. This is just the beginning. Let's walk a little.'

Clemmy had told him about Sam and her visit. The story of the Beautiful Boy had been more difficult, but Thomas had tried to understand.

*

He laid out five photographs on the table, the best of the bunch. He had been wanting to do this since he'd first seen her, apron on, pad in hand.

One was of Clemmy with her hands on her hips, head thrown back, the Clemmy she showed the world. Perhaps he'd found the real Clemmy in one or two of the others.

43

Helen tore open the envelope and something fell to the floor.

She picked it up, a ticket – *A Doll's House* by Henrik Ibsen. The Hackney Players and a London address. The date was for Saturday afternoon, 14th September 1996. She turned the ticket over, wondering who had sent it to her.

Her fingers felt something else in the envelope. She pulled out a newspaper cutting and unfolded it.

7th September 1996

A New Star at Local Theatre

The Hackney Players' production of A Doll's House by Henrik Ibsen has a new star. A moving story of a young wife and mother who leaves her husband and children, rather than endure as the cosseted wife/child/doll. The wife, Nora, is played by a newcomer to Hackney Players, Clytemnestra Richards, known as Clemmy, and she lives up to the Greek goddess's reputation for beauty. Clemmy Richards plays the role of Nora perfectly. Helmer Torvald, the insensitive husband, is also a pleasure but the performance is carried by a faultless and powerful Nora. Clemmy, aged 22, believes that acting is her life, believes it passionately.

Based on her performance as Nora, her future as an actress appears certain.

A matinee. Eleanor would drive her to the station. A train to London and Eleanor or Woodie would look after Sam for the day. But London, she had never been to London, never wanted to.

She was back in that other city, running from the gallery, searching the streets for Clemmy, certain she had been abandoned. And the strangers, standing in front of her painting. The admiration. Now Clemmy was the star and Helen had to be there.

She sat, a long time, breathing hard, her feet tapping. She had to do it.

She cycled into the town and took a bus to a larger one, to its most expensive dress shop, and chose a dress, blue with blobs of greens and a deep red leather jacket and new shoes to match.

'I'm going to London, the biggest city in the world,' she told Sam, making it sound like one of the stories she read to him. She waved her hands about. Sam opened his eyes wide. He'd heard about London at nursery. 'To see Other Mummy. She's an actress.'

'An actress,' he repeated, his voice full of uncertainty.

Eleanor organised it all for her, made sure she had train tickets and money for taxis, had offered to go with her. 'Mum could look after Sam.'

Helen shook her head. This was her pilgrimage. Jack would meet her back at the station, very late that evening.

Eleanor drove her to the train station, Sam in the back seat, then bewilderment on his face when she waved goodbye to him from her carriage, calling out to her, 'Mummy, where going, Mummy?'

She almost got off, instead made funny faces at him through the window. The train pulled out and, trembling, she sat down. 'Sam, my lovely boy,' she whispered to herself. 'I'll be back soon. Promise.' But she was afraid, asking herself if she would ever get back to him, to the forest.

The woman in the next seat kept talking to her and the train seemed to travel so fast she wondered if the driver had fallen asleep. She gripped the arms of her seat. 'Sam, Sam,' she cried to him silently.

*

London. She was afraid. Of crowds, buildings, everything rushing. Worse than that other city. The forest was her city, populated with trees and birds and animals, gentle, peaceful. She would never leave there.

She had to do this, for Clemmy and nothing could quite vanquish her excitement.

She stared so long at some people that some scowled at her and said words to her that she didn't always understand.

The taxi driver, a man who must be from some foreign country, was kind. 'Your first time in London, love?' he said, as she gave him the address of the theatre, written on a piece of paper.

'Yes.' She sounded abrupt and was sorry.

'Come far?'

She nodded, and he smiled.

The theatre was not even as large as the cinema she and Clemmy had spent hours, days, in. She had expected something much grander, something exotic. The taxi delivered her there just in time. It was filled with excitement, chatter and laughter. She wanted to laugh with them, would like to come here again.

A woman lowered herself into the seat next to her. 'Not seen you here before,' and a smile transformed her broad cheeks into two hillocks that almost closed her eyes. She fiddled with a coloured glass necklace that nestled on her overfull breast. 'I come to everything they put on here. We are so lucky to have them, but I almost missed this one, been away. I had to come. I hear that the girl that plays Nora is brilliant. She's been in a couple of other plays but small parts. They say she will be famous one day.'

The auditorium darkened, the woman sighed loudly and settled into her seat, taking over both of its arms. Helen leant forward, hands tightly clasped, and held her breath.

*

Clemmy waited in the wings, a small cramped area. The stage was no more than about twelve yards deep and a little wider – sometimes feeling the size of a large cupboard. She'd learnt her lesson about blocking and now moved confidently. Long gone were the sniggers, and playing Nora, she had earned the respect of the other actors.

She stroked her floral dress. It had taken a couple of rehearsals to grow into the costumes. The early Nora had believed that she knew what it meant to be an actress; this Nora now understood what a fool she had been. In that ankle-length floral dress, she was Nora, a happy Nora when she stepped onto the stage in a few minutes, to be excited by Torvald's pampering, her doll-like existence. For the moment, her courage was hidden. By the end of the last act, she would have rebelled, and the audience would have heard Torvald's anguished cry: 'She is gone.' She was excited and, as always, a little afraid so repeated to herself Will's words, her mantra: 'You are a brilliant Nora, believe in her.'

She would be Nora now and this evening, then Nora no more. Who would she be then? A different Clemmy to the one who had fled the forest. And Helen. She picked at her thumb, and quickly pulled her hands apart. That was the old Clemmy. She would stride confidently onto the stage, the dread and anguish of the first night gone. There had been praise, much praise. It was only a small amateur theatre, but it was a start. She would never forget Nora, but there would be different Noras, better theatres, there had to be. She grinned: New York, Hollywood. And Helen, would she be proud of her?

In the wings on the other side was Torvald. She had only ever called him that, even when they were in bed together.

She was unusually apprehensive and excited. The auditorium fell silent.

The curtains opened, almost noiselessly, and Nora walked onto the stage, humming.

This afternoon the audience were with her from the start, willing her on, believing in her. It was not always thus. And she was certain Helen was among them.

At the end of the first act, the audience remained silent a moment or two, then the applause, followed by the banging of seats and the rush to the bar.

*

Through that first act and the next, Helen closed her eyes many times and breathed Clemmy's voice into herself, where Clemmy still lived, and she was amazed to see the playful Nora/Clemmy.

With the final rapturous applause and Clemmy's last bow, Helen wrapped her scarf around herself, shivered, put her head in her hands and wept, looking up, hoping to catch one more glimpse of her.

'You all right, dear?' the woman said as she heaved herself up. 'She was good, wasn't she, Nora?' Then she stared hard at Helen and at the empty stage. 'I'm not good with faces and people really, but Nora, and you?'

Helen brushed her eyes with her hand, looked up at her and smiled.

A man came onto the empty stage then turned back toward the right-hand wing.

Clemmy ran out, peered into the auditorium.

'Clem,' Helen said, her voice transporting love.

'Hel,' Clemmy shouted, and ran off the side of the stage, up a few stairs, behind one row of seats, and another. To Helen.

'My Hel,' she whispered. 'My Hel,' and held her tight to her breast, their sobs becoming one, kissing her.

Others wandered onto the stage and stood, astonishment and smiles.

'Wait outside,' Clemmy said, so softly. 'I'll be five minutes, have to take this off.' She pointed to her make-up and dress. 'Take her off.'

'I'll come with you.'

'No. Don't worry, you won't lose me again, I promise. Two minutes.' She kissed Helen on the lips and ran back the way she had come.

44

Clemmy and Helen strolled along the London street in the late-afternoon September sun, arms around each other's waists, both wearing blue and green dresses and red leather jackets, Clemmy's slung over her shoulders. They had held their dresses and jackets against each other and laughed. 'Just like when we were kids.'

Helen gazed around, sometimes flinching.

'Don't be afraid. London's big, exciting.'

'Too many people, and…'

Clemmy laughed. 'I felt the same. You get used to it.'

'You couldn't live anywhere else now, could you?'

'New York perhaps.'

'Too far.' Helen pulled her closer.

'Let's stay away from people. There's a park nearby. With luck, we'll find a seat and get some peace.'

They sat close on a bench, undistracted by the shouts of kids playing on the swings some distance away.

'You were brilliant,' Helen said. 'A full house. I believed in Nora, in you – always have.'

'My Hel,' Clemmy murmured. 'It's a small theatre but that's my life now. One day I'll be on London's most famous stages. I have to be.'

Helen giggled. 'I'm so proud of you, Clem.'

Clem. The word hammered her, its ownership, its history, its love. She wanted Helen to say it over and over.

'And I am of you, your painting, Hel.' Clemmy had not expected those words, wanted to laugh, or was it cry, when she recalled the gallery, her words, her contempt. Had it been contempt of Helen's achievements or of herself? She knew the answer to that now, and that she still had a long path ahead, one filled with uncertainty. 'It's been too long coming, I know, but I am.'

They were both silent a moment or two.

'What now, Clem?'

'Oh, you know me, Hel, fame and glory.' Clemmy sighed. 'Drama school first, in a week. It took some getting into. Two turned me down. It was Will, the director at the playhouse, who got me in.'

'You can't be serious, back to school?' Helen laughed. 'You will be famous one day.'

'Yep. That's for certain.' Judi Dench was still the picture in her head. And Hollywood. 'It will be tough.' She squeezed Helen's arm. 'So, who is looking after my boy?'

'Eleanor.'

Clemmy threw back her head, still with its bun, still Nora, and her laughter shook the leaves of the nearby trees and some in the park turned and stared.

'Shorty. Is she still after you?'

Helen shook her head. 'She adores him, Sam adores her. She comes often during holidays and weekends or takes him to her mum. She came to me in hospital, took us home. I don't know what I would have done without her.'

Clemmy shifted a little on the bench, turning to face Helen. 'I have grown up, at last, well, I'm getting there, I hope. It's only been a few years but so much… Thomas helps me. Acting, that's what I want from life.' Her voice grew harder, louder. 'This play is just the start.'

'You will make it, Clem, I am certain.' Helen's eyes filled.

They sat quietly, for a time, their bodies joined, their selves complete.

'Life was almost perfect when I became Nora, except I had lost you. I'm still Nora, in my head. It will be a while before she leaves me. Perhaps I'll play her again, somewhere else. I'd like that.'

Helen smiled and she dug her elbow into Clemmy's side. 'That Torvald, a good-looking guy.'

'I wanted to know if he was Torvald in real life.' Clemmy's laughter caused some of those walking nearby to turn again and stare.

'And is he?'

'Not a bit.'

Helen's eyes spoke her question.

'I haven't changed that much, we are just lovers, it's the play, takes you over. He helped me a lot with the play, learning the lines was the easy bit. And with the others at the playhouse. He's an old hand at acting. This acting business, it's full of surprises, different every night. We all had good and bad days.' Clemmy turned to look into Helen's eyes. 'A bit like me. And stuff happens, your mistakes, someone else's. Torvald was always there. I could rely on him. After tonight I head off to my new life.'

Helen didn't bother asking if Torvald was married. 'Does Thomas know?'

'I hope not, he must not, it would hurt him too much.' Her voice softened. 'I would tell him the truth if he did, try to. It would be hard, really. Thomas and I love each other, will always be together. I feel safe with him. He's away a lot and I expect I will be, when I'm famous.'

Helen chuckled.

'I know, Hel,' Clemmy took Helen's hand again. 'That's me. Enough of me, your painting?'

Helen paused a moment or two. 'Murals. On the studio walls. Big.'

Clemmy's face told her surprise. 'Tell me more.'

'A story, our story.'

'Promise you'll show me, Hel.'

Helen nodded and looked in her bag. 'My train, I have to get back. Sam…'

'That's OK, I've got another performance tonight.' She wanted to show Helen the house, meet Thomas. There was no time. Later that evening Nora would leave her husband and children, for the last time.

Clemmy giggled. 'I can't believe it. Shorty.'

'She's great with him. When will you come? Home.'

Clemmy let the word rumble round her head. Home. Threatening and yet comforting. Wherever Helen was would always be that.

'Soon.'

They stood and walked, very slowly, through the park. Their clasped hands did the talking, words of tenderness, regret and love.

'I can't lose you again,' Helen said.

'You won't. I'll come to you and Sam. I can't let him forget me.' She carried inside her his small, perfect face and hopeful eyes.

*

'It was her, Jack, really her, Clemmy, she was a star, she's going to drama school, will be famous one day.' Helen clambered into his car, well after midnight.

'I expect she's always wanted that.' Jack's voice was soft.

In the cottage, she found Sam asleep and Eleanor also. She fell into bed.

The next thing was the sound of the front door closing, Eleanor's car starting and Sam's voice, 'Mummy, Mummy.'

Sam was sitting on the floor, beside her bed, Owlie in one hand, pencil in the other. She hauled him into bed with her and both slept on a little longer.

She crawled out of bed, dressed, not bothering to wash, stopping only to grab snacks for herself and Sam, and took him by the hand and led him up the narrow stairs, her excitement was mounting.

At the door, Sam pushed past her and rushed to the window and the sun, then back, running round the room, arms outstretched. In the sky, clear blue, a plane mimicked him, leaving behind its contrail.

He stood on tiptoe, hands pulling at the window ledge. 'Up, Mummy, up.' Helen held his back as he perched, nose and not-very-clean hands pressed against the glass. Then he turned his small, perfect face to her.

'Sam's oak, Mummy,' he shouted.

She held him fast while he wriggled and pointed.

He laughed and the bright late morning summer sun joined in and the baby clouds chased each other across the sky.

Later, he sat cross-legged at a small, low table, pencil held fast in his hand, lines, scrambled words that no one but he understood, scrawled across the paper, his tongue sliding across his lips, mimicking the brush's journey. At the same time, Helen's hand was moving over the freshly painted, bare white wall: quickly she dipped her brush in the paint. Sam dancing with his shadow, a small pack on his back, astonishment in his eyes. Her mind flipped to the next mural; it would be Nora.

Sam's pencil flew across the table and onto the floor. A gleeful giggle erupted. Mine ran over and pushed it with one paw.

45

It was over. No more skittish behaviour, Nora was free. Silence as the cast waited, while the audience breathed deeply, turning to hold their own loved ones, long seconds, until they found their hands to clap, their feet to stamp.

Clemmy gazed deep into the audience. Helen was gone, yet Clemmy bowed to her.

The applause was long, the audience sensing that they were the last privileged ones to experience something special. Perhaps they too had changed.

The actors left the stage, a little subdued. They would meet again at the bar, with Will, with the make-up girl, lighting, sound, stagehands, props, wardrobe, the prompt and others. They would party. Some would return tomorrow to dismantle the props, to transform them later into something else; new costumes would be made, new plays written and directed. The playhouse's life would continue and flourish.

Without Clemmy.

They gathered in the bar, shrieking and laughing.

Will hugged Clemmy, murmuring, 'Brilliant.' Jane did the same.

Torvald stood a little apart. She would go back to his flat with him one more time and both would regret parting, a little. Thomas would be asleep at home and would waken when she slid into bed beside him, ask no questions.

*

Thomas strode to the canal, breathing hard.

He had waited for her after the performance, dressed in new jeans and shirt, and had tied back his hair. He would surprise her. He had already seen the play twice. Wanting to share her triumph, he had slipped in the side door. She was in Torvald's arms, bodies entwined, mouths pressed, each to the other.

On the canal the darkness was fitful, uncertain, lighting up unexpected corners, blanketing others. Far away a few boats were still lit up and some voices carried. A mild night.

He did not lounge as he usually did, on the bench, but sat up straight, his arms across his chest.

He had not guessed. There was the excitement, the elation of the play, and he had ignored the very late nights. Coward, he spat at himself. He had never wanted to tame her but he had to trust her.

He had watched her become someone else, become Nora. And now with Torvald, was she someone else? He had been willing to sacrifice his photography for her, to abandon part of himself. For her. She had washed away the troubled, sad Thomas. He no longer searched out the poor, the abandoned, the vanquished. A different beauty now guided his fingers, his lenses. Until now.

Drunks, mostly young, stumbled by. How had he grown so old, so sad? He would never love like this again. She had changed him, love had, even his photography had begun to change: children on bicycles, people dancing in the streets, fun, joy.

He slumped. Straightened. The clock chimed 1am. He tried to light a cigarette but his hands shook and he threw it into the canal.

Clemmy's footsteps, fast, beating up the ground. Torvald and his Clemmy.

Clemmy had slammed through the front door, into the kitchen, the sitting room, and up the stairs and into the bedroom to fling herself on her Thomas.

No one. Why was he not there to share her triumph?

She ran out the front door.

She threw herself onto the bench beside him, still Nora. He did not turn towards her.

'My Thomas,' and she put her arms around him.

He pulled away.

'I came to find you, wanted to be with you. What a fool I am. All those late nights. This Torvald.'

In the dim light Clemmy could see his drawn face, and something she had not seen before: anger.

'Oh Thomas, what have I done to you? It was nothing.'

'Nothing. You didn't go to much trouble to hide it. Late nights. Do you love him?' He lit a cigarette, his hand trembling, then ground it out under his shoe.

'Torvald, of course not.' She took Thomas's hand. 'It was the play, somehow...' She couldn't find the words, any that would not hurt Thomas.

'What is his name when he's not on stage?'

Clemmy almost laughed. 'I can't remember, I've always just called him Torvald.'

'So, you and I, what are we? An act?'

'Never, Thomas. I love you. I don't why I did it. I will never see him again and I never cared about him.'

'So, it was just a fuck.'

Clemmy was silent. She took his hand. He tried to pull away. She held it fast.

'I would never betray you, never.' His voice so soft now that she could barely hear the words. 'Have I not shown you my love? I leave you, and you will leave me from time to time, that's what actors have to do. We have to be able to trust each other.' He freed his hand. 'Or part.'

His last two words slammed into Clemmy, blows, disbelief. She could not give Thomas up, never. She would give up the acting. Her breath slowed. She could not do that either. 'Forgive me, Thomas, forgive me.' She slipped down to the ground and knelt, in her Nora dress, at his feet, gazing up at him, real tears running. 'It was nothing. I promise, never again, only you.'

'Should I believe you?' His arms remained crossed. 'Is it finished?'

'Oh yes, Thomas, I beg you. I was wrong, so wrong. It was the play, the excitement. It just happened. Stupid, stupid, stupid.'

He wanted to say that nothing just happens, but that was not true. He was not sure he believed her promise but understood that she did. He pulled her up into his arms, kissed her, held her tight. He could not always guard her, treat her like the child she still was, although that was changing. There was something indefinable about her. He had captured a little of it on film and perhaps he would never capture the rest, never understand her fully. He had to go away again soon, on his never-ending hunt for something different. 'I go away a lot. I have to but I carry you with me. It will be hard, our life together.'

'I don't care how hard it will be. I love you, Thomas. That will never change. I'm not a good person, but I try. Torvald was part of the act. Stupid, stupid.'

'You are special, Clemmy, you must know that.'

Clemmy's eyes opened wide, as did her mouth and her heart.

'And the whole world will know one day.'

46

Helen's life softened after London. And Sam started school, making new friends, needing Helen a little less.

Woodie died. It was sudden, unexpected, perhaps too many of her exquisite cakes were to blame. Sam kept asking, 'Where's Woodie?' Helen tried to explain.

Helen took Eleanor in her arms and held her long. She too mourned Woodie.

The funeral was while Sam was at school. A few teachers from Eleanor's school attended and it was a brief service, nothing godly. Helen took Eleanor's arm to steady her and walked with her after the coffin. The undertakers organised a few eats and tea and coffee afterwards but no one stayed long.

*

Eleanor unearthed her travel brochures and gave in her notice at school. The Head permitted her to leave immediately. It was clear she could not face the children, indeed face anybody. Eleanor put the house in an agent's hands. It was too redolent of life with her mother, and she booked a train to St Petersburg. It would take several days to get there but she had a lot of them ahead. She would stay away some time.

'You and Sam brought joy and light into her life. And into mine.'

'We loved her,' said Helen. There was no need for more.

'I don't know when I will back.' They sat side by side in Helen's studio, holding hands. 'There's no hurry.' Eleanor smiled a little, the first Helen had seen since Woodie died. 'I will be back, will send you both some cards, fun ones for Sam, but you must promise me you will never give up your painting.'

Helen nodded, released Eleanor's hand and walked over to where a stack of unframed paintings lay. She picked up one and held it out to Eleanor. 'I want you to have this. My father left a very small one but I painted this, a goldfinch. It is small and will be no bother for you to take with you. It is my favourite creature of the forest.'

Eleanor took it. 'I have loved you, Helen, you know that. And Sam. Perhaps I always will.'

'And I love you, not in the way you want. I have Sam and he is enough. The time will come when I have to let him go, not for a while yet.' She leant over and kissed Eleanor, briefly, on the lips.

Eleanor had given Helen a small box of Woodie's ashes, so Helen went alone to the pond to scatter them among the trees nearby, murmuring, 'Goodbye'.

The trees, fully clothed, hid their bare limbs. Heavy rain, and some trees bowed before it, their branches swaying in the fresh water at the pond's edge, teasing and acquiescent until the level fell. The trickle at the far end, which fed the pond, grew fat on the abundance running off the hills and from the sky, and for a time, became a river of pride and tumult. The acorns were yet to fall, but some of last season's lingered, no longer fed to pigs, the right of pannage, and the male catkins had long since dropped. The oak was the king of trees, and hundreds of years old. A chieftain tree for the Celts so that the fine for felling a chieftain oak was the same as for killing a prominent person.

Late in November, a card arrived:

We are coming to you on Saturday. Your Clemmy.

Helen took Sam in her arms. 'Other Mummy is coming to see us, Sam.'

'Other Mummy?' His eyes opened wide, matching his smile.

Helen cycled into town to buy a feast and good wine, singing in concert with her turning legs. Sam had his own bike now and followed her.

She cleaned the house somewhat, made the sitting room habitable, and Mother's room.

*

In London, Clemmy had started drama school, and Thomas went away little.

She had meant to go to Helen sooner, but somehow it hadn't worked out so she scoured the shops and sent small presents: cards, scarves, a couple of bracelets, toy cars, games and soft toys for Sam to cuddle. Sent from Other Mummy to Sam. The shop assistants hurried over to her when she came in.

She didn't telephone.

It was Thomas who said, in his quiet voice, 'Time to go. Send her a note.'

So she went to the shop for a special gift for Sam.

*

The day augured well, as Thomas and Clemmy drove out of the city. Thomas was dressed, as usual, in jeans and shirt. Clemmy had bought a new skirt at the market, sky-blue, and had pinned the dragonfly on her blouse. Her hair sat loose on her shoulders.

'Love the forest,' Thomas said as they drove down the track. He held his camera in his lap.

'Helen loves it too.' It again seemed more amiable, even pleasing, in places.

They pulled up in front of the cottage. Thomas picked up his camera.

A small boy ran towards them, shouting.

Clemmy hastened towards him.

The boy stopped, swinging back round to Helen, who was some yards behind him, blue-skirted, hair loose on her shoulders.

Sam turned back to Clemmy. 'Other Mummy, Other Mummy,' his eyes wide.

Clemmy knelt on the ground and Sam flung his arms around her neck. 'Other Mummy,' he whispered.

She swung around, then back, placing a very large parcel

in front of him. His small hands struggled with the packaging so she helped.

Helen smiled and Thomas walked over to her and kissed her on the cheek. 'Helen, at last.'

'What it, Other Mummy?' Sam demanded. 'What it?'

'You'll see,' Clemmy said and helped him pull out a giraffe, almost as big as Sam.

Sam hugged the gift, looking puzzled.

'A giraffe, Sam. They are tall, almost as tall as that tree.' And she pointed to a birch about fifteen feet high. 'He comes from Africa. I'll take you there one day in an aeroplane.'

'Flying,' Sam said, and ran round and round Clemmy, with his arms outstretched.

Later, Helen and Clemmy sat in the garden, bodies touching, while Sam rode his bike up and down the track and Thomas was somewhere in the forest with his camera.

'This will surprise you: I teach a dozen women painting, in the local hall.'

Helen had met Muriel as she waited with the mothers after school.

'You are the painter,' Muriel said. 'Your son, Sam, tells everyone. I paint a little, badly. Would you teach me?'

And it had gone from there.

Helen did not mention the trip to the station, to him. She could hear Clemmy's scorn.

That evening, they stayed up late, even Sam for a time, his eyes moving from one Mummy to the other. When he could look no more, Helen carried him upstairs to bed.

Thomas was not what Helen had expected but she liked

him at once, his voice, his warmth and the kindness in his face. Very soon they were discussing light and colours, although Helen had never used a camera.

They supped the remainder of the expensive wine Thomas had brought and Clemmy's tales of her first weeks at drama school unrolled, as tumultuous as the deteriorating weather outside; her stories of hard work, confusion, tension and friendship. She had learnt to watch people, really watch; every hand movement, facial expression, especially the eyes, to read them. And to listen to what was behind the words. She found it tough and had occasionally despaired.

When the tales were done Clemmy said, 'I want to see your paintings, Hel.'

Helen bit her lip.

'I'll stay here, took some pictures earlier, might have a look,' and Thomas picked up his camera. 'You can show me another time, I do want to see them.'

Clemmy touched Thomas's shoulder. 'Leave him, he'll be happy.'

A strange feeling was suffusing Helen. When she returned from London, she had painted more pictures on the opposite wall: one of a small boy dancing with his shadow, the next, Nora and two copper-haired girls on clouds. Time would fill the rest. She almost told Clemmy but held back.

She stood, a little unsteadily, for she was not much of a drinker, and led Clemmy up the stairs, and across the studio to stand facing the painting of Sam.

They giggled together at Sam and the shadow and Helen's tale, and fell against each other and straightened up.

Clemmy put one hand out, towards Nora. 'I was good, wasn't I?'

'Brilliant, it was the play for you.'

Clemmy held Helen tight in front of the clouds and the two copper-haired girls. 'Us, always,' and, 'More, more,' she shouted, then swung around, gasped and turned back to Helen.

'What's this?' She pointed at the second mural on the opposite wall: copper-haired beauties, both big-bellied, one with blank eyes.

'You. I painted it just after you left. I believed, back then, that we would always be together, I knew no other love.' She paused. 'I was angry that you couldn't see what you had done to me, how blind you were.'

'What would I have done here in this dump?' Clemmy muttered. 'Of course, I loved you but…'

Clemmy moved towards the gold dress and flinched. 'Beautiful Boy, us,' she pointed to the hands clasped below it, ignoring the sparrow hawk with its determination, its ruthlessness, its freedom and its beauty. Her sobs bounced back from the wall.

Helen led her to the sofa and held her in her arms.

Helen took her hand. 'We understand each other, Clem, like no one else ever will, to our inmost core. You had to go, I understand that now, and I have my life with Sam. And this.' She swung her arm around the room. 'We are still one, and we are separate. That's what we had to learn. Our love has never changed, never will, but we are beginning to understand who we are, each of us. That will go on until we are no more.'

'That is the past, it's those there,' and she pointed to Nora and the other two, 'that are our lives now.'

*

Clemmy spent the next day with Sam, huddled together on the floor of his playroom, one time the dining room and now much covered with thick rugs and littered with his toys, in a basket and on the floor, and a special soft, plush bed for Owlie.

'Let's make up a story,' Clemmy said to the boy lying on the rug, his head in her lap and his body curled around the giraffe.

Sam nodded. He loved stories.

'Once upon a time…'

*

It had been a brilliant visit. Helen wanted to see more of Thomas, talk to him about his art. And she believed Clemmy was happy. As Clemmy was having a last dance with Sam, Helen gave Thomas a parcel carefully wrapped in brown paper. 'It is Nora.' She had struggled a little with the portrait. It was not the same Clemmy as in the earlier one of them both, and no longer quite the Helen in the mirror. The features were the same but Clemmy had lost her hints of vulnerability, her eyes strong and determined, dressed as Nora on stage, slamming the door as she left.

Thomas placed it carefully in the boot and kissed Helen on the cheek. 'She'll love it.'

As Clemmy was about to get into the car, London was calling, she dug in her handbag and took out a piece of paper. 'Mother, I bumped into her, outside my favourite dress shop. We had tea.'

Helen's hand went to her mouth, and she tore the piece of paper from Clemmy's hand.

'What was she like? Tell me, tell me everything.' She looked around, heard the engine running, Thomas sitting patiently in the driver's seat. 'Why have you left it until now? I could murder you, Clemmy.'

Clemmy grinned. 'Plenty of money, treated me at London's best tea shop. Her man has died. I expect left it all to her.'

'More, tell me more.'

'Not a lot to tell. I didn't stay long. She asked me to give you this. I think she would like to see you.'

Helen stepped back. She was never going to London again.

'Perhaps she'll come to you.' Clemmy kissed Helen and slid into the car, then she slipped out. 'I forgot. This.' She pulled from her handbag a lock of copper hair fastened at both ends. 'That night, when we crept downstairs and cut your hair, after mine had been chopped, I kept this, your hair. I take it on stage with me, wouldn't go on if I couldn't find somewhere for it. It's my good luck charm.'

47

A few days later, a photograph arrived at the cottage. She and Clemmy were perched on the fallen oak, wearing their blue-green skirts. Clemmy had on a blue sweater, Helen a green. Spreadeagled across their laps was a young boy, a cheeky grin on his face.

Every month or two, Clemmy arrived, usually unannounced, sometimes on her own when Thomas was away. She made up her mind, usually, at the last minute. She and Helen talked about their lives and Sam. And she spent much time with Sam, playing hide and seek on the edges of the forest, racing down the track and tumbling around the living room if it rained. She had done some dance classes so showed them to Sam and he clapped his small hands and tried to copy her.

Occasionally, if Clemmy could not come for a time, Thomas drove to the forest, to Helen and Sam, bringing his best work to show Helen and a surprise for Sam. They walked the forest, talking about light and colour, while Sam ran around, peeping out from behind trees. After a time, Sam demanded to hold Thomas's camera so he placed it in Sam's small hands, wrapping his own around them while Sam raised it to his eye and laughed. 'Cameraman,' he said.

Thomas was eager for the day when he could give Sam his own small camera.

Sam painted Owlie and Giraffe, and an oak tree or the pond and the ducks. Giraffe was too big to carry around so he waited for him on his bed.

Helen read Rudyard Kipling to him, his *Just So Stories*. Sam listened and was content to let the music of her voice send him to sleep. He was also reading his own stories. They found a baby rabbit in the fields and got bitten by mosquitoes. The swallows had gone. They went on an acorn hunt and found the keys of the ash trees hanging and the ground littered with hazelnuts. The wind caressed the trees, ruffling and tossing their branches about, the leaves dancing. Then it began to strip the trees and frost sparkled on many surfaces. Trees snapped in the storms and mourned their shorn branches.

The owl hooted and Sam held Owlie high with his still small arms so Owlie could listen and answer.

Spring came and the sky dimpled pink. Bluebells covered the forest floor with their glory and the wild garlic with its scent and white flowers.

Sam came home from school with stories of his best friend, Mikey, and asked could he show Mikey the forest. They ran out of the school gate together, satchels banging on their backs, excitement spread over both faces. Mikey dragged his mother over to Helen and Sam. 'I'm Janet, Mikey's mother. He does nothing but talk about your Sam and his stories of the forest where you live.' She was a small woman with a lively, happy face and constantly moving hands that reminded Helen a little of Clemmy.

'You must both come to us and we'll show you the forest. I too love it.'

The woman placed her hand on Helen's arm, her smile broad, 'We'll do that.'

Helen had her own car now – it took three attempts to pass her driving test. She and Sam drove into town, where Jack still insisted they sample his cakes.

'We are too old and our imaginations are not theirs; we carry different stories in our heads. Theirs are filled with hopes and dreams that we have long since abandoned,' she told Jack.

Clemmy finished drama school with accolades, and had some small parts in prestigious theatre productions.

A card for Sam lay on the mat. It had a giraffe on its front.

Sam stumbled over the words.

'*I'm coming to see you very soon, Other Mummy xx*'

'Why Other Mummy?'

Helen had been waiting for that question. 'We are one, Other Mummy and me.'

'One Mummy,' he gazed at her.

She bent and kissed his cheek. 'Yes.'

'When is Other Mummy coming?' Sam demanded.

'Soon. She'll be a famous actress one day.'

'How, Mummy?'

Helen explained that Clemmy had gone back to school. That confused Sam for Other Mummy was old.

'To pretend to be someone else, a story.'

*

Helen found the piece of paper with the address and sat at the kitchen table some time, biting her lip, until, finally, she wrote.

Dear Mother,

She smiled at that word. It was time. She was a mother too and it had taught her much and had carried her back in time, with some regrets.

I am still here in the forest. You met Clemmy in London. We are both happy in different ways. I am a painter, just like Father. I have had several exhibitions.

Clemmy is an actress. Perhaps that does not surprise you. You should be proud of us both.

And you have a grandson.

I have told him about you, his granny, and he asks constantly when you are coming to see him. He says will you bring him a present. His words, not mine.

She paused some time before the next word.

Love,
Helen.

Then Helen dreamt she saw her walking down the track, briskly, but tottering a little in high heels, dressed in beautiful clothes.

The next week she received a letter.

Dear Helen,
    I am coming to see you next week end. Please make sure your sister is with you.
    It's been a long time.
    Love
    Mum.

A strange word, Mum.

It had been difficult to get Clemmy to the cottage.

The two girls stood together, hands lightly held, and watched a woman step out of a taxi, a bright red handbag over her shoulder, a short black skirt and white blouse. She turned to look at the forest, wrinkling her nose, then at Helen and Clemmy. None moved until Helen bent down and whispered to Sam, 'Your granny.'

He ran to her, 'Granny'.

Mother knelt, with some difficulty, and put her arms around him.

Acknowledgements

I owe much to several authors. Two books that were invaluable were *The Wood* by John Lewis-Stempal, and *In the Company of Trees* by Andrea Sarubbi Fereshteh. Much of the forest in *The Other* is based on our local wood, Fishpond Wood. I hope I've done it justice

The Actor's Life by Jenna Fischer provided invaluable insights into the acting world, and *One and the Same* by Abigail Pogrebin was invaluable for understanding the psyche of identical twins.

I am fortunate to live in Pateley bridge in the Yorkshire Dales, a small town replete with talented, creative people: playwrights, and actors at our wonderful small playhouse, the model for my theatre in *The Other*, and artists, poets, photographers, and musicians, who have given unstinting help.

Sarah Garforth helped immeasurably with my understanding of painting and checked my script for idiotic errors. Thank you Sarah. And my thanks to another artist, Maureen Little.

And Ruth Dodsworth, Joyce Liggins and Sue Hickson at the Pateley Bridge Playhouse.

Rosie Szlumper for her stories of her identical twin mother and aunt.

Chis Henderson for unstinting help with IT problems.

My thanks to editors: Julie Gray, Jill French, and, in particular, Karen Mckellar, who stuck with me through several iterations.

At Troubador a raft of people to thank, most particularly Andrea Johnson, Beth Archer and Sophie Morgan, all experts in their fields, friendly and helpful.

And most of all, my thanks for the love and belief of my partner, Katrina.

This book is printed on paper from sustainable sources managed under the Forest Stewardship Council (FSC) scheme.

It has been printed in the UK to reduce transportation miles and their impact upon the environment.

For every new title that Matador publishes, we plant a tree to offset CO_2, partnering with the More Trees scheme.

For more about how Matador offsets its environmental impact, see www.troubador.co.uk/about/